PAINTING
LILY

MIMI SCHLICHTER

PAINTING LILY
Copyright ©2015 by Mimi Schlichter

First edition, Mimi's Art 2015

Cover design by Chrissy Caskey

Cover art from an original painting
by Mimi Schlichter

Nora Ephron quote with permission from ICM.

Schlichter, Mimi
PAINTING LILY
ISBN 978-0-9963308-0-0

Dedicated to lovely Evana.
With deepest gratitude for teaching me
to live with intention
every day.

* * *

"Above all, be the heroine of your life,
not the victim."
Nora Ephron

Once upon a time, when I was thirteen years young, my parents left me home alone on a Friday night. And I did that thing I did every night they left me home alone.

I sat at the piano for hours and played and sang at the top of my lungs, the same songs from "Cinderella" and "The Sound of Music" that I sang every time they went out and left me by myself. Oh, dear Cinderella, I was certain I knew exactly how you felt. My special alone place was a walk-in closet in my bedroom, my secret hideaway where my imagination was allowed to run wild. I'd disappear for hours, until my mother would yell up the stairs looking for me, and I would yell back "I'm in my closet." And believe me, she knew better than to expect me to come out any time soon.

When Cinderella and the Prince declared their love in a song, my heart sang right along with them. I couldn't help myself. If that was what love was like, real grown up love, well, I couldn't wait. I dreamed of the day when someone would look me in the eyes and sing to me like that.

It would be easy enough to blame Cinderella for my unrealistic adolescent expectations if I had left them behind when I grew up. But then along came Vivian Ward in "Pretty Woman." Replace Cinderella's rags with fishnet stockings and kick ass over the knee black hooker boots held together with a safety pin and it was the same story all over again. A wealthy, distinguished, and might I add not so tough on the eyes suit wearing executive drives up in his sports car and rescues the downtrodden girl from the street. Or as she declares in the final scene, she rescues him. It could happen, right?

I was a good girl, once upon a time.

Chapter 1

There. Across the room. It's definitely not love at first sight. He's not even my type. I don't find him all that handsome or remarkable in appearance, though he does wear his navy blue wool Brooks Brothers blazer and nautical striped tie with the ease of which I wear my favorite ripped out in the knees, paint splattered jeans. Oh, I suppose he's good looking, or at least good looking enough, but no, that isn't it. I just know deep down in the place where I sometimes know things that we must meet.

Three of my most recent paintings have been accepted into this alumni exhibit, an eclectic mix of pieces by well established, high priced successfuls hanging next to newbie artist wannabes like me. I have hopes of enticing a buyer or two to pay attention, perhaps tempting them to want more of what I have to offer. *Be careful, Lily. You might just get what you ask for.*

It's a funny thing, what people expect from an artist. They ask me "what is it you are trying to say with this piece?" And I never know quite how to answer. How do I explain to them that my painting topics choose me, not the other way around? A certain angle of light catches my attention. Or a juxtaposition of colors. Sometimes I simply feel the need to capture for eternity the way a child sits, or the look in an animal's eyes. But as for that great personal message to the world through art thing, well, it's just not my thing. Not yet.

I far prefer to ask the same question of others, because honestly it matters way more what a potential buyer thinks than what I do. I'm amused when someone tells me of a deeper message they get from my painting, particularly one I didn't intend. Maybe it is in fact the muse working through me and I don't know it. Or maybe they just want to sound intelligent by finding a message they assume should be there. In any case, it offers a good enough excuse to walk over and introduce myself.

The good news is that he is standing right in front of one of my paintings, so the approach will be easy. The bad news is that there is a woman standing next to him, perhaps a wife, or a girlfriend. She's just this side of stunning, wearing her St. John caviar knit dress, diamond stud earrings, and exquisitely applied makeup. Maybe she will turn out to be my premier collector.

"There's a certain gracefulness to her brush strokes, don't you think?" These are the first words I hear him speak.

"Oh, I don't know." She sighs. "I don't see it. They're just skies. You've seen one, you've seen them all."

"But look at how the light reflects in the water. She's captured it, the way it looks just as the sun is about to set." I think maybe it is an attempt to convince her. To suggest he is trying to enlighten her would be to go too far.

"You know I don't care for the water, Leo. That's your thing, with that damn boat of yours. Besides, I've never heard of her."

I take this as my cue to wade into their conversation. "Excuse me. Do you have any questions I can answer?"

They both turn to look at me. A broad grin spreads on his face. Though I'm not the only one who notices, and now my art isn't the only thing of which she disapproves. She turns and walks away without saying another word. She doesn't have to. Her body language speaks on her behalf.

He reaches out his hand to me. "Hello, I don't think we've met. I'm Dr. Leo Stocker. And you are?"

"Liliana Daniels. And these are my paintings. The ones you were discussing with your...wife?"

"Yes. But please don't pay too much attention to her. She considers herself an expert, though honestly, I think she's what you might call an art snob. Thinks most of these artists are beneath her standards."

He pauses, realizes the subtle insult he just dropped on me, and searches for the next right thing to say to fix it. "I'm sorry if you heard her criticize your work. Please don't take it personally. It's not about you. She just hates the water. In fact, lately she hates pretty much everything I enjoy."

"Oh, I'm sorry."

"You needn't apologize. If anyone should, it's me. I didn't mean to sound so..."

"Honest?"

"Yeah, I guess you could call it that. But hey, you do seem to have a knack for capturing light. Are you trying to show the tension of nature with..."

"No, it's just one of my favorite things to paint. They say you paint best what you are most passionate about."

"Passion. Now there's an idea I can relate to. Tell me more."

"Well, Pennsylvania is way too landlocked for me. I go north to the water whenever I can."

"And by north you mean...?"

"Cape Cod. Buzzards Bay, to be specific."

He pauses, then rocks back on his heels ever so slightly. His eyes haven't left mine. It's magnetic. And, to be honest, somewhat unnerving.

He says, "I'm moving there."

"Excuse me?"

"Well, not exactly there. And probably not for several years. But I have several friends at a museum in Boston who want me to join them. Truthfully, I wouldn't mind if it worked out that way. I have my own love affair with the water."

"Wow. Good for you. So, I've heard your name. You're a professor here in the art department, right?"

"Yes. Well, I was. Until they promoted me to department chairman. Unfortunately, that means I don't get to do much teaching these days. They send me out to schmooze instead." There's a slight sound of the south in his voice. I wonder if it is there simply for effect.

I ask, "So, is charming women to open their wallets also part of your job?"

He grins. "My, my, you certainly are direct, aren't you? Tell me, Liliana Daniels, why haven't our paths crossed until now? I mean, you're a product of this place, aren't you?"

"Yes, but I wasn't an art major."

"Oh? Do tell."

"Believe it or not, chemistry. One of the more stupid mistakes of my youth, but I didn't know any better at the time. I thought it would lead me to a good job. Instead it just led me to a terrible GPA and a disastrous string of waitressing gigs."

He chuckles. Pauses a moment, then says, "Well, you obviously love the paints, and from what I've seen so far, you have talent. So if it's not too personal a question, may I ask how you got from there to here?"

"Nope, not too personal a question at all. I've painted what seems like all my life, even studied privately for a while, but mostly kept it just for me, just for fun. I had a dad who hated his work, and I didn't want to end up hating my art. Then a friend offered me a nice sum of money to paint her old family place on the Cape. So I took her up on it. Found myself on the beach one summer day armed only with my paintbox and a camera, and, well, at the risk of sounding corny, I knew I'd found my one true love." I muse to myself *in more ways than one.*

"Your one true love. Aren't you a lucky girl. Some people spend their whole lives looking for that." He winks, then reaches into his coat pocket. Extends his hand toward me. "Here's my card. Call me. Maybe I can help you."

"Thank you, Dr. Stocker. That'd be nice." *Nice? Is that all the better I can come up with?*

"Wonderful. But you needn't be so formal. Please call me Leo."

"Okay. Thank you, Leo."

"I'm serious. I have all sorts of contacts. Gallery owners, independent collectors, and generally just people like me, or maybe I should say like my wife, who love to throw their money around in the name of helping poor starving artists."

"Well, that's me alright. The artist part, not the one throwing money around. Though I'm pretty good at spending it." *Shut up, Lily. You're babbling.*

"Ms. Daniels, you're a hoot. And obviously not the kind of artist who takes herself too seriously. I like that. And I'm truly glad we had a chance to meet, but I should go now. I need to find Lizzy before she buys something hideous. Or more likely hideously expensive. My number is on my card. Give me a call. Anytime."

"I will. And thanks again. I appreciate whatever help I can get at this point. Really I do."

"My pleasure," he says, with another wink.

That's two in less than a minute. *Is he flirting with me? Or does he just have something in his eye?*

Then he says, "By the way, please don't be too put off by my wife's comments. That's the way she is. If she likes something, you know it. And if she doesn't like it, well, the whole world knows it."

Oh, yeah. The wife thing. *Oh, boy. Here I go again.*

Chapter 2

"Why didn't you just go ahead and screw her in the coatroom?"

"Excuse me?"

"You know, the flirty artist with the awful sunsets. Did you think I didn't notice?"

"I was admiring her paintings, that's all."

"Admiring her paintings my ass. You couldn't take your eyes off of her."

"Drop it, Lizzie. I swear, you make things up that don't exist. Can't you just let it go for one night?" She constantly nags me. And accuses me of affairs that aren't real. Not that I haven't considered it, but I do try to behave myself. Honest I do.

"Why do we even bother, Leo? It's obvious to me and probably to just about everyone else that you don't care about me anymore. Remind me, please, why are we still married?"

"C'mon Lizzy, you know why. In the world we run in it just doesn't look right. And the kids would hate us. Besides, the financial ramifications don't make any sense at all."

"So, here's the thing, Leo. Fair's fair. If you get to have yourself a little hottie on the side, well, then, so do I."

Which is always her closing argument. And the one that annoys the hell out of me. Big time. Flirting with gorgeous women is just part of my job. What's her excuse?

Quite frankly, divorce is an expensive luxury I simply cannot afford. And I've never understood why people make the choice to pay lawyers rather than come up with an amicable arrangement between themselves. Lizzie and I have a clear understanding of our respective roles in the marriage. She takes care of the house stuff. Cooks, cleans, and picks up my dirty laundry, then puts it back in my dresser drawers, freshly washed and neatly folded.

Ah, who am I kidding? She pays some one to do it all, but honestly I don't care, as long as it gets done. Then she can do whatever else she wants. So let's just say she's a good manager. As for me, I go to the office every day. Work long hours. Bring home my minimal share of the proverbial bacon. It's like a wise business arrangement, each partner with a clearly defined job description. Nothing more. Nothing less. Works for me.

Sort of. Do you want to know the real truth? Divorce may make sense for her, but not for me, because after all is said and done, I'm the one with more to lose. Even as department chairman I don't earn nearly enough to sustain the lifestyle to which I've become accustomed, thanks to her money. No, correction. Oh, how I hate being cliché. Thanks to her beloved daddy's money. Yes, Frederick Roger Browning, III. He's my meal ticket. So why, oh why on earth would I ever consider the possibility of divorce? I mean, you don't just throw away a marriage because you're bored, do you?

If courting a little honey or two on the side makes life with Lizzy more bearable, then I'll just be discreet about it, and we can all live happily ever after.

Like I said. Works for me.

Chapter 3

I've stared at his business card on my desk for the past two days. He's a professor, but obviously there's more to his story, because the bling I saw on the wife is most definitely not from a professor's salary. He told me to call anytime, but I don't want to appear overeager. So I've made myself wait a few days. And not first thing in the morning, either. *Play it cool, Lily.*

Two o'clock. Feels about right. I dial his number. He answers on the second ring. "Dr. Leo Stocker." His voice smooth and sweet as honey to my ears.

"Hello, Dr. Stocker. This is Liliana Daniels. We met the other night at the art reception?" It occurs to me he might not remember me. Maybe he wasn't flirting. Maybe I imagined it all. Maybe...

"Of course. I've been waiting for your call. How are you?"

"I'm good." *He's been waiting for my call?* "The other night you suggested we might get together to talk about some ideas you have to help me. So, I thought I'd take you up on your offer, and see if we can set up a time to do that."

"Absolutely. Just let me take a quick look at my calendar. Can you hold on a second, please?"

"Sure." And the phone goes quiet. In the next thirty seconds or so of dead air space I question, as I have all weekend, my motivation. Am I calling him about his art connections, or is it because of the way his eyes stayed locked with mine? *I'm a married woman. Why would I...*

"Sorry to keep you waiting. I had to clear a few things with my secretary. Seems she knows more about my life than I do. How's this Friday sound?"

"Friday's great."

He says, "Why don't you come by my office around two?"

I say, "Perfect. It's a date." *Nice choice of word, Lily.*

He says, "See you on Friday. Oh, and one more thing."

"What's that?"

"Bring along a copy of your resume."

"My resume? Okay. Got it. Thank you again, Dr. Stocker."

"No problem. I'll look forward to it. And remember, please call me Leo."

"Yes, Leo. I'll see you on Friday."

After a week that feels like three, Friday is finally here. A fresh copy of my resume sits waiting on the kitchen counter. It's been a while since I've updated it, and I'll admit I was worried it would look too thin, but after just a few tweaks, I'm pleasantly surprised by the story it tells. Eddie doesn't earn a lot, but it's been enough to support us while I pursue my painting.

So, on to the more challenging part of this meeting. What to wear? I dress from the bottom up. Start with my favorite leather boots. I'll stand more confidently in them than if I try to teeter on a pair of heels. Next, a faux suede camel boot length skirt. Black turtleneck, silk scarf, and a pair of pearl stud earrings. Sweep my hair back and up in a bun. This should work. I do a mirror check. Far too conservative. I swap the sweater for a blouse, wrap the scarf at my waist, and let my hair down. Better. Then consider how many buttons to leave open, or not. Show only the tiniest hint of cleavage. Just a tease to pique his interest, but not enough to distract. I want those twinkling eyes of his to look into mine when we talk, not wander too far south.

His office is in the heart of campus. I wonder how many years he's been here. I don't know how old he is, but I suspect he has enough years on me for our time to have overlapped. Did I walk by as a student without knowing he was working there? It's happened to me before. Future significant people already exist in my life, I just don't recognize them. Like Eddie. I had a photo of him on my dorm room wall before I knew who he was. A group composite from a different guy I dated in the same fraternity. There was my husband to be, smiling at me from across the room while I made love with someone else.

I walk up the two flights of stairs to Leo's office. There's an elevator, but I think the walk will do me good, put a little flush of color into my cheeks, and allow me to clear my head for just one more minute. *Why are you here, Lily? What is it you want from this man?* I have a bad habit of taking an innocent flirtation and running away with it. *You're here for work, Lily. He's already got a wife, remember? And you've got a husband. Small details you seem to forget too easily.* Thank goodness nobody can read my mind, or I'd be in trouble. Big trouble.

He greets me in the hallway. "Liliana Daniels. Welcome to my world."

Now it's my turn to extend a hand to him. "Thank you again for agreeing to meet with me. And since you've instructed me more than once to call you Leo, may I suggest in return that those who know me well call me Lily?"

"Then allow me to correct myself. Welcome to my world, Lily." There's another wink as he says my name.

We go into his office. Sit down. I hand him my resume. He's quiet for a moment as he gives it a quick read, then looks up. "So, I have an offer for you," he says.

"Wow. So soon?" *Did I just say wow? Where's my college vocabulary when I need it?* "I'm listening. What do you have in mind?"

"How would you like to work for me?"

I say, "Uh, well, I don't know," which loosely translates to *what the hell is he talking about?* "I don't mean to sound ungrateful, I just wasn't expecting this. When you said you could help me with my career I thought you meant..."

"I know. You're an artist. So, here's the thing. They've put a lot of pressure on me in the past several years to find grants to help keep the department up and running, as arts funding has been, oh, shall we say, challenged? I'm quite good at it, but I'm not so good at keeping myself organized. That's where you come in. I'd like to hire you as my personal assistant, to help me keep track of where I need to be, and when, so I can spend my time on the road. It's a somewhat entry level position, but you'd at least have a chance to meet some of the art world, and learn the ins and outs of it at the same time. I could bring you along to meet some of the donors when you're ready. It'll be like getting paid to learn how to advance your own art career."

"Sounds great, I guess." I should be more excited. Ecstatic, probably. I'd get to work with him. And earn some money of my own instead of depending on Eddie. I'm just thinking about the luxury of the artist's life I've been enjoying, and I don't think I'm ready to give it up. Not yet.

He says, "It's only a half-time position, but I can pull some strings to make sure it pays enough to be worth your while."

I gather myself together, and fake my best enthusiastic voice. "Sure, I'd love to know more. But are you certain I'm right for this? You barely know me." *Nice self-deprecation, Lily. C'mon. Where's your confidence?*

"I did some asking around about you this week, from your professors over in the chemistry department. As to your lab skills, well, let's just say it's a good thing I'm not hiring you for those."

"I could've told you that."

"I know. But otherwise, they seem quite enamored with you, which is far more important to me. Apparently you have a way with people, which doesn't surprise me. I already figured that out for myself the other night. What I need is someone to help me build relationships. And that, Ms. Daniels, sounds right up your alley."

Build relationships. Ha! Little does he know. "Thank you, Leo. May I have a few days to consider it?"

"Of course. But let me know soon. Today's Friday. Maybe you can let me know by the end of next week?"

"Sounds good. And if I have any questions in the meantime?"

"You have my number. Just call me."

I'm surprised there isn't another wink. He stands up. Extends his hand. And I take it. "Thank you, Leo. You've surprised me with this, but I have to say I'm excited by the possibilities."

"Good. Excited is good."

Oh, my. The double entendres continue. But I am. Excited. More than he knows, and more than I should be. I just can't let him know how much, now can I?

Chapter 4

She's an interesting girl, Lily Daniels. I suppose I should call her a woman, not a girl, but she's so young, and seems so innocent. There's something about her. Can't put my finger on it. I mean, the other night, at the reception, she smiled at me like no woman has in years. And I got sucked in by it. Been thinking about her much more than I care to. Then today, when she came to my office, she was all business.

So, what's a guy like me to do? Well, the only thing I could do. I offered her a job. Yes, it was contrived, but I did it anyway. She'll add some quirky energy to this place. And it'll put her in closer proximity to me without crossing any lines of impropriety. Lizzie be damned. I'm not gonna screw this girl. Just, well, play a little. If she'll let me. A guy gets to have a few toys, right?

Chapter 5

Of course I accept the job. And while my original intentions might have been skewed toward the "let's play with the chemistry between us" sort of thing, I know enough to draw a firm line as soon as he becomes my boss. Besides, I was terrible at chemistry, remember?

We work well together. Even seem to have an intuitive sense of how to interact with one another. It's perfect. For a good long while. Until it isn't. But it isn't Leo's fault.

Friday the thirteenth. Nine o'clock.

Today is Leo's birthday. Around ten o'clock, we try to talk him into allowing us to take him out to lunch. He says, "I'm too busy."

I say, "Aw, c'mon. Cut loose for a change."

He says, "Is that any way to talk to your boss?" Then winks.

One o'clock. A group of us head out to one of our favorite lunch spots. I make sure Leo and I are seated next to each other. Meanwhile he, another he you haven't met yet and never will, is tying the knot.

Three o'clock. I'm back at my desk. The phone rings. "Hello. This is Liliana Daniels. How may I help you?"

"Have you talked to your father today?"

Oh boy, she's jumping right in. It's my mother. I dread when she calls me at work, because it always means drama. Her drama. And more often than not an argument, because in spite of the fact that my parents separated over a year ago, and I'm a grown up child, she still does her best to manipulate me to take sides. And I am in way too good of a mood today to deal with her stuff. I do NOT want this now.

I slip into the monotone voice Eddie tells me I use with her when I don't want to engage. "No. I've been at work all day."

"Well, we can't find him."

"What do you mean you can't find him?"

"He didn't show up at work today, and his boss called me a little while ago looking for him."

"So maybe he's sick."

"Well, we called the house, and he didn't answer."

She's such a drama queen. There's nobody here to witness it but I'm certain I just rolled my eyes. I say, "Then maybe he's out somewhere. Maybe his car broke down or something."

"Lily, he was supposed to be at work this morning at eight and nobody has heard a word from him. He's more responsible than that and you know it."

Why is she starting an argument with me over something out of my control? But I hear the fear in her voice. And now it begins to creep into mine, accompanied by the feeling that starts somewhere deep in your gut, when the facts begin to not make sense, and you start to believe something might be horribly wrong. Neither of us voices it out loud, but I know exactly what she is thinking.

She says, "I think someone needs to go by the house to see if he's there. But I don't want to do it by myself. And I don't want to bother your brother at work." *Gee, thanks, Mom. It's okay to interrupt my day, but not his?*

I say, "Well, I'm thirty miles away, and I'm at work, too, so what do you expect me to do about it?" I know I sound annoyed, even while I do my best to fight off the anxiety that's just set up camp in my bones. *Don't buy into her drama, Lily. You know everything's probably fine.*

She says, "I'm going to call Brian and see if he can take a walk down the street and peek in the garage windows to see if his car is there."

"Okay, fine. You do that if it will make you feel better. Call me, please, when you hear from him."

I sit back in my desk chair, absentmindedly rubbing my huge swell of a belly, not sure if it is meant to soothe the baby or me. Time slows to a dead crawl. I've just spent five minutes staring at the calendar on the far wall and if you ask me what the picture is on it, I will tell you I haven't a clue.

Four o'clock. I'm useless here. It's late enough now I can slip out unnoticed, but before I do, I dial her number. "I'm heading home. I'll be there if you need to call me, okay?"

"Okay, honey. I'm sure everything will be fine."

Then why the hell did you call me in the first place?

I call Eddie to bring him up to speed. He reassures me, but agrees to come home a little early so I won't be there alone. *Why is everyone creating such drama around this? I'm sure it's something simple. My father isn't beholden to have to tell us everywhere he goes. We'll be laughing about this by dinnertime.*

I gather up my belongings and head home. I am in the door safe and sound for no more than three minutes when the phone rings. *Here we go again.* I grab the receiver off the wall. She launches right in. "His car is in the garage, and the house is locked up tight." *Oh crap.* "So Brian called one of his police friends, and they're going to break into the house."

Talk about drama. "Do you really think that's necessary? I mean, maybe he's sick, and he's sleeping. You know, like maybe he's intentionally not answering the phone because he wants to be left alone. Maybe he took it off the hook. Maybe..."

"Lily. Stop."

And I do. Because I'm thinking the same thing she is.

She says, "He was supposed to move out today."

I'm quiet for a few seconds as I take in this new piece of information, then ask, "What are you talking about?"

"Our divorce. He was supposed to move out today, I'm getting the house, and I'm not sure he had a place to go."

I'm stunned. I mean, I knew they were separated, and he's been living in the house while she's been in a rented condo, but nobody mentioned divorce. I say, "What the *hell* are you talking about?"

She says, "Well, I didn't want to make a big deal of it, so I didn't say anything to you, but our lawyers got involved a month or so ago, and..."

"Okay, mother. Just stop talking, please." *I can't deal with this right now. I'm thirty four weeks pregnant and we were all together for a family dinner like about two weeks ago and nobody said anything about divorce and now my father has disappeared and...*

Her voice cuts through my thoughts. "Lily, I'm so sorry."

"Sorry for what?" I ask. Now on top of worried I'm angry. At her. For not telling me more about this sooner so that I could be there for him. "Please call me as soon as you know anything."

"I will. And Lily, I love you."

"Sure. I know you do. I love you, too." I say the right words, hollow as they likely sound.

We hang up. And I begin to wait, again. While my mind is reeling. I put the kettle on to brew a cup of chamomile tea. Remind myself to take slow, deep breaths. A divorce? She never mentioned that. *Don't jump to false conclusions, Lily.*

He's been dry for months. Could this have pushed him off the wagon?

Eddie walks in the door two minutes after I hang up the phone. "Any word yet?"

I fill him in on the last phone call. And we wait. Together. Until the phone rings, again.

We look at each other, not sure who should pick up. I'm terrified of what might be on the other end of this call, but I grab the receiver off the wall before he makes a move. "Is he okay?"

The voice isn't my mother's. It's Judith, Brian's wife. They've lived down the street for the past twenty five years, and known me since before I was born. Brian and my father grew up together half a century ago. He shouldn't have been dragged into this. "Lily, I'm so sorry. He's in a better place now."

Why do people say that? A moan leaves my lips, and Eddie reaches for the phone, but I turn my back to him. I say to her, "Tell me, please," and push the button that enables speaker phone mode.

"The police broke into the house, and they found your father. He made sure nobody else would find him. Lily, I know he loved you."

And there it is. My father in the past tense.

I'm an orphan at thirty-one. Like some sort of ill drawn Disney heroine, a hugely pregnant, quasi-happily-married orphan.

Chapter 6

I thank her for calling. Mumble, "I gotta go now." Hang up the phone. And wonder what one is supposed to do, or feel, after hearing a loved one just died by his own hand?

I feel... relief. For him. Which I am quite certain is NOT what one is supposed to feel. But it's real. His life had been so tortured for the past year. No, correct that. Years. Eddie and I often joked that if we had to live with my mother we would drink, too. But that's not fair. Not to her, anyway.

Think, Lily. What do you need to do? Before I can answer myself, the phone rings again. I don't think I can talk to anyone, not right now, but out of habit I answer. "Hello?" And then my brain kicks in, wanting to say something absurd like, *"This is Liliana Daniels. My father just committed suicide. How may I help you?"*

"Lily, I am so sorry." Those are my mother's first words to me, after.

And as reflex response to her, I say, "It's okay. It's not your fault." Which right now, honestly, is the furthest thing from the truth in my head, but we've always protected her, so why should this moment be any different?

She asks, "Are you okay?"

Stupid question. I say, "I don't know. I guess. Sure, I will be. Are you?" And it occurs to me for the first time tonight that there will be extra worry directed my way. So I add, "I'm home, and Eddie is here with me, and I'm going to call Mariann, my midwife, to let her know what is happening." Which I hadn't even thought of doing until this moment, but it does make sense.

She says, "Well, let me know if you need anything. I guess we'll need to get together tomorrow to make arrangements."

"Uh, sure, whatever." *Arrangements? She's going there already?* My mind is just beginning to attempt to wrap around the idea of him as gone and she's talking about making plans to bring closure. Probably her next call will be to the movers. *Insolent bitch.*

I say, "Call me tomorrow. I need to go now." Then hang up, look at Eddie, and realize he has been able to hear only half of the conversation. "She wants to talk about arrangements. But I just can't..." He reaches his arms out. I collapse into them, and the tears begin. "I need to call Mariann. I don't think she can do anything, but I at least need to be able to tell people that I did."

"One step at a time, Lily. Just breathe." Eddie isn't always my rock, but right now he's doing a fine job.

"No, let me call her. I need to DO something, not just sit here." I dial her number. She answers right away.

"Hi, Lily. You okay?"

"No, Mariann, I'm not. I mean, the baby is, but, it's, well..." Words fail me. I need to learn how to speak the truth out loud. "It's my father. I just learned, oh crap, I'm not even sure how to say this, but he's gone. I... I mean... he... well, I just found out he committed suicide today." There. It's out of my mouth.

"Oh, Lily. I am so sorry. Are you okay?"

Why does everyone keep asking me that? I say, "Yes, Mariann, right now, I think I am. I mean, you're the first person I've even told. It's all new and fresh and I just wanted to check in with you so that you know since I have a feeling there will be a lot of people worrying about me because..."

She finishes the sentence for me. "...because you are thirty four weeks pregnant and your stress level just went through the roof but let me remind you, Lily, I know you to be one strong woman, and you will get through this. Now, I'm going to give you advice that will surprise you. I highly recommend you have a glass of wine, and just do your best to relax tonight. If you want, I can come over and check you."

"No, that's okay. But thank you for offering. Can I call you later if I feel like I need it?"

"Of course. And Lily..."

"Yes?"

"You WILL be fine, and so will your baby. I know it, because I know you."

"Thank you, Mariann. I'll try to remember that. I need to go now."

"Call me if you need anything. I'm here for you."

"Will do. And thank you again." I hang up the phone. Look at Eddie. "Would you believe she wants me to have a glass of wine?"

He says, "Sounds like a fine idea."

And with that, we begin the next chapter of our lives.

If only I had known, I might have not gotten out of bed today, though it wouldn't have made a difference. The game changer was out of my hands. I breathe a silent prayer that I will be able to sleep tonight, then within minutes feel myself on the verge of collapse. I just want to close my eyes and disappear for a while. To dream something lovely to take me away from this slice of real life. I will never see him again. He's left me, alone, with my baby.

Chapter 7

Saturday morning. God must have heard my prayer last night, because somehow I did manage to sleep. Slept what I would under other circumstances call the sleep of the dead, but that is just too inappropriate today. He may be at rest, but our trials have just begun.

Tomorrow afternoon we will meet with the funeral director at my brother's house. I'm told that unbeknownst to me we were already meant to be there, for a surprise baby shower, now postponed indefinitely. Death is so fucking inconvenient.

Today will be spent making phone calls. Friends, cousins, aunts, uncles, co-workers. So many who need to be told. Thankfully it is a sunny day. Eddie makes me promise to try to stay as balanced as possible, so I agree to a fifteen minute fresh air break for every forty five spent on the phone. I am repeatedly asked for delicate details, and after about the fifth call, have crafted a rote response. "I'm sorry, I simply don't know. Perhaps in another few weeks." It's an honest answer. I myself haven't asked for details because I'm not ready to know. Not yet. Visually oriented as I am, I do not care to have pictures in my head. I hope he chose a peaceful, pain free way, and fear he did not. It's none of their business, anyway.

The day goes by quickly with all there is to do. Bedtime can't come soon enough. The second night.

Sunday afternoon. The funeral director speaks to my mother as the point person, and refers to her as his wife. I want to scream. *But they were divorcing! She pushed him to this!*

Of course it wouldn't be fair to blame her. Everyone knows that suicide is a personal decision. Many consider it to be a most selfish act, but I don't see it that way. One can only be pushed so far before feeling... pushed.

She produces a piece of paper, his all too cliché suicide note. Appears he was detailing his death while I was out celebrating Leo's birthday. The note states that he doesn't want a funeral, just cremation, and suggests we might toss his ashes into the sea. It's not a surprise. He was a simple man. And a sailor. We all agree on the cremation. Where the ashes will go is a detail that doesn't have to be decided today.

I argue for a memorial service, in spite of what he wrote. "It's for us, not for him. We need to be able to grieve, and feel supported by others who loved him, and love us."

My mother doesn't want to spend the money. I say, "It can be simple, and you know I have minister friends who would be happy to help." She acquiesces.

The date is set. Four days away. Because three days away would be the anniversary of my grandmother's birthday, and it just wouldn't be right to bury a man on his mother's birthday. Such are the details that draw our attention today.

The obituary will read "He died unexpectedly at home." I remember reading that in other obituaries, and wondering what it meant. Now I understand it is code, a secret shorthand used for suicide. Apparently it is okay to state the cause of death as cancer, or heart disease, or injuries sustained in an auto accident, but taboo to use the word suicide. I am now part of a secret clan who understands. But I didn't ask to be invited in. I don't want to be here. Though I suppose nobody does.

Thursday morning. We gather at the church. Get through the service. "When are you due?" is the question of the day, perhaps as distraction away from the obvious drama at hand. "Not for another six weeks. I'm fine," I say repeatedly, with a smile, when what I really want to say is, "Seriously, people? I'm NOT fine! My father just committed suicide, and my mother is playing the sad, deserted widow. They filed for DIVORCE! Did you know that?"

I stand beside her, and hear her tell person after person, "Oh, I'm devastated. We were just starting to be friends again." *FRIENDS???* My inner voice is screaming now, but I am too polite to do anything other than smile. I count the minutes until I can get away from her, have Eddie drive me home, and pretend none of this is real. If I wasn't thirty four weeks pregnant I would dive deep into a few stiff drinks, but I suppose that wouldn't be the proper way to celebrate an alcoholic's life. Or maybe it would.

There is no rule book at a time like this. We're making it up as we go.

Chapter 8

I want to go back to work right away, back to some sense of normal, but Mariann tells me I should take it easy until the baby is born, only a few weeks away. She tells me I don't need the extra stress. I compromise with a few half days, so that I can wrap up some projects still on my desk.

One month later, on the thirteenth, my daughter is born. There's no time for me to grieve. I need to revel in her birth, but honestly, it's all so hard. My father chose to exit in spite of my love for him. He didn't feel it. Or maybe I simply didn't do a good enough job of showing it to him. If I had, he would have stayed, wouldn't he?

I know. I've read the books and listened to the experts. Suicide is a personal decision. But seriously, if someone feels the love of their family, are they going to do that? I was thirty four weeks pregnant. Didn't he want to stick around to meet his newest grandson or granddaughter?

Grace. Look it up in your Merriam Webster dictionary. "Unmerited divine assistance given humans for their regeneration or sanctification." Oh boy, that's what I need, and then some. So I choose the name Grace, and Eddie agrees, so that every time I look at her I will be reminded that God loves me, no matter how much I do to try to get in my own way.

Life goes on.

That's another thing often heard around death and funerals. And we want to believe it even though at the time it sounds ridiculous. Life may go on, whether we want it to or not, but it is irrevocably changed.

Which is how, just shy of a miracle if you ask me, two years have passed, and I am the mother of a beautiful daughter, and I am not in the office. I originally planned to go back to work after the usual maternity leave time off, but I didn't. As soon as I held her in my arms, I knew I couldn't do it. And I needed to get back to the easel. It became my therapy.

On top of that, Eddie and I decided our marriage didn't work so well any more. The public story blames it on the stress that landed on all of us after my father's death, but that's not the whole story. There are some things best kept private.

One night at bedtime, Grace was only about six weeks old, Eddie was in the nursery alone with her and she wouldn't stop crying. He'd told me to leave them alone, he wanted a chance to get her to bed on his own. So armed with only a bottle, he tried. He really did. And I tried to stay away. But the hormones were still flowing, and after about half an hour, I couldn't listen to the screaming any more. I walked up the steps, and peeked into the room before he could see me. I expected to see a loving father doing his best to comfort his daughter.

Instead, there he sat holding Grace over his head, shaking her. I screamed. "Stop that! You'll hurt her." Rushed in and took her from him. He left the room in a huff. I sat down in the chair, put Grace's head to my breast, and we both sighed. Her tears stopped as mine began. I knew what I had just witnessed was wrong, even though nobody had ever told me about shaken baby syndrome. A mother just knows.

The next day, he accused me of overreacting, as other men have before him. And as I have before, I acquiesced and took the blame. Maybe it was my fault, because I nursed her to sleep every night, and she didn't take the bottle well. Or maybe I did overreact, still full of postpartum hormones. Maybe it wasn't as bad as I thought. Though for the first time I began to question our marriage. I prayed for direction. "Please, God, give me a sign. What should I do?"

Eddie grew depressed after my father's death. Did you catch the irony of that statement? HE grew depressed. Which left me, the daughter of the dead man, at home taking care of an infant, trying to hold it together for my husband, with no time or space for me to mourn. And while I began to think about leaving, the truth is I was afraid that if I did, or pushed for him to be the one to leave, that he might do as my father did. And I didn't want that one on me. No thank you. I was not going to repeat my parents' history.

I watched him put his fist through a wall one time when he was angry. You'd think I might have paid closer attention to that, but I didn't. Just prayed some more. "Please God, just one more sign. A clear and obvious one I can't miss."

It went on like that for another year or so. Until in the middle of an argument he pushed me. Didn't knock me down or leave bruises or anything like that, but when it happened, we both stopped, locked eyes, and knew. It was the last straw. He came to the edge of losing control, and I, well, I said, "Okay, God, I get it." I'd witnessed what his fists could do when provoked. I could handle emotional scars, but I wasn't going to stick around to collect physical ones. Grace and I moved out two weeks later. Our first ridiculously stupid move.

He should have been the one to leave. It would have been much more simple. Just him and his stuff, instead of me and my stuff, and my daughter and her stuff, and my entire painting studio. My lawyer told me (yes, by now I had a lawyer) to do my best to annoy him to the point that he would want to leave. I tried it for a weekend. But I couldn't do it. I wasn't going to push him to the edge. So on Monday I began my search for an apartment. Took less time than I thought it would to find one I could afford that included space for a studio. I strapped on my big girl shoes, took a deep breath (several, actually) and called Make My Day movers. The first time.

Chapter 9

Three months later, I find myself on the phone making a call I really wish I didn't have to, leaving a voice mail I'd rather not. "Hey Leo. It's Lily. I hope you are well. Wish this was a social call, but it's not. I don't know if you're in the loop of the latest gossip, but Grace and I are on our own now. And, well, I need to earn some money. Is there any chance my old position with you is still available? We haven't talked in a while, and I realize you've probably hired someone else by now, but I figured I'd at least ask. Please give me a call when you have a moment."

There. I did it. I hate to give up being full time mom and artist, but a girl has to do what a girl has to do. Now, I wait for his call.

Seven o'clock. Grace and I are in the middle of dinner. The phone rings. "Hello, this is Lily."

"Lily, it's Leo. How the heck are you?"

"Been better, been worse. I trust you got my voicemail?"

"Yes. And of course I'd be happy to hire you back."

"Wow. That's great news. I figured you'd have brought in someone else to replace me by now."

"Lily, there is no one who can replace you."

I start the following week. I'm not thrilled, but it gives me some financial security. Only three days a week, Tuesday, Wednesday, and Thursday, so I still have some Grace time, and paint time. Besides, it's good to be back with Leo. Familiar. Flexible. And only occasionally flirty.

Chapter 10

Six months later, I walk into the office on a Tuesday morning, and there are balloons. "What did I miss?" I ask Debbie, Leo's administrative assistant.

"Big announcement yesterday. He's leaving."

How did he get this one past me? Were there signs I didn't notice? My heart sinks. Yes, I know I said it's been strictly professional, but deep down I enjoy working with him more than I care to admit. And at the risk of sounding selfish I'm not certain my job will exist for me without him.

"Is he in?" I ask.

"Nope, he left this morning for a few days in Boston." Now it makes sense. The museum job he mentioned the night we first met.

"Oh. Well. Okay. I'm just surprised. He didn't breathe a word of it to me."

"Yeah, he's pretty good at hiding things when he wants to. Kept it secret from all of us until it was a done deal. But hey, he asked me to have you call him when you got in. Said you should call him from his office, so he can tell you more of what he has in mind."

"Sounds like I'm being issued a secret mission or something."

"You know him, he likes to keep a little mystery in his life."

Mystery? Didn't take me long to discover Leo keeps secrets better than anyone I've ever known. Decided to move to Boston and never breathed a word of it to me. Not that he owed me an explanation. Apparently my mistake in thinking we were closer than we are.

I walk into his office. Close the door behind me. I sit down in his chair. HIS chair. I look at the pictures on his desk, from his perspective. There are the obligatory family ones. The wife and kids. And one of his boat. The one he promised I might see some day, but never did.

I open a desk drawer. While the top of his desk is neat and tidy, the inside of the drawer is a jumble of, well, everything. I open another. It's full of papers. Not in organized file folders, just stacks of them, intermingled with old magazines, and newspapers. I swivel around and open a credenza drawer. More piles. Impeccably groomed to the outer world, right down to his manicured fingertips, while his inner world is a mess. He keeps it well hidden. I've been working side by side with him, organized his work life, or so I thought, and somehow I hadn't a clue about his true state of affairs.

I'm spying into a world where I don't belong, but that never stopped me before, so I go back to the middle drawer for a closer inspection. The one most people use for pencils, rubber bands, and paper clips is a jumble of empty pill bottles, loose change, and receipts. I'm tempted to clean up his mess. But he hasn't asked me to do it, at least not yet, so I close the drawer, pick up the phone, and dial the number Debbie gave me to his hotel room.

He answers on the first ring. "Leo Stocker."

"Hello, Dr. Stocker. This is a voice from your soon to be past."

"Well, good morning, Lily. I was expecting your call."

"Yeah, I bet you were. I can't believe your secretary knew about this before I did. Pretty sneaky of you."

"I know. Kinda sprung it on you, didn't I?"

I'm guessing he winked involuntarily when he said that. "Not nice, Leo. I thought we had a closer working relationship than that."

"Yeah, well, some things are best kept discreet. So, now you know. What do you think?"

"I suppose I'm happy for you. I mean, it's obviously a great professional move, and you did tell me when we first met that eventually you were going to head north. You just caught me by surprise, that's all."

"I know. So listen, here's the plan. I gave notice last week. I'm here for a couple more days, then when I come back I'll clean out my office, tie up a few loose ends, and head north."

"Sounds awfully fast."

"It is. And I'm going to need your help with a few things, if you don't mind."

I take a deep breath. Still can't believe this is happening. "Sure. What can I do for you?"

"Well, you told me you have some experience around boats. Mine's still in the water out at the lake. Can you help me pull it?"

"Okay. I guess I can."

"And you're welcome to start cleaning out my office before I get back. You know my files better than anyone."

If I hadn't just seen what a mess his desk is, I would probably respond with an enthusiastic yes, but not now. I say, "How about if you and I do that together when you get back?"

"I'd be much happier if you'd just do it for me. I'm not so good at cleaning, and terrible at making decisions about what to keep and what to let go of."

Yeah, he's got that one right. "Okay, I'll do it. Maybe I can come in for a little while over the weekend."

"No, just do it during regular work time. Remember, Lily, I'm still your boss, at least for a little while."

I am tempted to answer with a curt "yes, sir!" but think better of it. My mind races another few steps ahead. "Do you have any idea who I'll be working with after you leave?"

"Wow, you do move on quickly. Thought you'd be sad for at least a little while without me."

"Of course I will, Leo. You know that."

"I would hope so. Thought you and I worked quite well together."

"Yes, we do, and we have, but you're still leaving me, and I need to think about my future, right?"

"Yes, you do. Though I must say you surprise me, Lily, when you show your pragmatic side. Honestly, I don't know the answer to your question. I'm sure there will be a new head of the department, but I was thinking of recommending you to be the one to take over at least some of the things we did together. Might even have a nice promotion to go with it."

I sigh. I know I *should* be ecstatic, or at the very least, grateful. "Leo, you know I only want to work part-time. There's Grace, and my painting, and..."

"I know, Lily. Let's just wait and talk about it when I get back. How's lunch sound, this Friday? For the work stuff. My treat. And then maybe we can find some time over the weekend to pull the boat."

"You know I don't usually work on Fridays, but I'll see if I can find someone to take Grace for the afternoon. I'll let you know later about the weekend." I try to sound enthusiastic, but I've never been adept at hiding my feelings.

"It's going to be okay, Lily. You'll see. Trust me."

"I do, Leo." *My first mistake?* "I'll see you on Friday. Have a good week. Boston's a great city. Maybe I can come visit you there sometime."

"Or you could just come work for me."

"Now there's a thought. But not likely. My life is here."

"Never say never, Lily. You never know where life might lead."

Chapter 11

Boston. The big city. Might have been better if it was Fort Lauderdale, or Miami, or just about anywhere the sun shines more than the snow flies, but at least I'm getting away.

Lizzie's thrilled. All she can talk about is finding a place for us to live in one of the posh suburbs. Like Wellesley. Or Newton. Anywhere reeking of status and country clubs and society luncheons. As for me, I'd rather be right in the heart of the city and campus. Feel the pulse. Cruise the coeds. God, I can't wait to move.

I've suggested to Lizzy more than once in the past week that we could use this as the perfect excuse to separate our lives. I mean, think about it. She could tell her friends, "Oh, Leo's got himself a great new position. He's excited to move, but Boston's just not my kind of place. So I'm going to buy a condo in Washington." A long distance relationship of convenience. A lot of couples do it nowadays. It would get me away from her without having to separate from her Daddy's money. Sounds like a perfect plan to me.

But she's not buying it. Told me, "I'll come with you on your next trip, and while you're working, I'll venture out with a realtor or two." Wouldn't be how I would do it, but what the heck. Let her Daddy buy us another big fancy place. If it's what she wants, and it lets me keep what I want, then so let it be.

Except then there's Lily. Sure will miss the girl. Would love to re-hire her and move her to Boston with me. Though after working side by side with her as we did, well, let's just say I now know I want more from her than she can give. So, maybe it would be better if we just say goodbye.

Always more fish in the sea.

Chapter 12

Friday. Lunch day. We meet on the sidewalk. Go inside together. Sit down in a booth in a quiet corner and place our orders. We discuss his transition schedule. He tells me more about his new position, at a prestigious museum in the city. "Come work for me," he says. Tempting as he might be, I say no thank you.

It feels different today, like the chemistry I thought I felt the night we met has resurfaced. We ignored it after he hired me, except for the occasional wink in a meeting. Or both of us lingering after hours at the end of a work day, and ending up in his office discussing life. But we never crossed the line to inappropriate. Now, with him leaving, it becomes the elephant in the living room, or in this case, the dining room.

We talk more about his new work. Which morphs into a discussion about careers, and moving on, and life choices.

"Have you ever been in a long-distance relationship?"

His question catches me off guard. *Why is he asking? Okay. I'll go with it.* "Yes, in fact, I have. My first truly serious relationship was after my freshman year in college. A summer romance. Then we went our separate ways back to school, and saw each other only on occasional weekends."

"And how did that work out?"

"Oh, I don't know. At the time it seemed pretty rough. Then I transferred colleges to put myself closer to him."

"And I assume that was Grace's father?"

"Nope. A different guy. We broke up just a few months later. Apparently we worked better far apart than together. So, why do you ask?"

"I'm trying to convince Elizabeth to stay here rather than move with me. You know, keep her close to her friends, and her social life, rather than start over somewhere new. But she's not buying it."

"I suppose some couples are able to do that, but I think you have to have a pretty strong marriage to begin with. Honestly, I think I'd want my husband to be with me. I like having someone in the bed next to me at night."

"Yeah, well, we've not been doing so well in that department lately, so maybe some distance would be good for us."

"Leo, I'm not sure I should wade any further into this conversation with you."

"Why not?"

I respond with a look. Direct. Eye to eye. It starts as a serious one. Then we both grin, simultaneously. Not another word is spoken. The waiter shows up at the table, asks us if we want anything else. Leo says, "No thanks, we're all set here. Just the check." He manages to maintain eye contact with me through the entire exchange.

"Leo, we need to..."

"I know, Lily. Let's go." He pays the bill. We walk outside and down the sidewalk together. There's his car. A white turbo Porsche 911. It's gorgeous, even if on the edge of cliché for a man his age.

I ask, "So, is this your mid-life crisis car?"

"My goodness, Lily, you are blunt today."

"I'm sorry. I thought by now I could speak my mind with you."

"It's okay. You just amuse me."

"So answer my question."

"No, the car's not a mid-life thing. And she's not compensating for anything either."

"Excuse me. She?"

"Yes. I said she. The car. Surely you know all cars and boats are female."

"I know it about boats, but I don't think I ever considered it for cars. Though I do name mine. Does this one have a name?"

"Of course. Lily, meet Angel."

"Angel?"

"Well, it's my hope that she'll protect me and keep me out of trouble."

"Ah, I see. Nice thought. How's that worked for you so far?"

"So far so good. One day at a time." He winks.

I ask, "So what's the story?"

"Well, you know I had a heart attack several years ago."

"Yes, and I've often wondered about it. Aren't you a bit young for that? Was it bad genetics?"

"No. Just too driven. You think I'm a mess now, you should've known me then. Caged up in the hospital like I was, all I could think of was heading out on a stretch of highway and driving way beyond the speed limit. Promised myself that if I got out alive I'd treat myself to something sleek and fast. Life's far too short to always play it safe. About a week after the docs let me out, well, here she is. So hey, I need to do a quick trip to Walmart for a few things. Care to ride along?"

I check my watch. Two o'clock. Grace is with the sitter until three. "Sure. Love to."

He opens the door for me. "Your carriage, ma'am." *Seriously? A carriage? Are there mice hiding somewhere to turn into horses, too? Oh, stop it, Lily. You're getting way ahead of yourself.*

I settle into the front seat. As we pull out of the parking space, he reaches for the stick shift, and the side of his hand grazes my knee. I jump from the shock of his touch. Chemistry be damned. This is electricity.

Long underwear. The thermal waffle weave type. I know, it's neither romantic nor sexy, but there is a display of it in Walmart. As we walk past I say, "Hey, Leo, check this out. You might want to grab a pair of these. New England winters can be tough."

"Yeah, you're right. I'm definitely not looking forward to that part. Wish I was headed to Florida instead. I'm not so much into the cold." He laughs, but ignores my suggestion.

Three blue plastic bags full of odds and ends later, we are back in Angel.

He says, "So, how does your schedule look for the weekend? Any chance you can help me with the boat?"

"Let me check with Eddie, see if he'd be willing to take Grace for a while in the afternoon. Otherwise I might have to bring her along."

"That'd be fine. She might enjoy it. I'll call you tomorrow."

The drive to my apartment is short. I open the door, and without thinking, lean over and give him a quick kiss on the cheek. Then exit the car as quickly as I can, and walk away without looking back. I wonder if he is watching me. Hope he is. Though why should it matter? He's married. And moving. And I'm just dreaming. Indulging a fantasy I stuffed away when he hired me. Guess sometime in the past several days I allowed it to sneak out of its box where I had tucked it away, neat and tidy and out of sight while we worked together.

Maybe it would be more accurate to say it was partly tucked away. While I maintained a professional demeanor with him on the outside, I'll admit I still on occasion fantasized on the inside. Sometimes late in the evening I would go for a walk across campus, look up, and see his light on in his office. That's what men do who aren't happy at home, isn't it? Well, one of the things they do. They spend a lot of time in their office during the hours when nobody else does. What he was doing there, I can only guess. The good Leo version would suggest he was working. The other version might allow for there to have been another woman before I ever thought of becoming the other woman.

And there were a few photos of him I kept in my desk, buried deep in a file. Nobody knew I had those. I stole them from one of the public relations department's files. When I needed to dream a little, I'd study them, and wonder about this man who fascinates me so.

Though honestly, why he does, I'm still not sure. But I'm getting ahead of myself.

The boat, Lily. The boat.

I'll see him again tomorrow. He wants me to help him pull his boat, or as Elizabeth so lovingly refers to it, his damn boat.

Chapter 13

"C'mon Grace, let's go. We don't want to keep Dr. Stocker waiting."

"Okay, Mom, I'm coming, but I can't find my navy blue headband."

"So just wear something else. We need to go. Now."

"But I need that one."

"And why does it matter?"

"Because it's the one with the fish on it."

"We're not fishing today, Grace, just helping him take his boat out of the water."

"But Mommmmm..."

How is it my dear young child has already perfected her whiny voice?

We arrive about five minutes late. He's down at the dock.

"Welcome to Leo's heaven," he says.

I say, "It's not the north Atlantic, but at least it's water." I'm a little concerned there might be some awkwardness after my kiss on the cheek yesterday, but if there is, it's not apparent.

"So, before we pull the boat, shall we take her for one last spin around the lake?" he asks.

"Sounds good to me. Grace, you get on first. Dr. Stocker will help you."

He reaches out his hand, and she takes it, then steps down into the cockpit.

"Pretty confident young lady you've got here," he says. "Takes after her mother, I see."

"Thanks. May I join your party?" I ask.

"Absolutely. Let me help you on board." He reaches his hand toward me, and I take it. Not because I have to. I'm quite capable of boarding a boat by myself, thank you. I take his hand because I want to. And for those few brief seconds, as I step onto the boat, I am keenly aware of how good my hand feels in his.

I keep to myself how amused I am by the size of his boat. Not sure what I pictured, but it's definitely smaller than I expected, and I know better than to say anything about it. Never, ever, say anything about the size of a man's boat, unless it's a big one, and you can honestly say something like "my what a big boat you have" but if it's a little one, well, you know what I mean.

I've been around boats since I was younger than Grace is now, but I allow him to tell me what he wants me to do, ever the boss in control, and I do as I am told, ever the obedient employee. Except I forget, one time, when we first get back to the dock after our boat ride. Without thinking about it, I grab the line, hop off, and tie a perfect hitch around the cleat.

Leo notices. "Wow, where'd a girl like you learn to do that?"

"Oh, this? My father. He was a sailor. Taught me how to tie all sorts of fancy knots."

"Well, pardon me. I just never saw a woman do that."

"Oh, Leo, there are a lot of things I know how to do that might surprise you."

"I bet you do."

Oh my. *Stop it right now, Lily. Focus. Your daughter is with you.*

Grace thinks this is all great fun. I think it is, well, not exactly the fantasy I'd hoped for. But maybe if I'm patient something wonderful will happen... a knowing glance, or a stolen embrace. Of course it doesn't. Not with Grace here with us. It's simply not appropriate, and he's wise enough to know that. No fairy tale this time. At least not until the wicked witch shows up. I was unaware she was on the invitation list for today.

Elizabeth. Such a beautiful name for such an unhappy woman. She's just pulled into the driveway, and is standing hands on hips looking our way. I thought the look she gave me the night our paths first crossed at the reception was bad, but it was nothing compared to this. Apparently it doesn't matter to her that my daughter is with us.

"Stay here. I'll handle this," he says. He walks across the lawn to her. She gestures repeatedly toward me. I cringe every time she does, and try to keep Grace distracted away from seeing too much of it. How is it possible to feel guilty for something I haven't even done? Has she read my mind?

She's in her car now, leaving. Leo's walking back down toward us, here at the dock.

"Well, that looked uncomfortable," I say.

"Not at all. I'll tell you about it later," he says, as he nods toward Grace. "How about we get this boat out of the water, then I'll buy my two helpers some ice cream."

The following week is spent cleaning out his office, just two professional colleagues working together. And then we say goodbye, quite unceremoniously, at the end of the day on a Thursday afternoon. I wish him well. We share a professional hug. I go home to Grace. On with my life, with my new job. Let him go on with his. All's well that ends well.

Or so I think. Until the phone rings on Saturday afternoon. It's Debbie. "So, it turns out Leo isn't actually leaving town for another week or two. Some of the other faculty members decided to put together a last minute going away party. I know you don't usually work on Mondays, but do you want to come and say goodbye?"

I thought I already had. But what could it hurt? "Sure. I'd love to. What time?"

"Starts at two."

Of course I go. Bring on the drama.

I walk into the party. It's already in full swing. I scan the crowd for him. There he is, his back to me, in the middle of a group of eight or ten others. I walk over and stand next to him, silently. He doesn't look at me, but there is a shift in his body language, a slight move toward me, like he feels me here. We stand next to each other, without sharing a word, while others come over to say their goodbyes. They're used to seeing me by his side, but I can feel something different in the air. Like a premonition. Do our souls know something we do not?

Our goodbye is simple. A hug, but no kiss. He leaves the next day.

He did as he said he would. Carved out an expanded set of responsibilities for me to continue within the department, with a sizable increase in salary. The search is on for his replacement.

Over the next several months we lose touch, mostly. We exchange occasional emails, or I call him with work questions, but the chemistry thing dissipates. Without him here, I don't enjoy my job as much as I used to. It takes up too much of my time. And my painting time is once again compromised. A stifled creative is not a pretty thing. I grow grumpy. And impatient. At the risk of appearing ungrateful, I'm starting to look for a way to leave this job, even though I have grown accustomed to the salary. It's a paycheck, and a pretty good one at that.

Life is fine. I'm okay. Honest I am. Lonely and bored and creatively stuck, but okay.

Chapter 14

Saturday morning. Grace and I are decorating our Christmas tree. The phone rings. Grace answers it in the kitchen. Then yells to me, "Mom, it's for you."

"Who is it?"

"I don't know. Didn't ask."

I don't appreciate the interruption into our morning, but try to sound cheerful anyway. "Hello, this is Liliana Daniels."

"Good morning, Lily." My heart leaps involuntarily at the sound of his voice.

"Oh! Good morning to you, too, Leo. To what do I owe the pleasure of your call?"

"I have an offer for you. One I think you can't refuse."

"Oh? That sounds like fun. What's up?"

"I've talked the museum into creating an assistant's position here, like what you did for me back at the college. Interested?"

"Leo, you know Grace is too young for me to move her away from her dad."

"Aw c'mon, Lily, you need to at least come for an interview."

"But you know my funds are tight for travel…"

"Oh, did I forget to mention that the museum would pay for your trip?"

"Really? It's one of those interviews?"

"Yep. This is the big city. We do things right here. Pay pretty well, too."

"Okay. Now you've got my attention. So tell me more. When, where, how?"

"Next week, if you can make it."

"But it's the week before Christmas, Leo. Are you serious?"

"Absolutely serious. I'll have my secretary book your flights. All you need to do is get yourself onto the plane."

"Alright. Let me see if Eddie can take Grace for a few days. And I need to arrange for time off here."

"Nope. Won't be necessary. You still have Fridays off, right? I'm thinking you can fly up Thursday evening, we'll run the interviews on Friday. You can stay over until Saturday and be back home before the end of the weekend."

"It sounds like you've thought of everything already, Leo."

"Is that a yes?"

"Let me check with Eddie about Grace and I'll get back to you."

We hang up. I call Eddie. He's delighted to have extra time with his daughter. *This is way too easy.*

I call Leo. "I'm all set. Go ahead and buy those tickets. I'm not promising anything, but I certainly could use some time away, so why not at least give it a look."

"There you go. Good plan. I'll send you the details."

"Thank you, Leo."

"No problem. I'll see you at the airport. And if you'll let me, I'll buy you dinner."

"That would be lovely. I'll look forward to it."

Well now, I didn't expect this turn of events when I got out of bed this morning. A trip to Boston, dinner with Leo, and a day of interviews. Time to dust off the resume and tweak it into shape.

I haven't been to Boston since the time I went to the Cape to spend the week with Sarah. She's the one who helped me discover my true love of painting. And a few other things.

Chapter 15

Sarah and I were close friends back in college. Super close. No, not in that way, even though we were physically closer than most women in those days, or at least more than any I'd known. Back then it wasn't like it is now. Women didn't touch other women. And they certainly didn't fall in love. Not in the conservative college town where I was. I don't think I even heard the word lesbian until I was about eighteen. And then, any who were, well, they were all what one might call butch. No such thing as a lipstick lesbian back then. Besides, I couldn't imagine doing anything like that. Or maybe I just didn't know it was an option.

I never questioned why, just knew I felt more comfortable with Sarah than with any other girls, or guys. We'd lie on our backs, up close to each other on the single bed in my dorm room, and talk for hours about the boys in our lives. About how they continually disappointed us.

Sarah had this long brown hair, reminiscent of a luscious mink coat. And she was an athletic, outdoorsy type, so she always had a tan, especially on her back and shoulders. I'd sit behind her and brush her hair, or I'd rub her shoulders for her when she was tired. I suppose I might have occasionally kissed the back of her neck, but it was more of a 'poor baby' sort of kiss. An 'I'm sorry you're sore' gesture. Not sexual. At least I didn't know it was, if it was.

She married soon after graduation. Married well, too. We stayed in touch with the occasional phone call, but I didn't see her after her wedding day. Because as I stood there in my bridesmaid dress and watched her walk down the aisle I battled a fierce case of jealousy. And I didn't know what to do with it. So I did the best thing I could at the time. I walked away. No, correct that. I ran away. From my feelings.

Until a few years later, Sarah calls and invites me for a visit. "I've heard you're painting more, and would love for you to come to the Cape and do some of our views so I can take them with me to Florida this winter." Of course I say yes.

The first two nights her husband is with us. A proper wealthy Bostonian he is, James Anthony Madison. Provides everything she wants, and then some. Gorgeous Cape home on the water. Barn in the back for her horses. Except he doesn't let her out of his sight. At least not while I am there. I think he knows. Or maybe he hopes we will do something in front of him. But we don't. *Sorry to disappoint you, James.*

On the third day, he is called away on business. We have the house to ourselves. Sarah cooks a classic lobster dinner to celebrate the completion of the paintings. And opens a bottle of champagne. Then another. We laugh our way through dinner.

"Did you ever think we'd end up like this?" she asks.

"Like what?"

"I don't know. I always thought you'd be the one with all the money. World famous artist."

"And we know how well that one has turned out so far."

She says, "At least I was wise enough to know I wouldn't amount to anything, so I married James. Found myself a safety net."

I say, "You are way too hard on yourself, Sarah. But I gotta admit you do have a wonderful life here. AND you have a piece of lobster in your hair." I reach up and pluck it. *There it is. Her hair.*

She reaches her hand up and takes mine before I can pull it away. Then looks me straight in the eye. "Have you ever wondered what might have happened if we knew back then..."

"Sarah, that's the champagne talking. I don't think we should go there."

"Why not? I'm serious."

"You're seriously married, Sarah. And besides, that's not who we are."

She lets go of my hand. "I guess you're right. I'm sorry."

"No, don't be sorry. I'm flattered. It's just not..." I don't know what to say. But I realize there is no barrier. And I wonder, is it considered infidelity if a married woman takes on another woman as her lover?

Sarah breaks the awkwardness by standing up and starting to clear the dishes. The moment passes.

I bump her away from the sink. "Here, you cooked. Let me do that. I'll load the dishwasher. You refill the wineglasses. And how about you put on some music?"

"Anita Baker okay?"

"Love it."

I'm at the sink. Humming. It's sultry. Sarah is standing behind me now. Rubbing my shoulders. Close. So close. I move back into her, not realizing what I'm doing. The bubbly. Must be it's gone to my head. Except that's not the part that's taking control of me. She reaches her arms around me. It feels so natural. I take a deep breath, then say "Sarah..."

"Shhhh. Just turn around. Look at me."

I do. Now her hands are on my face. And she's kissing me. I've been kissed by a variety of men, but this is quite different. Her lips are smaller. More delicate. I feel like I'm kissing a baby bird. She feels so fragile, yet at the same time powerful. I pull away, say nothing, just look in her eyes. She takes my hand. Leads me upstairs to her bedroom. Not another word is spoken between us. She lights a candle. Then a second one. I'm standing in the middle of the floor, unsure how to do this. Yes, definitely too much champagne. My mind has taken a vacation, leaving my body alone with this gorgeous creature, knowing full well what it wants. She unbuttons my blouse. Lets it fall open, but does not touch me. Not yet. Then she does the same with her own. Removes her bra. Her body is as beautiful as I had imagined it would be. She takes my hand again, walks backward toward the bed, and pulls me down on top of her. I am stunned by how easy it is to be with her. There should be a part of me screaming that this isn't right. But this, this is... beyond words. I marvel at the feel of her body beneath my hands. So strong, yet pliable to my touch. I kiss her belly. Then work my way up to a breast. Her breast. I cup it first with my hand, then move my mouth to her nipple. It grows hard in my mouth. What a surprising sensation. I had no idea. Hands, mouths, candlelight, soft skin moving together in the candle's glow. Time spent as a single woman, learning how to pleasure myself, has taught me how a woman wants to be touched. She climaxes first. Then turns her attention toward me. She's bolder. Willing to do things I am not yet. Makes love to me as no man ever has. After I finish, she moves up and kisses me.

We lie on our backs here on the bed, side by side, just like we used to.

And I start to giggle.

"What? Did I do something wrong?" she asks.

"Oh, no, not at all. You did everything just right. I'm not laughing at you. I was just thinking back to all those hours we spent lying together on my bed in my dorm room. If we only knew then what we were missing!"

"Lily, you know that..."

"Shhhh. Yes. I do. James comes home tomorrow."

"I can't leave him. It's not the marriage I would have envisioned for myself, but my life is here."

"I know. I didn't ask for anything from you, Sarah. We've been long overdue for this. It can just be what it is, just this one night. Probably best that way. I'll go back to my life, and you stay here in yours. But do promise me one thing, please."

"What's that?" she says.

"I want you to always smile when you think of us, like this."

"Of course. You, too."

"Well, duh!"

We giggle again, then lie in the quiet for several minutes, my fingers entwined in her hair, marveling at the gentleness of the moment.

"So, Sarah, I do have one more favor to ask of you."

"Sure. Name it."

I kiss her neck, then whisper "one more time, please." And she does. And after, we fall asleep in each other's arms. Sweet dreams. If only we'd known then what we know now.

The next day, everything seems normal again. She's already up and dressed when I wake. James returns. Sarah and I share many smiles and knowing glances, but nothing more. The paintings are complete. Time for me to go home. There is just one problem.

Somewhat predictably, I've fallen in love. No, silly, not with her. With the Cape. The sand got a little too deeply into my shoes this time, and I am caught, hook, line, and sinker. I will need to return, someday. I'm just not sure when, or what, it will take to lure me back.

Chapter 16

When is now, and Leo is the lure.

Thursday evening. Wheels down at Logan airport. I'm excited. Yes, I know, more than I should be. But I'd be lying if I didn't admit it.

I'm wearing jeans for travel, with a grey wool turtleneck sweater, and a black French beret. Want to feel and look the part of the artist.

There. He's leaning up against a wall, talking on the phone, his back to me. Without a word I move in behind him, and lean against the wall, mirror image to his stance. Then nudge back until we touch. He turns around ready to scowl at whoever just bumped into him, sees it is me, and grins. "I gotta go now. Talk more tomorrow." He ends his call. "Well, Lily Daniels. Aren't you a sight for sore eyes!" He offers his arms in a broad welcome hug. *Oh my, he smells wonderful.* "Love the hat. You're adorable!"

I like how this is starting. Back in the front seat of Angel, driving into the city, he reaches over and puts his hand on my knee, says, "So, what are you hungry for?" and winks.

Here we go again. "I don't care, Leo. Something simple is fine. Maybe there's a restaurant in the hotel where I'll be staying."

"Oh. About that. You're not in a hotel."

"I'm not?"

"No, the museum has a great little apartment in the Back Bay that's usually occupied by visiting artists, but it's empty this week, so close to Christmas, so you're staying there."

"That's different. But it sounds like it could be fun."

"Tell you what. How about if I take you there first. You can drop off your things, and then we can walk over to Newbury Street and find dinner."

"Sounds perfect. Thank you, Leo."

The apartment is delightful. A second floor walk up in a brownstone on a side street. A short block's walk and we're on Newbury. Twinkle lights everywhere, the stores decorated for the holidays. No other way to describe it. It's magical. We find a little bistro. A table for two. Way too much romantic potential.

He says, "Looks like life is agreeing with you."

"Thanks, Leo. Yes, life's been treating me quite well."

"Oh, do tell. What's his name?"

"No, it's not that. Just found a great balance between the job you left for me at the college, and time to continue to paint." It's a lie, but I want to sound positive about my life, not desperate.

"Well now, that IS good news. So are you ready to move to the big city?"

"Not yet, Leo. You see, here's the thing. I'm happy where I am right now. I'm afraid to shake things up too much." *Seriously, Lily? Where did those words come from?* I'm lying again, but it seems like the right thing to say.

"Maybe you could consider it building on what you've already done. Think of the opportunities the city presents. World renowned galleries..."

"Oh, you do flatter me, but I'm just developing my style. I'm not ready to go there. So, let's take it one step at a time. I haven't even interviewed yet. They might not want me."

"THEY don't have to want you. I get the final decision on who's hired as my assistant. So as far as I'm concerned the interviews tomorrow are just a formality. You already knew that, didn't you?"

"Uh, no, but I guess I do now."

"Oh, Lily, you still have the capacity to surprise me with how naive you can be."

I'm not sure whether I should be offended or not. "I'm not naive, Leo. Just not as experienced as you are."

"Well, in my book, I call it naive."

"Okay, then you win. I'm naive. But it still seems like a waste of people's time to spend the day interviewing."

"No, not at all. Think of this as your opportunity to get to know my staff. You need to make the decision of whether or not you want the job. I already know I want you."

He wants me. Oh, how I'd love to run with that statement, but I let it go. "Alright, Leo. I'll keep an open mind."

"Good. Be open to the possibilities, Lily. That's all I ask."

We finish dinner. I have only one glass of wine. Need to stay in control. I may be naive, but not stupid.

He walks me back to the apartment. There's an awkward moment before he leaves, when I wonder if he might try to kiss me, but his phone rings at just the right moment. Or wrong moment, depending on how you look at it. It's Lizzie.

After a brief conversation, he hangs up and says to me, "I need to go now. Are you sure you can you find your way to the museum on your own in the morning?"

"Yes, I'm all set. Looks like a pretty easy ride on the subway."

"This is Boston, Lily. We call it the T."

"Okay. On the T. We're meeting at nine?"

"Yes. In my office."

"Remember, Leo, no promises."

"I understand. At least enjoy your time in the city."

It's an interesting life to contemplate. I am delighted to be in this apartment, rather than a hotel room. It allows me to try on what a different life might feel like. Not sure how Grace fits into this picture, but we can determine the details later. And it's just over an hour to the Cape. And Sarah. Oh boy, I do like to complicate my life, don't I?

The interviews go well. I'm intrigued, but not convinced. And wondering if I get another evening with Leo.

So far today it's been all professional.

He asks, "Can you find your way back to the apartment on your own or do I need to take you there?"

"I'm sure I can find it. Though I was thinking maybe I could buy you dinner tonight, as a thank you?"

"Not necessary, and not even possible. Our office Christmas party is tonight. Command performance."

"Oh." I try to hide my disappointment. "So, this is goodbye?"

"For now. Until you move up here. Are you ready to accept my offer?"

"No, Leo, I'm not. It's quite generous, and truly exciting to consider, but I need some time to think about it. And about what it means for Grace. Then there's her father to deal with. I'm not sure what he would say about me moving her away from him. I didn't tell him this was an interview when I asked him to take her for the weekend. He thinks I'm here on a consulting assignment."

"Alright. Well, please don't take too long to decide. Can you let me know by Monday or Tuesday? My office shuts down for two weeks over Christmas and New Year's. I'd like to be able to bring you up here early in January."

"You've got to be kidding. That's way too fast."

"You know me better than that, Lily. I don't kid about work things."

"Okay. Well, I should go. You need to go home and get ready for your party. Thank you for everything. I'll be in touch early next week. And please tell Elizabeth hello from me."

Chapter 17

Tell Elizabeth hello from her? Is she serious? What Lizzie doesn't know won't hurt her. More accurately, what Elizabeth does know could hurt her. Could hurt all of us. Lizzie's been suspicious of Lily from the first night we met. Went absolutely bat shit when she heard I'd hired the girl. And remember the day she found us out at the lake? Well, she still throws that one in my face. A good thing we moved away.

And now I'm supposed to tell her I might be moving Lily north to work with me again? No sir. At least not yet, not until it's a definite thing. And even then I might fail to say anything for as long as I can get away with it.

I still wish Lizzy had decided to stay in Washington, and let me have my own life up here. I mean, I appreciate the house she's bought us. And my new fishing boat. Had to name it after her. The Lizzy B. She thinks the B stands for Browning, her maiden name. But I know otherwise. It's that other B word. The politically incorrect one. My own private joke. Every time I look at her name on my boat, I smirk. Like I said, what she doesn't know won't hurt her.

Chapter 18

The apartment I found charming last night is bad for my psyche just twenty four hours later. Friday night alone, and it's too much in my face that Leo is still with Elizabeth. If I was considering this move as a way to be closer to him for any reasons beyond professional ones, well, tonight is a clear sign I should not. *He's still married, Lily. Remember that small detail?*

I wake up Saturday morning in a frigid apartment and notice I can see my breath. I put my hand to the radiator. The metal feels like the inside of a refrigerator. I turn on the light next to the bed. Nothing happens. Great. Just great. The power is out. So much for my cozy getaway.

My plane doesn't leave until two, so I have time to kill this morning. I'm not going to be able to make a cup of tea, so I bundle up to head out for a walk. There must be a breakfast place on Newbury Street where I can treat myself to something lovely. I notice a gentle snow is falling. Already about two inches on the ground. The neighborhood is transformed. If I thought it was magical on Thursday night, now it has moved beyond into the realm of fairy land. Notice I didn't say fairy TALE land. No man or woman to share it with me this morning. But that's okay. I'll find a way to be content to enjoy it on my own.

My need for food is replaced by a fascination with the shops on Newbury Street. First, a used book store. The sign over the door says Avenue Victor Hugo. Creaky wood floors. Musty smell of old volumes. Perhaps a few bats hanging in the rafters. Old books have never been my thing. I prefer crisp, new pages. Exit quickly from there, cross the street, into another. Trident Booksellers and Café. Perfect. The smell in here is an interesting mix of cinnamon, incense, and vanilla, swirled with morning coffee, and baked goods fresh from the oven. There is a magazine rack more extensive than I've ever known could exist. And books. Including a complete section devoted to erotica, a secret indulgence of mine. I treat myself to a new volume to keep me company on lonelier nights back home.

I sip a luscious chai, nibble an almond croissant, watch the street scene unfold before me. Yes, I could get used to this part of city living. Then I notice it. There. Across the way. A sign with rainbow colors on it. And something about paint. Another place I need to explore.

I finish eating, then head back out to the street. Catch a few snowflakes on my tongue. Yes, I've found my way to contentment on my own this morning, thank you.

I cross in the direction of the rainbow. Look up at the sign. Johnson Paint Company. I walk inside. Here on the first floor it's the 'paint your house' type of paint store. But there's more waiting up the stairs. Okay, now I truly AM in heaven. It's the other kind of paint store. Art supplies. Pens. Papers. Canvases. Tubes of oil paints. A toy store for artists. I select a few colored pencils, a small sketch pad, and some new brushes to carry back home. I've been considering all morning whether or not I should take the job with Leo, but this store reminds me of the commitment I made several years ago to pursue my art. The part time job back home has interfered enough. If I move here, it will be a full time position. Sure, the money would be good, but at what cost? I've been looking for a sign. And I think I found it. *Pay attention, Lily. Don't give up on who you are meant to be.*

I venture down the street a bit further. Pass several art galleries. One in particular beckons. The Copley Society of Art. I walk inside. Pick up a brochure. "The oldest non-profit, artist member gallery in the United States." I speak with a woman named Helen. She tells me of the application process for what they refer to as professional artist membership. I decide it is a worthy goal, but I'm not ready. Not yet. Maybe some day.

Though I am ready to make my decision. No need to wait until Monday. It's time to call Leo and tell him thanks, but no thanks. This girl wants, and needs, to paint. And I need to go home. Now. It's been a fun fantasy, spending time here in the city with Leo. But it's only a fantasy. *Click your heels three times, Lily, and repeat after me. There's no place like home. There's no place like home. There's no place like…*

Chapter 19

Home. Like the old English fairy tale, where the teeny tiny woman lives in a teeny tiny house in a teeny tiny village. Well, that's me. I'm living a teeny tiny life in a teeny tiny town at a teeny tiny job. Maybe I am ready to move on to something larger.

I am recommitted to my paints. And I find in doing so, it's as if the muse is recommitted to me, too. Leo wasn't happy with me when I turned down his job several months ago, but he'll get over it.

And Sarah called me yesterday. With an even better offer.

"Lily, do you remember that adorable house next door to me? We found out a few weeks ago it was going on the market, and James and I got a jump on it before the realtors did. We're buying it to protect our property, and planning to make it a rental. Not sure why, but I thought of you. You ready to shake up your life a bit? Would you like to be our first tenant?"

"Sarah, do you think that's such a good idea? I thought we agreed to put space between us."

"Well it's not about you and me, Lily. Honestly it's not. I just thought it might be a cool place for you to live, if you're ready to get more serious about your painting. Just imagine living here on Cape year round. We could convert the loft over the barn into a studio. It's got a sink, and a bathroom. We had plans to turn it into a small apartment but never got around to finishing it. We only store old furniture up there now."

"Sarah, if I move to the Cape it means I give up my income from the job at the college. I'm not sure I can afford to rent one place, let alone a studio, too."

"Don't worry, Lily. We'll come up with something reasonable on the house, and throw the studio into the deal for free. It's not like we need the money. Consider me a benefactor."

"Then I'd feel like I owe you or something."

"Not to worry. We can work that out."

"That's what I'm afraid of!"

"No, I don't mean that, Lily. Let me do something nice for you, please? It would make me happier than you can imagine to see you successful with your painting. Look, I just want to do this for you, just because. What good is it to have money if I can't share it with my dearest friend?"

"Sarah, you're being incredibly generous, but what about Grace? I don't think her dad will let me move her away like this."

"Lily, stop putting up roadblocks to your own success. Do you want to grow, or don't you?"

"C'mon, Sarah, that's not fair. You know I do."

"Well, then, quit making excuses. There's a wonderful private school here that Grace would absolutely love. I know several people on the board. I can pull some strings for you, see if we can find some financial aid. Then Eddie won't be able to argue with you, because it will be too good of a move for Grace, too."

"No, Sarah. I mean, thank you. I don't want to sound ungrateful. It's just that, well, I need to know I'm okay doing it my way. You understand, don't you?"

"Sure. But please think about it, Lily. We pass papers on the house tomorrow. The place is pretty much in move in condition. Could use some fresh paint and polish, but other than that it's ready for you. You could be here within a few weeks. It's time for you do something wonderful for you and Grace."

"And now you're pushing me. I don't know that I can do this so quickly. It's a huge decision."

"Just try, Lily. Try. What's that thing you always say, about God closing doors and windows opening?"

"Yes, I know. You don't have to remind me. So, maybe email some pictures of the place to me if you'd like. I'll talk with Grace and her dad about it this weekend. And if you can send me information about the school that'd be great, too. It IS the right time of year to make a switch. Though I don't know if we can get into a private school with such short notice."

"You can if you will allow me to help you. Please, Lily. Put a plan in motion and see what happens. Give it a chance. What have you got to lose?"

"Okay, I hear you. Maybe we could move before the end of summer, so Grace could start in with the other kids on the first day of school?"

"There you go! Now you're thinking positively! Oh, Lily, it would be so much fun to be next door neighbors, wouldn't it?"

"I don't know. Is there a fence between the properties?"

"I'll put one up if it will make you feel better. Just give it a try, please?"

"Okay. I will. I'll call you in a few days. And Sarah, one more thing."

"What's that?"

"Thank you. You know sometimes I need a kick in the tail to get into action."

"There will be no talking of your tail. Unless..."

"Oh, Sarah!" We both laugh. This could be fun. I mean, why not? Maybe it's time for a change.

I find it astounding how sometimes things fall into place in spite of my best attempts to get in my own way.

The talk with Eddie is a breeze. His new wife is all too happy to get us out of town. And when I go in to work on Tuesday morning, I'm told my job is being terminated due to budget cuts, and I'm offered a three month severance package. So I now have a financial buffer while I get re-established. This is way too easy. I guess I don't have any choice in the matter. We're moving, whether I want to or not. *Fear and doubt, please step aside. Cape Cod, here we come.*

Chapter 20

We're moving. Again. I've moved so many times in the past several years that I've become far too good at it. Not because I wanted to, but because I had to. I'm reminded of a favorite saying of a friend of mine. *Never become very good at that which you do not truly enjoy.* Yes. Guilty as charged on that one.

First was the divorce move, out of the family home. The time when I left Grace's dad and the house with the white picket fence. Gone my dream of a traditional happily ever after, that move was the toughest. Moving out with my toddler daughter, one cat, and all of my belongings, from a three thousand square foot home I loved with all of my heart and soul into a seven hundred square foot apartment. Now get this. It had the same house number as the one we left. I took it as a sign that it should be our next home. I'm always looking for signs. Because they appear when I feel lost and ask for direction. Though maybe I just tell myself they are pointing me the right way, because I want to believe they are. We see what we want to see, don't we?

I remember lying with Grace one night after prayer time, in the room with the hideous brown indoor-outdoor carpet, staring at the peeling paint on her bedroom ceiling, and saying out loud to her, "We won't live here forever. We'll find a better place." I fought back my tears, because I didn't want her to see me cry. We made it home, and filled it with love, laughter, and friends, but deep in my heart I knew my daughter deserved something better. It just never occurred to me that I did, too.

We stayed there longer than originally intended, because it was what I could afford at the time. Eventually my prayers were answered. After I went back to work for

Leo and had some income of my own, which turned into even more income after he moved away, I was able to move us into a three bedroom brick duplex. It was more than we needed, but it felt good to be able to stretch out. There was a bedroom for Grace, one for me, and a third I turned into my studio. Hardwood floors. And no cracks in the ceiling. The house had been on the market for several years, but the owners agreed to rent to me because they figured it might be another few years before they found a buyer. Well, I must be some sort of good luck charm, at least for other people, because a month after we moved in, it sold. We were allowed to stay another three months. Then it was time to move. Again.

Are you ready for this one? We found an apartment over the marina at the lake outside of town. The boat Leo left behind when he moved north sat on its trailer beneath my bedroom window, right where we'd put it the day Elizabeth found us. I was comforted by its presence, as if he was looking out for us.

A voice inside my head taunted me as I carried yet another box of books up the stairs. *Maybe we should just live out of a moving truck. It sure would be easier than all of this.* I wondered how long it would be until I carried those boxes back out, and where that move would take us.

It brought us to today. The big move. The four hundred fifty four miles away move. This one is by far the most difficult, because everything, and I mean everything, except what will fit into Vivian Volvo, needed to be wrapped and boxed. Everything had to be ready to go on the moving truck, except for some house plants, a few fish, two cats, a couple of suitcases of clothing, and a cooler full of refrigerator stuff.

This is also the most joyful move, the one where I escape my old life, or maybe I should call it my ex-life, to make a new start for us. Cape Cod, Massachusetts, vacation haven to the rich and famous, and the contractors, landscapers, and artists like me who cater to their needs. Sarah is charging me ridiculously low rent on the house. I accept it for the gift it is. That, plus my severance package, and some money I managed to save during the past year, will provide enough for us to live on for a few months while I attempt to make my mark on the Cape art world. I am drawn to the colors of the ocean and sunset skies. I hope my creative spirit will soar when given the opportunity to run free.

I've planned this move so that we will have time to settle in to our new home before the truck arrives. Sarah offered us her guest room for a few days, so we will have time to clean, and paint bedrooms. Grace will start school, and I will get the house ready and set up my studio. I have devised the perfect plan.

It's Saturday morning. Today we will drive to the Cape in one long haul. Eddie agreed to meet the movers at the lake on Monday, so they can load the truck after we leave, then follow us up later in the week. There is something to be said for remaining on friendly terms with the ex.

The alarm goes off at six. By eight I am ready to throw the aquarium fish into the lake. But Grace will cry if I do that, so I try my best to be patient, and pack them into the car in Mason jars of water. Next, drug both cats and put them in their kitty crates. And away we go.

Grace is my copilot. The cats are comic relief. First there's Kit, the hyper feral kitten who adopted us while we lived at the lake, the one who never allows us to hold or even touch her. Lord knows why we keep her. The drugs that are supposed to make her sleep for the nine hour drive just make her more crazy than usual. She passes out, then wakes up once every half hour or so, runs around in tight circles inside her crate, howls, collapses, and passes out again. Then there's Georg. He's the mellow stoner cat, who sits still in his crate like a zen master and stares out with a stupid hazy look in his eyes. We play some Grateful Dead tapes for him, and that seems to work just fine. Helps me a little, too. Though not enough.

By one o'clock we've traveled about two hundred miles, not even halfway yet, and I'm not sure I have the stamina to go on. We pull into a rest stop somewhere along Route 287 in northern New Jersey.

Dear God, please help me get through this. Praying is what I do when I feel stuck, or on the verge of an anxiety attack, or need a sign of what to do next. This time I'm not in search of a sign, just the energy to finish the drive. Turning back isn't an option.

"Mom, you never let me drink soda, but it's all they have here," says Grace. I doubt it's true, though right now a super sweet cola does sound good to me.

It appears my prayer was answered through the miracle of a wonder drug called caffeine. Sometime after dark we pull into the driveway of our new home. Sarah and James greet us and help unpack the car. We put Kit and Georg in the basement, lock up the house and call it a night. Grace and I fall into bed together in Sarah's guest room, a room nearly half the size of our first apartment. Mother and daughter both sleep twelve hours. I treat us to a sumptuous breakfast in Woods Hole, the town where the ferries depart for Martha's Vineyard. We feel like tourists on vacation, while starting to re-invent ourselves as locals. We can relax, and take our time for a few days to settle in before the moving van arrives with the rest of our things.

But you know that saying, about how if you want to make God laugh, tell God your plans? Cue the laughter.

Chapter 21

Tell me you have good news and bad news, then ask me which one I want to hear first, and I will always, without exception, ask for the bad news. Because I figure after I hear the bad news it will only get better, and I live for the better parts.

Tuesday morning. Showers, breakfast, then drive Grace to school. It's her second day, and she's excited to return to her new friends. I get back in my car and head toward town to buy curtains. The voice of intuition interrupts me. *Stop at the house.* I want to shop first, but I've learned that when my intuition speaks, I should listen. It's not a sign thing, more like a little voice inside my head that tries its best to get my attention and keep me out of trouble. Yes, I have just admitted to hearing voices. But they're good voices. Helpful voices. Maybe you hear them, too, you just don't want to admit it.

The phone is ringing as I turn the key in the knob. The neighborhood where the house is located is notorious for bad cell coverage, so I had a landline phone installed, but I don't remember giving the number to anyone. I answer. "Hello, this is Lily."

"How's your weather up there?"

"I'm sorry. Who's this?"

"It's Dave. From Make My Day."

"Oh." *Of course. The movers.* "To answer your question, we've got blue skies and gentle breezes. Why do you ask?"

"Well, we have a little problem."

Never a good thing to hear in the midst of a move. I sit down on the step behind me. Everything I own is on that truck. "Okaaay," I say, then take a long, slow, deep breath.

"I've got good news and bad news. Which do you want first?"

"The bad news, Dave. What's going on?"

"Well, we took directions from some locals last night, outside of New York City, after we stopped for dinner. I'm sorry, but there's no easy way to tell you this. We ended up on a road we shouldn't have been on. And there was this low bridge, and we saw the sign that told us we shouldn't be there, but we thought we could make it, and, well, we were wrong. We didn't get stuck, but that bridge was just low enough to peel the roof back off our truck like the top of a sardine can. Funniest thing you've ever seen."

His attempt at finding humor in the situation is wasted on me. My heart starts to pound as I envision all of my belongings scattered on the side of a highway somewhere in West Chester County.

"So, what's the good news?" I ask.

"The good news is the truck held together, and your stuff is okay. But we heard there's rain coming, so we're going to drive straight through. Should be at your place around three this afternoon. We gotta get that stuff off the truck before it gets soaked."

Okay. I can handle this. They're coming early. No big deal. Heart rate back down. Resume normal breathing. Until he starts to talk again.

"Oh, and there's one more thing."

Uh oh.

"We're kinda concerned about the weigh stations. If we get stopped for inspection, they'll send us back to Pennsylvania with a huge fine. Then we'll have to off load onto another truck and start all over."

Who needs an aerobics class? My heart rate shoots back up. So, now it's full speed ahead. Maybe. The truck will either be here in six hours, or another several days. And even if they do make it today, how much of my stuff is blowing out of the truck with no roof while it makes its way up Route 95 through the northeast corridor?

Oh well, stuff is stuff. We're here. So if I lose a few things along the way, it won't be the end of the world. They say loss is a good thing. Builds character. Lightens the load. Makes room for new and better things. I'm ready for a fresh start. And I still have my daughter, my cats, the damn fish, and a sweet home in which to live. I exhale again.

Forget the shopping expedition, it's time to move into high gear. I call Sarah and let her know about the truck's early arrival, then grab a broom and start to sweep the living room floor. We had planned to polish and wax it this afternoon. No time for that now. Five hours and counting. Maybe. Hopefully. Hurry up and wait. The story of my life. I no longer have the luxury of taking my time with this. New life starts a day sooner than planned.

Two-thirty. I get in the car to drive to Grace's school to bring her home. If I hurry, I will be back here before the van arrives. I imagine what it might be like to witness the truck when it comes across the Bourne Bridge, the bridge that spans the canal separating Cape Cod from the mainland. To those who love the Cape, the drive across the bridge is like a passage onto holy soil. It will be a sacred event when whatever is left of my stuff arrives. The camera sits next to me in the front seat, just in case I might be able to capture the moment, even though I know that trying to take a photo while maneuvering rotary traffic at the base of the bridge would be nothing short of stupid. Besides, the odds of that timing are pretty slim.

I'm almost to the rotary now. Just a few more seconds. I glance up. A white box truck. I read the red lettering on the front. Make My Day. Unbelievable. My worries about the topless truck vanish. A more simple thought replaces them.

It's here. I'm home now. I forget all about the camera, and instead whisper "thank you" out loud, hoping God is listening.

I continue on to the school, grab Grace's hand at her classroom door, and hurry her out to the car. "We gotta go. I just saw the truck come across the bridge. Can't let them get to the house before we do!"

She gives me an odd look, then says, "But I thought that wasn't until tomorrow, Momma?"

Oops. She doesn't know. *Deep breath, Lily.* "Yeah, well, they called me this morning to tell me the truck went under a low bridge last night and got the roof ripped off. So they drove up here as quickly as they could, and hopefully can get everything unpacked and inside before it rains."

"Is our stuff okay?"

"Honestly, honey, I'm not sure. I guess a few things were damaged when the truck hit the bridge, and I hope nothing more blows out. But yes, it's okay. We just have to wait and see. They're here. It's all just stuff. It's going to be fine." I'm not sure which one of us my words are meant to convince.

We get home just in time to see the van pull into the driveway. I thought ahead and secured the cats in the basement, so all I have to do now is prop open the doors.

Dave gets out of the truck. "So sorry about this, ma'am."

"It's fine. Really. How can I help?"

"Just stick around to tell us where you want things. We need to get this stuff off the truck real fast. There's rain coming."

"Yes, I know. We'll stay out of your way."

I go inside to pour glasses of iced tea. Look out into the living room just in time to see one of the guys walk in with an upholstered chair. Perched on top is a stuffed polar bear with a red scarf tied around its neck.

"Oddest thing, ma'am. You and your daughter need to go take a look inside the van right now."

I'm frightened by the thought of what I might see. How many broken pieces of furniture, crushed boxes, damaged goods? I take another deep breath. Seem to be doing that a lot today.

I walk up the ramp. Look inside. Things are disheveled, tossed about from the accident. Here, there, and everywhere, though not necessarily two by two, are animals, stuffed animals, in all varieties of sizes and shapes.

I turn to face Dave, who is standing right behind me, waiting for my reaction. "I guess you had them packed in plastic bags," he says, "and we'd tossed those bags on top, up near the front. When the roof ripped, so did the bags. Scattered the animals all over."

I wonder what the grin looks like on my face right now. Noah's ark. Maybe later there will be a rainbow. Signs of hope, of God's promise and blessing. The roof may have been ripped off, but I know we are right where we are supposed to be.

"C'mon guys. Let's get this van emptied out before the rain gets here. I'll toss a batch of brownies in the oven, and put out a few other snacks and cold drinks for you. You have no idea how happy and grateful I am you made it here safely."

I'm giggling. They must think I'm crazy. It's possible they may be right.

I say, "You see, if this had happened at the other end of the trip, I'd be a mess right now. But I'm so glad to be here it just doesn't matter."

Three guys take four hours to unload the truck. Pieces of broken furniture show up on the lawn, but nothing tragic. And on every fourth or fifth load carried inside, there's another animal, grinning at us in that way that they do. It's a parade of cartoon characters from Grace's youth. Barney the purple dinosaur. Opus the penguin. Snoopy and Woodstock. Our own ark. The storm hits Boston, soaks it hard. There's a rain delay at Fenway Park, and thunder in the distance, but here at my house, it's calm and clear.

All is well. Until the phone rings. Again.

Chapter 22

"Well, hello, Lily. I thought I'd try to find you before you get caught up in moving day."

"Excuse me. Who is this?"

"It's Leo. Forgotten me already?"

And I stop. How could I possibly not recognize his voice? I'd written to him about my move, told him the date, and shared my phone number. But somehow with all else that has been going on today I have managed to push thoughts of him far enough aside to be caught off guard by his call.

"Oh, hi. Sorry about that," I say. "Yeah, well, we had a slight change in plans. In fact, the moving truck is here right now. You won't believe it when I tell you what happened." I pause. Catch my breath. *Calm down, Lily.* "I do want to talk to you, but I can't right now. I'm sorry. May I call you back tomorrow? What time is good?"

"Around seven, I guess. I just wanted to let you know I'm planning to come down to the Cape on Saturday."

"Oh?"

"I hear the fishing's good down there, and I'm thinking of looking for a place to put my boat next summer. Thought maybe you could show me around. I'll buy you lunch. We can catch up on each other's lives."

"Sure. That'd be great. Come on down and I'll show you my new world."

"Great. And good luck with the move. Can't wait to hear your story."

"Thanks, Leo. And thanks for calling. It's great to hear your voice. I'll call you tomorrow night. We can talk then about Saturday."

I hang up the phone. Grace looks at me. "Mom? Are you okay?" She knows me all too well. I snap back to reality.

"Yeah, sure, I'm fine. I'll tell you later. Anyway, let's get back to this moving thing."

I can't believe I didn't recognize his voice. Or that he's coming here in four days. Here, to the Cape, and he wants me to show him around. And he's not my boss anymore. *Breathe, Lily, breathe.*

Chapter 23

Prince Charming. I'm still holding out for him. The one who will sweep me off my feet, set me up in his beautiful castle, and make love to me like the swarthy swashbuckler on the cover of a romance novel. Not that I read that kind of book. I don't. But those movies with the sappy endings? Well, let's just say I haven't given up my adolescent delight with them. I have watched *Pretty Woman* enough times in the past several years that I can quote almost the entire script. Named my car after Julia Roberts' character. Vivian Ward.

Then there's the newer Disney version of *Beauty and the Beast*. I still want to believe a grumpy guy can turn into a handsome prince if the right woman loves him in just the right way. I look for the good and ignore the ugly. Crazy, huh?

And last but most certainly not least, there's my old friend Cinderella. She's the one responsible for this mess, isn't she? Rags to riches. Glass slippers.

Whoever wrote those fairy tales should be shunned from any and all future contact with women. They're all such a set up for disappointment. Just once I'd like to see the heroine end up content to be on her own.

And for the record, I don't recall that Prince Charming was already married to someone else when he held out the glass slipper, now was he?

But I'm getting ahead of myself. The simple fact remains that somewhere along the way I did buy into the fairy tale happily ever after no matter what the cost with the perfect guy dream. I just did an awful job of picking the perfect guy.

Ray. He is the first one to catch my eye. Or rather I suppose I catch his eye, but if someone shows interest in me, well, I'm going to pay attention. He is the first one, unless you include my teenage heart crush on David Cassidy, but he didn't even know I existed, so never mind him. I meet Ray at a county fair. Sounds corny, doesn't it? Anyway, he is a friend of some friends.

He holds my hand, a first for me. I am petrified. Sitting in the bleachers, watching the parade of cows, with my hand in his, and I have no idea what to do. I'm thinking I couldn't, or rather shouldn't, move a muscle. *This guy is holding my hand! Woo hoo!* For the first time in my life, I feel desirable to a man. Well, okay, a boy. I'm only fourteen, but I'm hooked.

An hour later, we've walked behind the bleachers, and now he's kissing me. Talk about having no idea what to do. This is my first real boy kiss. Now I am beyond hooked. I think maybe I could fall in love with this guy.

A couple months later, he invites me to his high school homecoming dance. My mother doesn't want me to go. He is, after all, three years older than me, but I guess I've whined enough, and she's given in. She delivers me to his home late in the afternoon. My mother, the country club set wannabe who lives to be impressed by money and appearances, pulls up in front of his house in the country with the junked cars in the backyard. She gives me one of those looks only a mother can properly deliver. In return I roll my eyes, get out of the car, and march on up to his front door. My mother is absolutely freaked out, but I don't look back.

I'm wearing a dark green velveteen dress with white lace trim. He gives me a corsage, a single white carnation. To me it is the most beautiful flower in the world. Off we go, to the ball.

Time for a slow dance. I'm swooning. He pulls me in real close, and now I'm just confused. Because there is this, well, thing. He presses his hips against mine, and there is this hard part of his body that he seems quite intent on pushing against me. I try to back my hips away, but he follows me. Nobody told me anything about this, or what to do about it. Honestly, I have no idea. It feels like he has a roll of hard candies in his pocket or something but I don't know what it is.

The night ends. I go back to my life in a different school than his. And wait for him to call again. And wait some more. A bad, disappointing, lifelong habit acquired way too young. Waiting for the phone to ring.

Fast forward a year later. We're back at the fair. He's holding my hand again, and leading me out back behind one of the barns. The good girl in me knows this is a bad idea, but nobody ever told me how to say no, so I'm going with him, because maybe he just wants a quiet place to tell me how much he has missed me and wants to be with me. He starts to kiss me. I remember how much I like this part. But now his his hands are inside of my sweater, and he's unhooked my bra, and his mouth is on my breasts and he seems to be quite enjoying himself, and I have no idea what to do or how to tell him no. Or whether I should tell him no. I just know it's not doing much for me, what he's doing, and something in my mind thinks maybe it's not right, but I am getting attention from him, and he seems to be quite happy, so maybe this is what it means to be in love.

Now he's trying to put his hands in my pants, and I somehow figure out how to stop him, because even I know this is going too far behind a barn at the county fair.

And he never does say anything about missing me. Maybe he just wants to show me, by kissing me and the other stuff. That's how guys show they care, isn't it?

A quick goodbye, back to our separate schools, and on to more waiting for the phone to ring, hoping for more signs that he might love me.

Fast forward a few more months. We're together again, after a football game at my high school. He says, "hey, there's a cool place down by the river that's pretty in the moonlight" which sounds perfectly romantic to me, so of course I say yes. We're in the front of his pickup truck, and he's kissing me *(you know I like the kissing part)* but he's got his hands in my sweater again. And now somehow, I don't know how, but he's got me pinned on my back underneath him in the front seat of his big old white Chevy pickup trick, you know, the kind with the huge bench seat for a front seat. And he's got my pants down to my knees *(how and when did he do that and where was I when he did?)* and he's opened his own pants and the thing that was hard when we danced is exposed. And I have no idea what to do now because nobody told me what to do and he says to me "let me just put it near you and I promise I won't put it in" and finally something surges up in me and I push him away and yell NO. So now he's angry with me, and he zips back up and starts to drive me back home. I'm crying a muffled cry, there in the front of that Chevy pickup, but I still desperately want him to love me, so surely I can't show him how upset I am.

Thank goodness he has the radio on. Except it's this song that keeps repeating "I love you" over and over again and I'm so confused, because I love this guy, and I thought he loved me, but I'm too upset by what just happened, and now I have to get myself under control because I don't dare let my parents see how upset I am or surely they will never allow me to see him again. I'm not even sure what it was that just happened, but I know, in my gut, that it wasn't right, and he probably doesn't love me, but I don't know what to call it.

Date rape. I know, you don't have to correct me, technically speaking in the strict definition of the word it wasn't, because he didn't, well, you know, but as far as I'm concerned, some twenty years later and hopefully a little bit wiser, it still was. He coerced me into doing things I didn't want to do, and it's nothing short of a minor miracle that it didn't go further.

Yes, those were the words I was looking for, but back then, we didn't have the words, and I guess we still don't, but I know for certain it was wrong. I remember I'd sit in health classes, when we'd have the sex talk, and the teacher would ask us if we had any questions. One time she invited us to write our questions on pieces of paper and turn them in without our names so we could ask anything we needed to ask. I remember I wrote something like "how do I ask a guy to stop when I don't want him to touch me a certain way but I love him and I want him to love me so I don't want to make him angry by asking him to stop?" I remember she read my question, and I guess we were told to just say no, but it didn't help me.

Somewhere along the way I finally stopped seeing him. Until one time in college. He had gone off and joined the service. When he came home he wanted to see me. Now, one would think he would have matured by then, or I would have known better than to allow him back into my life. Maybe I thought he wanted to apologize.

He comes to visit me in my college dorm room. We sit on the floor, because I have only one chair. And within minutes, I have no idea how it happens (*I never did*) but here I am pinned on the floor beneath him and he's trying to do it again. The difference is that now I know what the hard thing is, and I know I don't want it from him, and I push him off of me, and yell NO. Just like I did before. Except this time, I also say "if that's the only reason you're here, there's the door, use it." And he does.

I can't stop shaking for at least an hour, maybe two. What part of me says "doormat" that he thinks he can still try to get away with such a thing? He's a disgrace to his uniform. I guess he was absent the day they taught respect.

I have still to this day never confronted him about what he did to me. Maybe I'm still looking for the right moment to tell him what a horrible thing it was. I was so ill equipped to deal with his advances. Maybe I'm still hoping he'll apologize.

Except I bet he wouldn't even remember any of what I've just told you. And I still remember the damn love song on the radio. And the sweater I was wearing, the first time he put his hands under my shirt, at the fair. Brown, with a horse embroidered on the front. Kept that sweater for years, as a memento. Yes, I know, ridiculous, like Monica cherishing the dress she wore, oops, I mean, allegedly wore, with you know who.

I wonder how many other young girls have allowed themselves to be put in the same sort of situation for the sake of something we think is love. How many of us allow a man to use our body in the hope it might mean something more than it does? Do we let ourselves do things we know in our heart of hearts aren't authentic to who we are, or what we want to do, all because we are not willing to say no, because we fear he might walk away? What man who would do that is worth keeping around? That's not love, is it? I like to think of myself as a smart woman. Though apparently not when it comes to men. Nope. Temporary blindness induced by fairy tale dreams. Smart woman making stupid choices.

So, here I am in my new place full of boxes and stuffed animals, four hundred fifty four miles away from the only place I ever called home. Single woman poised on the cusp of a fresh start, and I've just set myself up again. Leo wants to come see me, and I'm getting all excited, because once upon a time *(did I actually just say once upon a time?)* I had a crush on this guy, and he's coming on Saturday, and...

He's still married, Lily. What's the point?

Chapter 24

New routine starts today, our first morning in our new place. We set up our beds last night before the movers left so we could sleep here rather than in Sarah's guest room. I share a quick breakfast with Grace, pack her lunch, then drive her to school. Drive myself back home. I am to call Leo tonight at seven. Time now to get to work. The next ten hours will crawl by unless I focus my attention on other tasks.

Adrenaline charged, I begin to unpack boxes. Move pieces of furniture. Create home out of chaos. Except there's too much time to think, and too many questions. He'll be here in three days. We haven't seen each other since the day I interviewed with him in Boston. Where should I take him? Will there still be sparks? Yes, I know, when he called he said it was about boat stuff. But maybe there's more to it.

I assume he's still married, so there are respectable limits to how far this fantasy can go. I'm a good girl. I don't do things like that, like what you are thinking. I go to church every Sunday. I value honesty and integrity. I say my prayers, and ask God for guidance. Look for signs. Listen for voices.

The good girl thing? I was taught at an early age to not take something that didn't belong to me in perhaps one of my mother's finest parenting moves, though I doubt she remembers it. I was, I think, about five. We were in an old fashioned general store, except back then it wasn't old fashioned, it was just a store. And it had this wonderful display of penny candy, right at my eye level. I knew if I asked my mother for some of what I wanted she would say no, but nobody was watching me, so I helped myself. I mean, what difference would it make? Three pieces of bubble gum, those hard little pink rectangles of colored paper with the mini cartoon inside wrapped around the gum. It wasn't much. What would it matter? Nobody would notice they were gone, would they?

Until we got home, and my mother found them on my dresser. Guess I hadn't yet learned how to hide things well. After she scolded me, she made me go back to the store with her, take it all back, and confess to the owner exactly what I had done. I think he was nicer about it than she was, because I don't even remember talking with him, but I do remember her making me do it, and the mere thought of it still gives me shudders. Confession may be good for the soul, but it's hell on the nerves. I learned my lesson. Maybe.

Seven o'clock. Dinner is finished. Grace is in her room, doing her homework. It's time. I reach for the phone, dial his number, not even sure what I will say. Why, oh why, am I making such a big deal of this?

He answers on the first ring. "Leo Stocker."

"Well, hello, Dr. Stocker. This is Liliana Daniels." I feign formality. He seems not to notice.

"Hi there. Give me just a second." I hear the sound of a computer keyboard. "Just finishing up an email. So, how are you? Sounded like a crazy day yesterday."

I envision him pushing back from his desk, maybe putting his feet up on it, stretching out. Does he still do that? I don't know. Though I am quite sure he's dressed in a starched cotton shirt, probably white, or maybe blue or pink, striped tie, and dress slacks. Likely there's a navy blue blazer on a hanger on the back of his office door.

"Yeah, I'll spare you the details, but hey, I'm here." I pause, uncertain what to say next.

He's still in work mode. "So, I got your letter, and sure, I'd be happy to help you make some gallery connections up here. Even though you rejected me the last time I saw you."

"You're never going to forgive me for that, are you?"

"Nope. But I need to head out shortly to a meeting, so how about if we make a plan for Saturday, and we can talk more about all of this while you show me your Cape."

"Okay. That works for me."

"I hear it's going to be quite a day," he says. "Indian summer. I'll leave here around nine thirty, so where might you be, oh, let's say around eleven?"

"How about if I email directions to you so you can meet me at the beach?"

"Sounds great."

"Oh, and Leo, this is the Cape. I probably don't have to tell you, but we're a casual bunch down here. You can leave the starched shirt in Boston."

"Got it. You're still a hoot, Lily. You've been living there for how many days and you already sound like a local."

"Yup. You know me. I'm a sand in my shoes girl. I'll look forward to Saturday."

"Me, too," he says. We hang up, rendezvous plan in place.

Chapter 25

Saturday morning. After three days of rain, the serious, heavy, thank God the truck arrived on Tuesday not Wednesday or everything I own would have been destroyed type of rain, the sunrise is spectacular. I know because I am awake early enough to see it.

I find myself lying in bed wide awake at six o'clock. Rather than fight it, I get out of bed. Throw on an old sweatshirt and a pair of jeans. Make a cup of tea and bring it outside with me to my backyard oasis. I settle into my favorite green rocking chair and watch the morning sky grow brighter, trying to be in the moment, rather than rushing another day.

My anticipation for today is way out of appropriate proportion. *He's a married man* becomes my mantra with each inward breath. *Let go of the fantasy* on each exhalation. *Nothing good can come of this* overrides both.

I snap back to reality. Maybe this is just a simple reconnection with someone from my old life. Nothing more. A time to show him the water. Share the places I love.

So why do I play out fantasies of our hands touching, or of an accidental embrace? No, stop right there. Look at those two words together. There'd be nothing accidental about it. Or, maybe, our first kiss. What will his lips feel like? We managed to avoid it when we worked together, but I'm no longer his employee. One barrier removed. It's a new place. A new start. Remind me, please, what does he smell like, up close?

My mug of tea is empty and my musings are getting me nowhere, so I go inside and shower. Time to focus now on what to wear. A pair of denim shorts, basic black V-neck T-shirt, sexy in a subtle yet relaxed way. And my favorite navy blue fleece pullover, the one with the zipper. Plain gold hoop earrings. Sandals. Totally me. Relaxed. Comfortable. My hair is pulled back in a ponytail, one he can let down later, when he tilts my chin toward his to kiss me. *No, Lily. Stop it. He's still married.* Or maybe he isn't. We fell out of touch again after I turned down his job offer. Who knows what changes might have occurred in his life.

Wardrobe issues resolved, I slip back into mom mode. Wake up Grace. We share breakfast together. Her new friends have invited her to spend the day and stay for a sleepover. I didn't orchestrate it. Honest I didn't. It just happened. She has her play date, and I have mine. I wonder how long he plans to stay. We didn't talk about the end of the day. Just the beginning.

It's ten-thirty. We agreed to meet at the beach at eleven. If I leave now, I'll have a little time to settle in before he arrives. One last check in the mirror, and I'm ready to head out the door.

Lucky for me the beach is within walking distance. I could drive, but if I walk we can leave the beach together in his car.

I lay my blanket on the sand. Lie down. Try my best to look casual, while subtly sexy, in an innocent sort of way. Attempt to drift off for a short nap, so he'll have to wake me up when he gets here. *Nice try, Lily, but no way you're gonna sleep now.* My ears are on high alert for the sound of Angel.

The rhythmic lapping of the waves does its best attempt to lull me to sleep. Then I hear it. He can't sneak up on anyone in that car. Should I get up to greet him, or stay here and pretend I'm unaware of his arrival? *So coy, Lily.* I opt for the latter.

I hear his footsteps approach across the sand. Then the voice. "Excuse me. Is this spot taken?"

I sit up. "Well hello, Dr. Stocker." I motion for him to sit on the blanket next to me, but he remains erect, um, I mean, standing. It feels awkward to have him hover over me, so I stand up, too.

"So, this is Cape Cod?"

"Yup. Welcome to my world." We grin at each other.

"Well, you look great, Lily. How've you been?"

"I'm good. It's been a wild week, but I'm happy to be here. Can't begin to tell you how happy."

He pauses. Looks at me, perhaps for a few seconds longer than he should. "It does look good on you. Really good."

I hope I didn't just blush. I say, "So tell me what you'd like to see first."

"Well, how about a little drive around the coast? Give me the big picture on what's here. Then maybe I can buy you some lunch and we can talk about your next art steps in this new life of yours. You got a car here?"

"Nope. I walked. But I'd be happy to drive your car." I don't expect him to trust me with his baby.

With a wink, he tosses me the keys. "Sure, have at it. You ever driven a car like this?"

I mumble something sounding almost like yes, though the truth is I haven't.

We spend the next hour driving along the shoreline, me getting used to the feel of the twin turbos, and him being uncharacteristically patient. Cautious driver that I am, I'm surprised at how alluring Angel's power is in my hands and underfoot.

"*C'mon. Drive me faster, harder. You can handle it.*" Is that Angel talking or my own subconscious? In my mind I give her a new name. *The Temptress.* Just like me.

We end up in Woods Hole. I show him the ferries to Martha's Vineyard.

"Should we go now?" he asks.

I'm confused by his question. Does he have to head back already? I hoped for a lot more time together than this. Disappointment rushes in. "Okay, but I didn't know you'd have to leave so soon."

"What? No. I mean, should we go on the ferry? To Martha's Vineyard? We could eat lunch over there. My treat."

Disappointment flies away. Excitement fills the gap.

"Sure! I haven't been there in a long time. I'd love to!" I probably should try to be more aloof, like my mother trained me to be. *Just stop talking, Lily.*

On the ride over, Leo offers me a cherry Lifesaver. A little bit of sweetness I will now forever link to this man.

The boat puts us off in Vineyard Haven. We wander into a restaurant overlooking the harbor. The Black Dog Tavern. Just about everybody who has ever been to Martha's Vineyard has passed through this place, so why shouldn't we? Some claim you're likely to see someone wearing one of their logo t-shirts in just about any airport around the globe. Our lunch conversation turns professional. I ask questions about how his work is going, of more interest to me now since I met some of his colleagues when I interviewed. He asks me what I hope to do with my career, here in Massachusetts. I dig for proper answers, but haven't given much thought in preparation for this discussion. It isn't where I want the focus to be. Not today. Afterwards we take a walk through town, a main street of t-shirt shops, art galleries, fudge and ice cream stores. The season is winding down. The town feels sleepy. Relaxed.

Sure wish I was.

On the ferry ride back, we watch a beautiful sunset. Bookends to my day, the sunrise and sunset. Over the public address system, there's a marriage proposal. She says yes. Everyone applauds. It's quite romantic. I wonder if maybe it is a sign, for us, for our future. *Oh my gosh, Lily, get a hold of yourself.*

We're back in his car. He drives this time. He says, "How about a quick dinner before I head home?" Apparently he's not in a hurry for our day to end either. Seems like we just ate lunch, but maybe it's been longer than I think. Time flies when you're having fun, right?

I suggest Gill's. Not too fancy, but dependable. A place where the locals go. Driftwood walls. Nets on the ceiling. So cliché. We sit in a booth. He orders a glass of Chardonnay. I stick with water. Nothing that might loosen my inhibitions. Not tonight. I must stay in control. I don't trust myself.

Our day together is winding down. We've been well behaved. Nothing has happened he couldn't report to Elizabeth, even though I know she already distrusts us both. I'll admit the setting for today was a romantic backdrop to our innocent meeting. Did I say innocent? Well, perhaps that's not accurate. But we haven't touched. There's been no embrace. Not even a friendly hug. Not yet, anyway.

Though right now I am mesmerized by this thing he's doing with his middle finger, running it in lazy circles around the top rim of his wine glass. No doubt an unconscious movement on his part, but my mind wanders, thinking what it might feel like were he to draw the same lazy circles on my body, on my skin. Perhaps across the nape of my neck. Then languish in ever smaller circles around my breast. Just barely graze across the nipple with each pass.

Move lower, in ever smaller circles between my thighs. Move closer to...

"Lily! Hello? You still there?" His voice interrupts my fantasy.

"Uh, yeah. Sorry." I have no idea what he might have just said to me. *Oh my. I'm in trouble.* We need to say goodbye, soon. I fear I might say, or worse, do something I might regret. Thank God I had the good sense not to order any alcohol.

Dinner over, he hands the keys to me again. "Here, you know the way." I take a detour, drive us back to the beach where the day began. A full moon offers sufficient light to walk out on the short jetty. We don't say much, just stand next to each other for a little while at the end of the rocks. Breathe in the peacefulness of the night.

I turn to walk back across the beach toward the car. He's just a footstep or two behind me. With no forethought, I reach my hand out behind me, and he takes it. We walk back to the car in silence. His hand in mine feels so natural, like it belongs there. No words are spoken. None required. Nothing to break the spell of this moment.

We get in his car. Drive to my house. He's left his sweatshirt inside, so he will need to come in at least for a minute, before he heads back to Boston. *Back to his wife, Lily.* Yes, I know. I don't need to be reminded. Well, maybe I do, but right now I don't want to hear it. I'm quite aware how dangerous it is for him to come inside the house with me. Skating on thin ice. Playing with fire. Choose a favorite cliché and insert it here. It's just a bad idea. And at the same time, oh, so deliciously lovely an idea. I assume he's feeling what I am, but I could be wrong. Might just be my fairy tale brain running away with me.

We stand together in my kitchen. Utter mumblings of goodbye. Stay in touch. I'll let you know about the job thing. Blah blah blah. Electric air passes between us. Simultaneously we reach out for a hug.

Now his lips are on mine. Polite, not pushing, yet lingering. A moist, full lipped kiss. As many times as I have fantasized about this moment, I'm still caught off guard. And it's even better than I imagined it would be, or could be.

Then he's gone. Out the door, into the car. Angel flies away down the road. I'm left standing alone in my kitchen. In shock. I can't move. He just kissed me. He fully, live in the flesh, not a dream kissed me. I remember the moment in *The Sound of Music* when Rolf kisses Liesl for the first time, out in the garden gazebo. He catches her by surprise, then runs away. She's left standing with empty arms, then lets out a shout of glee. Yup, that's me right now. Romantic fantasy fulfilled. *Now what am I going to do?*

Though I miss Grace on nights when she is not with me, right now I'm grateful to be home alone with my questions and all too wild imaginings. I toss and turn all night, haunted by the memory of the feeling of his lips on mine. Sleep eludes me.

For the second morning in a row, I find myself wide awake too early. I get out of bed, throw on sweatpants and a sweater, grab a notebook and pen, and head back to the beach. Back to the jetty, now and forever our jetty. I need to think this through, something I often do best on paper. Words become my companion.

The water is quiet, while my soul is not. There's more rain in the forecast. An entire week of rainy days, and we were blessed to share the one beautiful one in the middle of it. Fog has moved in, like a protective cocoon around my memories of yesterday, and of last night. I'm torn between my fantasies, my longing for what feels oh so right, and what I know is wrong.

I am surprised when I remember it was me who took the first move to physical contact. I reached my hand out for his. It just happened. And he took hold of it so naturally in return. Then there was the kiss. What did it mean? Much as I want to indulge in imagining the possibilities, my conscience, annoying little bugger, is speaking to me. *He's a married man. This can't possibly go anywhere good. Run, do not walk, away from it, from him. Now. You're a good girl, remember? Walk away now and nobody gets hurt.*

I know the obvious right thing to do. Do NOT let it go any further. If only I had the strength to heed my own advice.

The good news is if I do decide to walk away, I have a lot in my life to keep me busy and distracted. Grace has a new world to discover, a new school, and new friends. I need to find ballet classes for her, and a piano teacher. Find a church for the two of us. Yes. Church. Do the right thing. Don't break any more commandments. I'm resolved now. I'll behave. I'm ready to leave the beach, go back home, and get on with life. Drop the fantasy.

And I'm good with my decision. Or at least I think I am. Until I walk into my kitchen. My new home has already been touched with an unforgettable memory. I wanted to say it was blessed with a memory, but honestly, I'm not certain yet if this will turn to be a blessing or a curse.

When I check my email, there's one waiting for me from him, sent about an hour ago. I guess he's also had time to think about things.

"Dear Lily," he writes. *"It was a pleasure to speak with you the other day about career possibilities that might be suitable for you to pursue in the Boston area. You know I have always respected the positive attitude and diligence you bring to your work, and*

admire you as a highly capable, bright woman. I will keep you informed of any other opportunities as they may cross my desk." Signed, "*Dr. Leo Stocker."*

End of document. Boy, was I ever off base. How can he be so cold, so distant, so darn professional? Maybe I did imagine the whole thing. Apparently the kiss was an unremarkable passing moment. Got my hopes up for nothing. I no longer have a decision to make. He's made it for me.

I brew a cup of tea, then settle in with pen and paper for the second time today. It's time to create a to-do list to keep me busy so I don't continue to obsess about him. What a fool I've been. *Get over it, Lily. If you were looking for a sign, his email certainly gave you one.*

Then I hear the computer ding. Another new email. I look. It's from him. The subject line is simple. *"P.S."*

What? More rejection? I got the sign, God, I did. I don't need another one. *Just read the damn email, Lily.* Get it over with.

"P.S. Thank you also for taking the time to show me around your new world. It is truly enchanting, as are you."

Chapter 26

Self control. It's never been my strong suit. I'm cautious, yes, but that's more about fear and risk. I may try to convince myself I have self discipline with certain things, but there is far too much evidence to the contrary. And if you throw in a hint of a promise of romance? Forget it. I'm a lost cause.

My man of starched shirts and tailored suits just called me enchanting. Whatever I thought the initial sign was, this changes everything.

The ball is now in my court. He's served up two emails. The first one formal and easily disregarded. Good cover for the day, if anyone else is paying attention to us. The second one speaks volumes. Or maybe not.

I put the water on to boil for another cup of tea. So much for my to-do list. This is way more fun. And challenging. I can choose to respond only to his first email, and ignore the second. Or maybe just write a short thank you for the second. I know in my heart I need to do more. No, change that. Needing and wanting are not the same thing. I want to do more. I'm just not sure how much more.

The tea water is ready. I cut up a lemon. Go with chamomile this time, for the calming effect. Drizzle a little honey into the cup. My hand trembles slightly as I stir the spoon in slow circles. My mind wanders back to the memory of his finger circling the rim of his wine glass. *Shake it off, Lily. Don't go there.*

Back to the computer. I have no idea what I'm going to say, so I try out a few possibilities, careful to not put his address in the "to" line just yet. The last thing I need right now is to literally send the wrong message.

First attempt. *"Dear Leo. Thank you so much for taking the time to consider professional opportunities for me, and for coming to the Cape this past weekend to meet to discuss them. I look forward to any further suggestions you may have for me to pursue."*

That was easy. Professional. Then I read it again. I catch the double entendre at the end and laugh out loud. I add his address, and send it anyway. Ta da. Good enough.

Now, what about the second email? I read it one more time to make sure I'm not making an incorrect assumption. His choice of word. Enchanting. So uncharacteristic of him. What can I possibly say in response?

First, let's try honesty. *"Dear Leo, The warmth of your kiss lingers on my lips. I must see you again soon."* Yeah. Right. Honesty my ass. Backspace. Delete.

Bring the good girl in to write the next attempt. *"Dear Leo, One day of enchanting is not worth destroying a marriage, or a family. Though it was most certainly a lovely day, I do think it is best we not see each other again. We're playing with fire."* Yup, definitely the right thing to say. But who ever said I want to do the right thing? Backspace. Delete.

Third time's the charm? *"Dear Leo, Enchanting indeed. You know where to find me. Princess Lily."*

I smile. It's perfect. I add his address and hit the send key. Then cringe. What did I just do? I open the sent file, and read it again. It's intriguing. Intelligent. Playful, with the princess thing making it seem almost comical, so if I become too embarrassed, I can say I was just being silly. In any case, through the miracle of email, I can't take it back.

I go about my day, checking the computer every five minutes. The cyber silence is deafening. Maybe I was too forward. I should have waited. Given myself time to think it through.

Eleven o'clock. Time to call it a day. I leave the computer on for a few more minutes, just in case. It used to be that I waited endlessly for the sound of a phone call. New technology now has me waiting for incoming email. I'm not sure which one is worse.

I go into the bathroom to brush my teeth. Hear the computer. *Ding.* I know better than to get my hopes up. Already did that too many other times today. Wish there was a way to assign a specific sound to his emails. It's probably not even from him. *Seriously, Lily. You're a mess. Get over yourself.*

I will allow myself to read the one that just arrived. Then I'll go to sleep. I promise.

Oh my. There's his name. *Read it, Lily. Just read it.* Nothing in the blank subject line to give me a clue.

"Dear Princess, Believe it or not I have to come back to the Cape a week from Saturday. May I call you tomorrow?"

The thought of seeing him again makes me start to tingle, and I don't mean in my fingertips. Without hesitating for even a second, I hit the reply key. Type one word.

"Yes."

Chapter 27

My thoughts have boarded a runaway freight train called desire. Here I am at the beginning of another day I will need to wade through to wait for another seven o'clock phone call. I do my best to stay distracted. Hang curtains. Organize the linen closet. Unpack paintings, photographs, all sorts of framed things to hang on the walls. What's this one? The Serenity Prayer, given to me by a boyfriend years ago. Maybe it's another sign. Is God trying to get my attention?

God grant me the serenity to accept the things I cannot change. Yes, I know. He's married.

The courage to change the things I can. Hmmm. My own reactions?

And the wisdom to know the difference. Wisdom. Not the problem. I know without a doubt what the wise thing is to do. Nip it in the bud. End it. Now. Don't open up a door I can't close.

But back to the courage thing. Can I muster enough of it to walk away, to trust there can be something better, more honest for me on the other side of this decision? How did I even allow myself to get to this point? This move was supposed to be my fresh start. In far too short a time I've created yet another mess.

I watch the clock. Go through our new routine. Pick up Grace from school. Hear her excitement about her Cape Cod friends. Prepare dinner. Sit with her to eat. Wait for seven o'clock.

"I'm gonna do my homework now, Mom, okay?"

"Sure. Maybe we can spend some time together reading when you're done." I try my best to sound normal.

"Whatever." She heads upstairs to her room. I clear the dishes, and begin to wash them. *Deep breaths, Lily. Relax.*

I'm making something way too dramatic out of this. Maybe it's not another romantic rendezvous. Maybe he wants to see me to talk about doing the right thing. Have I considered that? Though why would he even bother? I know what I should do, but am not sure I will.

The phone breaks into my thoughts. I let it ring once, twice, a third time, then grab it. "Hello, this is Lily."

"Hey you." There it is. His 'sultry without even trying to be' voice. I melt. All resolve of today gone away with two words from him. I'm in trouble now. *God, help me. Please. I think.*

Can I honestly say I want God to help me, or would I rather dive headfirst into my fantasy? And just who am I in this fairy tale? The beautiful princess, or a more sinister character, out to steal away another woman's prince?

"Lily, are you there?"

Oops. Lost in my melting and musing. "Yeah, sorry. Just momentarily distracted. How are you?"

"I'm good. More importantly, though, how are you?"

It occurs to me these are the first words we've spoken since our kiss.

"I'm good. Thanks for asking. Been busy getting Grace settled into her new routine, and trying to figure out what my new life up here is going to look like."

"Good. Well, I'm calling to follow up on our discussion from last weekend. I've done some checking around, and I do have a few gallery leads for you, if you'd like them."

Thud. *So this IS just about work?* "Uh, sure. That's great. Thanks. Should I grab a pen or do you want to just email them to me?"

"Well, that's part of what I wanted to talk to you about. It wouldn't hurt for me to pay a visit to some of these folks myself, so I was thinking maybe next weekend we could head out to Chatham together. If you'd like to join me, that is."

Wheeee! We're back on track. Maybe. Compose yourself, Lily.

"Sure. Sounds great. Thank you. I need to make arrangements for Grace, though I think I can make it work." There. I've given myself a way out. *Yeah. Right. Like I'm going to want one.*

"Good. Oh, and one more thing. I may decide to say through to Sunday, to take some time to explore the area as long as I'm driving all the way down. I can help you find a place to stay if you'd like to join me. Or we can take separate cars and meet there, so you can drive home Saturday night on your own."

"I understand." *Frankly, I haven't a clue.* "I'll see what I can do. Can I let you know, oh, is tomorrow soon enough?"

"Yes. That'd be great."

"Good. And thank you, Leo. I do appreciate you thinking of me." *More than he knows.*

"Sure thing. Have a good night. And tell that beautiful daughter of yours I said hello."

"Okay. Bye."

Now I'm more confused than before. Did he just invite me to spend the night with him? I need to be careful not to read too much into this. Maybe it just is what it is. He wants to introduce me to some gallery contacts he has. He wants to help me along with my painting career. *Yeah. Right. Are you that naive, Lily?*

I say a quick prayer. *Dear God, please help me with this one.* Except I'm praying with my fingers crossed behind my back. It's obvious what God will tell me to do, isn't it? Walk away. Now. Resist the temptation. But honestly, I don't want to hear it. Because I'm praying to the God of fairy tales, hoping for my happy ending, the one where my prince sets me up in his castle. Except for one small detail. What about Queen Elizabeth? What does God plan to do with her?

Grace walks in. "Hey, Mom, who was that on the phone?"

I hesitate, just a second, then say, "Remember Dr. Stocker, my old boss?"

"Yeah, the guy with the boat?"

"Yep, that's the one."

"Why did he call?"

Wish I knew the real answer to that question. *Stick to the facts, Lily, this is your daughter you're talking to.* "He lives in Boston now, and he knows I'm trying to get into some galleries up here, and he's offered to help me. He asked me to say hi to you, too."

"Cool," she says, looking in the freezer for dessert. Pulls out an ice cream sandwich and looks my way for approval. I nod yes.

How much more do I tell her? I don't dare draw her into my drama. Haven't said a word to her about last Saturday.

"He's invited me to tour some galleries further out Cape with him next weekend. Thinks there might be some good contacts for me to make there. Though I'm not sure if I'm going to go or not."

"Uh, Mom, why wouldn't you?"

Oh, dear child, let me count the reasons. The ones I can't tell you. "I don't know, Grace. It's next weekend. You and I made plans to spend time together. Don't you want me to be here with you?"

She's smiling. "Mom, we've been spending a ton of time together. And, well, I hadn't asked you about it yet, but Kylee's having a bunch of girls from my class for a sleepover."

"Okay, but why is this the first you've said anything about it?"

"I thought you might be disappointed, since we'd already made plans, and I was just there last weekend. But can I go now?"

"Sure. If that's what you want." This is coming together way too easily. My excuse for getting out of a sleepover of my own has just been taken away from me.

She lights up. "Cool! Oh, and Mom, one other thing."

"What's that, Grace?"

"I know it's still a few weeks away, but I need to come up with a Halloween costume for school. We're supposed to pick something from a fairy tale."

"Of course you are," I mumble.

"What did you say?"

"Nothing. Never mind." *Oops.* I need to be more careful about what I say out loud. "Anyway. Sure. Sounds good. What do you want to be?"

"I don't know. Can we talk about it tomorrow? You said you wanted to read together. And I need to go to sleep soon."

My wiser than her age child. We settle in together. The book we choose does a poor job of holding my attention. Too many visions of my own fairy tale dance in my head.

We read a little. Say prayers. I kiss her goodnight. Spend some quiet time with her. Her bedroom has freshly painted walls, and beautiful hardwood floors. I remember the night in our first apartment when I looked at the flaking ceiling paint and said, "it won't always be like this" and now here we are. We made it to something more beautiful. I utter a silent prayer of thanks.

Then I go back to my laptop. Click the "new" button and a fresh email screen appears. On the "to" line, I type in

Leo's name. Now it wants a subject. I type "Chatham galleries." Safe enough.

"Dear Leo, Thank you for your invitation to help me do some networking next weekend. I wasn't sure if it was going to work, but my daughter just informed me she's been invited to a sleepover, so it appears I'm now free. Please let me know details of time, what to wear - will you be in casual weekend wear, or a suit as usual? When and where to meet you. And again, thank you in advance for all of your help with this. Lily."

Professional, and clean enough in case someone else reads it.

Time to go to sleep. Or at least try to sleep. I need to let go for a while.

Getting ready for bed, I mentally rerun the day. Wouldn't have predicted this. Stunned the hell out of me, truthfully. I thought he'd be the wise one, the married one, the rational one who would end it. I never dreamed instead he would invite me away for the weekend. What does it all mean?

I realize I don't know enough about this man to answer my own question. Is he a good man, one hundred percent committed to his marriage, loves his wife, the kiss merely an accident at the end of a beautiful day we shared? Or is he a horrible womanizing cad who takes advantage of young female colleagues on a regular basis, and I'm just gullible enough to fall for him? My guess is the truth lies somewhere in the middle.

Of course I should probably be asking the same question of myself. Who am I that I would consider running off with someone else's husband? Doesn't exactly say good things about my own character.

I go to bed fully expecting it to be a futile attempt at sleep, certain I will torture myself all night with questions of right and wrong.

Instead there is now sunlight streaming through my windows. I must have exhausted myself. I'm face to face with the new day.

This is ridiculous. I am not going to waste another day obsessing about him while I wait for the phone to ring. I clean the house and go into town. Groceries. Bank. Carpool. Dinner. Bedtime. Nothing new yet. Maybe my email didn't demand a response. I told him I would join him. Only things yet to be determined are the specifics of time and place.

The weekend comes and goes. I'm disappointed every time I check the computer and find nothing. My ears are on constant alert for the sound of his phone call, but it never comes. I comfort myself with the thought that at least I have next weekend to look forward to.

Wednesday. A whole week without a word. Dinnertime. Then Grace goes to her room to do homework. I'm grumpy around the edges. Damn him for getting my hopes up, though I suppose I did that all by myself. The phone rings, and I grab at it. I'm tired of people calling me who aren't him. Tired of the disappointment. I answer without bothering to look to see who it is. I'm terse, and I don't care. "Hello?"

"Well, hello to you, too. Did I catch you at a bad time?"

"Oh, no, sorry." I soften. "How are you? Gosh it's good to hear your voice." *Oh crap. Too honest?*

"Well, I thought I should get back to you about this weekend. I'm sorry I didn't call sooner. I've been overwhelmed here this past week with meetings."

Of course. So much worry on my part for nothing. Another bad habit. It wasn't about me. It was about his work. He says, "I can be in your driveway around eleven, which I think will put us in Chatham a little after noon." Apparently he assumes we're driving out together.

"Sure, that'll work. I think I can drop Grace off at her friend's place around ten thirty. It's a sleepover, so I'm all set if we decide to stay the night." I wince when the words leave my mouth. Didn't mean them to sound quite so obvious.

"Cool. Good to have options." Nice save on his part. No assumptions.

"Anything else I need to know?"

"Nope. I'm setting up some appointments with the gallery owners in the afternoon, then the evening is up to us. We can play it by ear whether we end it there, or stay until Sunday."

End it there. An odd sounding choice of words. Is he talking about the visits, or us? Good grief I do get ahead of myself. *Back on topic, Lily.*

I say, "Great. And thank you again for doing this for me, Leo. I appreciate it more than you know."

"Don't give it another thought. I'm not doing this just for you. I have my own reasons for going there."

Yeah, I bet you do.

I say, "Thanks anyway. I hope I won't be slowing you down by coming along."

"Heck no. I wouldn't have invited you if that was the case."

"Okay. Do we have a plan? Eleven in my driveway?"

"Yes. It's a plan."

Thank goodness he doesn't say "it's a date" or I'd blush right through the phone.

A weekend together in Chatham. Not just a day, but the potential for a night. No assumptions. Just fantasies.

Oh boy, now which packing box holds my ethics and morals?

Chapter 28

Saturday morning. *"Dear God,"* I pray, *"what am I getting myself into?"* I'm pondering adultery, contemplating the violation of multiple commandments. *How dare I pray about this?*

I think I want God's guidance, but wonder if I truly do. Am I willing to walk away? I can fool myself by saying it's about work, but I know in my heart it's not. If I was doing this for the professional opportunity, I wouldn't be so obsessed about what to wear, what to take to sleep in, or what best way to shave my legs.

It's a few minutes after eleven. I go to the bathroom to check the mirror one more time. Add a touch of makeup so my eyes are bright and shiny, my cheeks rosy, but who am I kidding? All I have to do is think about him, about his kiss, and I blush. I'm dressed in a black, draped neck knit tank top, with a lightweight soft and flowing black cardigan. Beige linen cropped pants and sandals. Artist with a professional slant. I even took the time to polish my toes. Fall weather is approaching, but the forecast says it will be warm enough to get away with sandals. Another perfect weather day on Cape Cod, just for us.

Then I hear Angel pull into my driveway.

Should I go out, or wait for him to come in? I decide it would be best to avoid an awkward moment alone in my kitchen to start the day, so I go outside. No need to return to the scene of the crime, uh, I mean the kiss. Not yet.

He's standing next to the car. His face broadens into a grin when we make eye contact. "Well, you look ready to take on the world."

Noncommittal, safe greeting, and a gentle compliment. Good. I'm not ready for high drama this early in the day.

Then I realize I have an overnight bag in hand and wonder if it looks too forward of me. Should I have assumed instead we were coming home tonight? Would it make me look less...

"Oh, good," he says. "You've come prepared." *Whew.* He opens the door and I get in. Awkwardly. A sports car may look sexy, but this one is far too low to the ground. Getting into it gracefully is an acquired skill I have yet to master.

We're on our way. I fall quiet. Something I do when I get nervous. Well, I either fall quiet or run off at the mouth, but that can be just plain annoying so I'm erring on the quiet side today. Call it shy and coy.

He says, "I hope it's okay I went ahead and booked a room for tonight." *So much for no drama before noon.* "I'm not making any assumptions, so don't worry. I made sure to ask for two queen size beds. I'd have booked two rooms, but the rates were a lot more than I expected. We can share a room like two professional adults, can't we?" I'd believe him, except for the way he casually puts his hand on my knee when he delivers the news. Thank God he doesn't wink when he says it. That would be downright cheesy.

I don't say a word. Just look at him, and an uncontrolled grin spreads over my face. "Uh, sure." *So much for being coy, Lily.*

The silence broken, my nervous chatter begins. We talk about, well, I don't even know what. We stop at the Wendy's on the rotary in Hyannis for lunch. This man loves fast food. I eat it maybe once a year. But today doesn't appear to be a day I'm big on self-restraint, so what the hell.

Angel's GPS points us in the right direction. We drive down the quaint Main Street, then head north along Shore Road back out of town. Chatham sits on what many refer to as the elbow of the Cape. We've turned the bend. Possibly in more ways than one.

"Holy crap." The words jump out of my mouth. Thought we'd stay at some oversized motel conference center. Well, it's oversized alright, but this place is what I would call an old grand dame of a hotel. The Chatham Bars Inn. I half expect Gatsby and Daisy to wave to us from the front porch.

It's plush. Elegant. Waterfront. Angel looks perfect parked in the circular driveway. Vivian would look like a servant had parked in the wrong place.

Leo winks at me. He says, "Wait here. I'll check in and find our room." Now it's our room, like we're a couple or something. I don't know whether to be excited, or to throw up and run away screaming. I'm about to get what I've been wanting, but now I'm not so sure. Two beds, remember? No reason to be worried. We're adults. This is all okay.

He comes back to the car. "We're in one of those cottages across the street." We drive over, take our bags out of the trunk, and walk up to the door. Room 3A. Three. My lucky number. Good things come in threes. Though I'm still baffled how this has gone from "does he even remember our kiss?" to "now we're checking into our room together." And I think how little I know about this man outside of work. Am I safe with him? I guess I have to just trust it's all okay.

He opens the door, and stops. "Oops."

Chapter 29

I'm behind him, so it takes me a few seconds to catch up with why "oops." I look into the room. Count one king sized romantic as hell looking bed, and a couch. Talk about awkward. Where's the second bed? There's either been a mistake made by the hotel, or Leo planned it this way all along. A tiny slice of fear clenches my stomach.

He looks at me and shrugs his shoulders. "We can look for a room somewhere else, but they're sold out here. Some big festival going on I didn't know about."

"It's okay. I can sleep on the couch." We squabble for a few minutes about who should sleep where, but who are we kidding?

I change the subject. "When is our first appointment?"

We go through the motions of the afternoon. He introduces me to his contacts. Maybe this actually is the reason we're here. Maybe my fairy tale brain has just run away with me yet again. I should be grateful to have the gallery introductions. This could be huge for my career.

Other than his hand on my knee when he told me about booking the room, there's been no physical contact. Not even a hug. Certainly not a kiss. Nothing inappropriate, though I'm certain Elizabeth would not approve of us sharing a room.

Dinner time. Time to clean up, then we will go into town and find a restaurant. Leo brought along a bottle of his favorite Chardonnay. I'd prefer red, but this is not a time to be choosy. I take a glass into the bathroom with me while I get dressed for the evening.

I emerge wearing a jade green floral dress. Hair up in a bun. Not the tight librarian type, more like a slightly elegant up do, to make my neck appear longer, more graceful. To offer easier access for him to kiss the spot at the nape of my neck that makes me crazy, just before his lips move across the top of my back, peel the wide neckline down off one shoulder, and move toward... *wake up, Lily!*

He looks at me. There it is again. The broad grin on his face. "Wow. You clean up real good."

"Why, thank you, kind sir." I do my best imitation of a curtsy.

"Shall we?"

We walk into town. He offers me his arm, and I take it. Oh, what the hell. I decide to indulge, just a little. Is it such a bad thing to allow myself to feel appreciated? I like this, having my arm through his. Not so intimate as holding hands. Just, well, cozy. Protected.

There are waiting lines everywhere for dinner. "How about this place?" he asks. The Chatham Squire. Half tourist restaurant, the other half a locals' bar. License plates on the wall for all to enjoy. The hostess tells us it will be a thirty minute wait for a table in the dining room, but if we can find two chairs in the bar, we're welcome to take them. There's a couple just leaving a two seater in a quiet corner. Perfect. We grab it.

The menu boasts the typical seaside bar offerings. We order stuffed quahogs. Then pasta with shrimp. And more wine. *Be careful about the wine, Lily.*

Now we are back in our room. *Our room.* Should sound so happy to my ears, but honestly, I'm scared. How did the day go by so quickly? I realize we never discussed whether or not we'd stay tonight. At some point it simply became assumed we would. Now here we are, dinner's over, and we've walked back, and I don't even remember doing so. Maybe it was the wine. What have I gotten myself into?

Chapter 30

I keep saying I'm a good girl, but the whole truth is that that statement isn't the whole truth. Maybe instead I should say I'm a relatively good girl, which then begs the question, "relative to whom?" And if I am, then what am I doing here, in this hotel room with a married man, contemplating whether or not the couch will be used tonight?

Leo says, "I need to call home for a few minutes. Do you want me to go outside and use my cell?"

Talk about a reality check. It's bad enough Elizabeth exists, but now he's invited her into our evening. So I lie. "No, it's okay. I could use some fresh air. I'll go check out the stars and give you some privacy. Just let me know when you're done."

I grab the open bottle of wine, the Chardonnay we shared before dinner, and head outside. There's a brilliant full moon. This would be romantic if he wasn't on the phone with her, in there. God is giving me a sure sign, in response to a prayer for help I hadn't consciously spoken, but I'm not paying attention. Because I don't want to. There could be a neon sign in the midst of those stars right now that says "sleep on the couch" and I'd ignore it.

Leo's 'just a few minutes' phone call turns into half an hour. The half full bottle of wine is now empty.

The door opens. He says, "Mind if I join you?"

The wine answers on behalf of both my brain and my body. "Sure."

He settles in with me in the lounge chair. I lay back against him, resting my head on his chest, his arms around me, as if it is the most natural thing in the world for us to do. I can feel his breath on the back of my neck. Smell his after shave. He nuzzles my hair. I wonder how he shifted gears so quickly after the phone call.

But it doesn't matter, because now his lips are back on mine. I've spent the past two weeks wondering if our kiss felt as good as I remembered, and in a split second I know. Yes, it did, and it does. In silent agreement, we stand up. Move back inside the room. We're on the bed now, taking our time, undressing each other, our lips barely ever breaking apart. He reaches his hands to my face, placing one on each cheek as he kisses me. My hands wander further down. As do his. My brain has left the room, run away hand in hand with my conscience. I touch him, there. Caress him. He lets out a moan, and in an instant, is finished. Not a word has been spoken. Intimacy shared, though not fully consummated. We fall asleep in each others arms.

I wake up. It's light in the room, and my head feels like it's in the middle of a giant marshmallow. It takes me a minute to remember why. Oh, yeah. The wine. Images begin to surface in my brain. Moon. Stars. Bed. But he's not here next to me, so maybe I dreamed the whole thing. I look over at the couch. He's not there, either. Then I realize I'm naked. I roll over. He's sitting in the easy chair beside the bed, coffee in hand, big grin on his face. "Good morning, princess."

Oh my. Talk about awkward. I moan. Well, more of a groan. Then I remember his moan, last night.

"There's a gorgeous day going on outside," he says, "but you looked like you could use the sleep, so I didn't wake you. Want some coffee?"

What I want is to slink away into the closet, or someplace equally dark and hidden so I don't have to deal with this dance of the morning after, embarrassed and wondering what we do next.

"No thanks, I don't drink coffee. Just decaf. Or is there tea? Tea would be good. Or maybe some juice?" I notice the carton on the bureau next to him.

"Sure. Please yourself."

I think *no, sir, I believe you were the one who pleased me last night* but am wise enough not to speak it out loud.

He hands his glass to me. I guess after last night there are no boundaries on drinking from the same cup.

On to the next challenge. I'm naked. And while he saw me naked just eight hours ago, there's a huge difference between naked while intoxicated in the dark at midnight and naked wide awake and sober in the morning. I have to reconcile it right now because it will be a lot more embarrassing if I wet the bed. Oh, what the hell. I decide to just go for it. The bathroom, not wetting the bed. I toss the covers aside and walk to the door.

I say, "Back in a minute. Don't go anywhere."

I close the door behind me. Who knew a bathroom could provide such safe haven? I sit on the toilet, head in hands. In a flash my mind goes from sleepy hangover into full alert crisis mode. *What the hell did you do, Lily?* So I got what I wanted. A night of passion with this man. Well, sort of. Now what?

I'm going to have to face him, and then there's the hour car ride back home which could prove to be oh so uncomfortable, so we're going to have to talk about it. Or maybe not. If it goes to a "where do we go from here" discussion, I don't even know what I want. There's another woman involved, who honestly I don't want to hurt, but his kisses, oh my, they're like an illicit drug. And I want more, even as a different part of me, a more rational part of me, is screaming I should not.

The facts remain. I'm still naked. And he's still out there in the room. I have to leave my ceramic tiled cave.

But maybe not quite yet. I yell through the door. "Hey, I'm gonna take a quick shower, okay?"

"Sure. I'll be here."

I've just bought myself a few more minutes delay, time to get my head together before we talk. I turn the water on, a little hotter than usual, like somehow it will steam away my sin and clarify my choices.

I know, of course, what I should do. Say thank you. Then blame it on the wine. "I apologize. I was drunk and tired. I don't blame you at all, but we both know this can never happen again." Good girl's plan A. Good girl's only plan.

Though now in the shower, as I start to wash my body, my soapy hand passes over my breast, and I remember his touch, here. It passes down, between my legs, and I remember him there, too. The spark re-ignites. I think, well, as long as we're still here, maybe just a little more would be okay, as long as we end it after I go home today. Good girl has just mutated into only sort of a good girl, on the verge of allowing bad girl to take control.

I'm a lost cause. I want more of him. I finish my shower. Walk into the bedroom wrapped in the adorable fluffy hotel robe I found behind the bathroom door. Drape myself across the bed, and allow the robe to fall open, grateful for all the miles I've logged in the pool in the past several months. My ass has never looked better, and I do believe he just noticed.

Playing with fire pretty early in the day, aren't you, Lily? Can't blame this one on the wine. I look him in the eye, and smile. "So, now what?"

"Now, we get you back home, young lady." *Ouch. Did he really just call me that?* I pat the bed next to me. He moves over. Sits down. He's fully dressed. I'm still not. He picks up my hand, and kisses it. He's the one who says it first. "Do we need to talk about any of this?"

I take my time to respond. He's being the wiser one, thinking more clearly, while I remain totally in feeling mode. "Yes, we do. Just not yet, please?"

He winks at me. Leans down to kiss me. Takes me in his arms, and we're in it again. Here, in the morning light, round two begins. Even better than the night before. This morning, I am fully awake and fully aware of every move. Gone is the urgency of last night. With eyes wide open, we take our time this time. His hands explore my breasts. I remove his clothes. My body becomes the wine glass from two weeks ago, his finger moving in gentle circles around parts of me only imagined before.

Now he's on top of me. A line is about to be crossed. It's decision time. Our eyes lock together. He asks, "Is this okay?" My response is to put my arms around him, and pull him into me. It's not perfect, at least not right away. We're like two dancers, together for the first time. We need to find each others' rhythms. His more punctuated, mine longer, and deeper. Then we find it. We're in synch. And we can't stop. Won't be stopped. Until we finish. Together. Exhausted. Exhilarated.

I roll over. He spoons in behind me, wrapping his arms around me, finding that spot at the nape of my neck that I had dreamed of him kissing. But I'm wide awake now, and this is real.

And I start to giggle.

Chapter 31

"What's so funny? What did I do?"

"Oh, you did just fine. I was just thinking of your last words. So much for talking about it."

He starts to laugh, too. And in this joy filled moment it is in fact all okay. For right now, neither the past nor the future seems to matter. We are unashamedly happy in each others arms.

Until he playfully smacks me on the ass, and says, "Okay, you temptress. We have to be out of this room in twenty minutes or it's gonna cost me big bucks."

So much for the joy filled moment. Reality is back. First, another shower, a quick one this time, not to think but purely to be washed clean, if that is even possible now.

In the car, we're headed home. We stop at Dunkin' Donuts. A raspberry jelly filled one for me, with a hot cup of tea to help chase away the hangover. Then back into Angel. His hand rests on my leg. And it feels perfectly fine for it to be there.

He says, "This is just a temporary phase, you know." *What? What is he talking about?* "You'll find some galleries who love you, and then you won't need my help."

Without bothering to acknowledge what he just said, words pop out of my mouth. "So tell me, Leo. Where do we go from here?" My hangover must be interfering with my filter.

"What?"

"This. Us. What happened last night. And this morning. I need to know what you're thinking."

He doesn't answer right away. I manage to stay quiet, to allow him time to speak. "Well, Lily, you know I'm married.

And I don't have any desire to rock the boat." Thud. It's the sound of my heart hitting the floor, crashing through my stomach on the way down.

He reaches over and takes my hand. Tries to smile at me while keeping his eyes on the road. I take my hand back, and wrap my arms tightly around my body. I stare straight ahead, working diligently to start building walls around my heart. This is not going well. And we've another forty five minutes until I can escape. I feel a wave of nausea hit. I go on the offensive.

"So then what was this?" I ask. "Just a random fling with a former colleague?" I slump down further into my seat. Stare out the window. Now I'm pouting like a ten year old. I don't dare show him my true feelings.

"No, Lily, you know better than that."

"Do I? For all I know, you do this sort of thing all the time. And now I look like a damn fool for playing into it, and feel like I've made a huge mistake."

I've hit a nerve. I see the tension in his arms, in his grip on the wheel.

"What do you expect from me?" he says. "Do you want me to throw away my marriage and my family after one weekend together?"

"Two," I mumble.

"What?"

"I said two. Two weekends."

He lets out a long, frustrated sigh. Neither one of us speaks. I stare out the window, watching the landscape. The beauty of autumn, just yesterday the backdrop for fantasy, love, and potential, the lure of new romance, now betrays muted sadness.

Minutes feel like hours while I muster the courage to answer him. "Of course I don't expect you to throw that away. And I don't want to hurt anyone, not your wife, and not your family. I don't know what I expected. We knew we were playing with fire, and now's the part where I get burned." I stop for a moment to catch my breath, and my thoughts.

Then I say, "I just want you to know, no, I need you to know, that I don't usually do this sort of thing. It's just, well, it feels to me like we have, at the risk of sounding trite, a special connection. Felt it the first night we met. But I've been an idiot to allow myself to build some sort of fantasy around it. I get that. It just seemed so magical, that day we spent together two weeks ago. You kissing me in my kitchen. And then last night, the moonlight over the water. The wine, and the stars." *Shut up, Lily. You're digging your hole even deeper. Don't tell him you have fantasies of him. What kind of stupid are you?*

He pulls over to the side of the road. Shuts off the engine. Turns toward me. Touches my cheek with his hand. Looks me in the eye.

He says, "You are not an idiot. And please don't belittle what just happened. I'm in this, too, you know. If it makes you feel any better to think I'm a terrible person, well, then do that, but you need to know I don't do this sort of thing either. Of course I feel the connection, or I wouldn't be here with you." Now he pauses. Lets out another big sigh. "But I'm a practical man. And I'm sorry if I hurt you. You need to know that's the last thing I want to do."

I need so much for him to kiss me right now, to make it all better. But it wouldn't be right.

"Lily, look at me, please."

I obey.

"You are...amazing. And I don't know what I'm doing here, or what to do with you in my life. What I do know is that I have a wife waiting for me at home in Boston."

"Yes, I know. You don't have to remind me."

"Lily, you're not making this any easier for me."

"Oh, I'm sorry, I didn't know I was supposed to make it easy for you." I feel the need to make him squirm a little. I want to punish him for what I'm feeling right now, even though I know it's not his fault. I did this to myself. But it's easier to blame him.

He says, "That's not what I mean and you know it. But you also know, and I know you do because you're smart, that we should just walk away from this, right now. It's not what I want to do, and I don't think you do either. I want to see you again. The question is, with all my baggage, do you still want to see me?"

I speak. It comes out slowly, each word a measured sentence of its own. "I. Don't. Know."

He sighs. Again. My words have hit their mark. How did we in less than an hour move from sweet lovemaking to this?

He starts the car. Pulls back on the highway. After a few minutes of silence, he reaches over and takes my hand. Squeezes it.

"You know, this isn't something I do."

"I know. You said that already."

"No. Not that. I mean this." He squeezes my hand again. "I don't hold hands. Never have before. It's just not me. But for some reason I feel like I can't let go of yours."

Against my better judgement, my heart reopens, just a little. Just enough. There's a sliver of light under the door.

I look over at him, and allow myself to smile. "Well, now, that's a good thing, isn't it?"

My hand stays in his the rest of the way home. We say nothing, each lost in our thoughts. Savoring, or at least I am, our remaining moments together before we have to say goodbye.

We're back in my driveway. He helps me out of the car, and walks me to the door.

I ask, "Do you want to come in for a few minutes before you leave?"

He says, "I think maybe I better not. Not right now. I might do something to confuse us even more."

I want so much for him to do just that, but I know he's right.

I say, "Will you call me, please?"

He says, "Of course I will." Then pulls me in for a hug. Followed by a gentle kiss on the lips. Then another, planted on my forehead. Tips my chin up to look me in the eye. "You are...lovely. I don't know what we're going to do, but please don't forget this, okay?"

I nod. "You should go."

There's one more hug. He walks toward his car, turned away from me. I say, "Hey. Thanks for the weekend. Maybe I'll find some work from this after all." I laugh, just a little. I do my best to sound light and relaxed. I don't think I'm successful.

He stops for just a second before he gets into the car. Turns toward me, smiles, then winks. That darn wink.

I motion him away. "Go. Get outta here." I walk inside the house, but linger by the window to watch as he backs out of the driveway. I listen as Angel flies down the road.

I'm back inside my nest. It's time to start to shake off the fairy tale, and return to real life. I need to shift into mom mode. Grace will be home any minute.

Yet I do so with the warmth of his kiss lingering on my forehead, and the smell of his aftershave around my neck. The scent of my prince, of making love in the morning light.

Snap out of it. Lily. Fairy tales are just made up stories. They never come true.

Chapter 32

The days, weeks, and months following the Chatham weekend are a roller coaster ride. I live for the moments when we can steal away together. Summer is best. He keeps his boat nearby, so Elizabeth doesn't suspect a thing. And we don't have to worry about her wanting to come along with him, given how she feels about 'his damn boat,' as she referred to it the night we first met. Sure, it's a different boat now, but I'm guessing her feelings haven't changed.

Winter is more of a challenge. No good excuses, just lies. We're lying out loud to our friends, to our family, to ourselves.

The courtship continues in spite of the obstacles. Okay, courtship is the wrong word. *Call it what it is, Lily.* Our affair continues. Stolen moments, when he can get away and come to the Cape. Or on rare occasions, when he travels to New York City for work, he pays for me to take the train to meet him for a night of passion in a five star hotel. He leaves a key for me while he is out wining and dining. I wait in his room until he returns. After some small talk, there's an embrace, and a kiss, and I melt, and we end up in bed. Round one is charged with the intensity and urgency of time spent apart. Afterwards, we lie in the afterglow and catch up on each other's lives. It's not like we don't know everything already. We talk on the phone nearly every day. Yet somehow when I am in his arms there is always more to say.

We lie there, and talk, and rest. Until one or the other of us becomes aware of our naked bodies touching, and begins to stir, and round two commences. Relaxed now, we take our time, until he is on top of me, looking down into my face, both of us with eyes wide open. He says, "I can't get close enough to you." Is it possible to get closer than this?

After we make love in those fancy hotel rooms, reality sets in.

He heads into the bathroom. Leaves me to lie alone, the sheets still warm from our bodies. I look around at where I am, and think about who he is, and remember how wrong it is for me to be here. I am with another woman's husband. Anxiety creeps into my bones, into my stomach. This is a man with a weak heart. What if he has a second heart attack, tonight, right here in this hotel room? What will I do? Call Elizabeth? Or call an ambulance and then disappear? The fairy tale turns into a horror story. I feel panic. Sheer panic. I MUST stop this. This isn't right. *How can I possibly have allowed myself to get into this situation? This is WRONG.*

I use every trick I know to fight the anxiety. Focus on the good. Say prayers. Breathe. Say some more prayers. Breathe again. I stop short of promising God I will never do it again if I get out of it this time undiscovered, because I know I will. Scared as I feel, anxious as I am, wrong as I know this to be, I won't stop. I will meet him again. I will convince myself all will be fine in the long run because of our love for each other. This is just a hurdle we need to get over to prove our love to one another.

We are so damn cliché. A voice inside my head screams at me. *THEY NEVER LEAVE THEIR WIVES.* I've heard it said in movies. I've read it in magazines. Yet I still believe he will. Someday. Because my fairy tale is real.

I still wonder how I can keep doing this. Have I built the fantasy too large to let it go? Or maybe it serves me well. Here is a man with whom I can be wildly in love, or perhaps more accurately crazy in lust, share the fairy tale weekends, minus the downsides of domestic life. We never argue about who will take out the trash, or who leaves their dishes in the sink.

Though I did leave him alone in my place, one weekend.

Big mistake.

Chapter 33

Trust. It's a funny thing. She says she trusts me, enough to leave me here alone in her house this weekend while she travels to Pennsylvania to reconnect with old friends. For me, it's a fishing weekend, but I'm not so happy about her plan. Old friends? More like old boyfriends. And the ex-husband. She tells me I should trust her. Says I don't have reason not to, except for what she's done with me. Yeah, right.

She told me a while ago about a videotape she made with her ex. Apparently they got randy together one weekend and made a movie. Yes, one of those. She told me it's hidden somewhere here in the house, then gave me explicit instructions to under no circumstances try to find it. Which of course was exactly the wrong thing to tell me. I love a good challenge. I'm going fishing alright. Or maybe I should call it hunting.

Eureka! It's ten o'clock on Saturday night, and I am holding it in my hand. Found it in the bottom back corner of a trunk full of sweaters, wrapped in a brown paper bag (she's so predictable), with the instructions "do NOT watch" written on it in fat black Magic Marker scrawl. Now all I need to do is pop some corn, pour myself a shot of Jack, and let the show begin.

Oh no. This wasn't what I expected. I'm not sure how I thought I would react, but frankly, I am disgusted. It's like passing a car wreck on the highway. I can't turn away. I know I shouldn't watch it, won't like what I see, yet I can't help myself. I have to look. And then do my best to rid my eyes of the images I've seen.

It's not what you think. It's not the images of them naked together that bother me. No, it's the other ones on the tape, the far more intimate ones, that they shot before they got to the sex part. Scenes of the two of them showing off their new home. Newlyweds, right down to the white picket fence. They had hope for a life yet to be enjoyed together. They didn't have a clue how tough it could be.

They were simply happy. Together. There in their home. Those are the images that bother me. Evidence of her love shared with another man who she will most likely spend time with this weekend.

Just wait until she comes home. Won't she be surprised. Though maybe I shouldn't tell her I saw it. I should just put it back where I found it.

Yeah. Right.

Chapter 34

I walk into my happy Cape house, tired from traveling all day.

He says, "Welcome home."

I can smell the whiskey from across the room.

"What's up, Leo? It's Sunday afternoon and you're already half in the bag. What's going on?" He's sitting in my favorite recliner chair. The one he knows is meant for me and only me. The one Eddie and I bought when I was pregnant with Grace, that perfectly conforms to my body after countless hours spent there, nursing my baby.

"How was your trip down memory lane? See anybody interesting this weekend? Rekindle any old flames?"

"What the hell are you talking about? I told you I had business to attend to, and yes, I saw some old friends, but I wouldn't call them flames."

"How's Grace's daddy-o?"

"What the heck are you talking about? I didn't see him."

"Aw, c'mon. What's old Eddie boy up to? You can tell me."

"There's nothing to tell, Leo. What's going on? What the hell's gotten into you?"

"I saw the tape."

"Excuuuse me?"

"You know, the one you hid so well."

"You mean the one I specifically told you not to look for?"

"Yup. Watched every minute of it. Learned a lot about you."

"But Leo..."

"Don't but Leo me."

"I trusted you here in my house alone. And now you dare to be angry with me? I told you what was on the tape."

"Yeah, you told me it was a sex tape."

"Yes, I did, and I distinctly remember asking you to not look for it. It's private. You've violated me."

"No, Lily, you're the one who's violated me."

"Are you seriously going to turn this around on me when you're the one who turned this place upside down to find it? How dare you be upset with me?"

"You painted a horrible picture of your life with him. Well, obviously you skipped a few details. I saw you two together, there in your cozy little home, all full of young dreams. You looked happier than I've ever seen you."

"Oh, Leo. I can't believe you did this."

"Found you out, didn't I?"

"No, Leo. There's nothing to have been found out about. Yes, obviously I loved him, we loved each other, or we wouldn't have gotten married and had a child together. I'm sure we appeared to be happy together in those early days, because we were. But then life happened. And it did fall apart. And we got divorced. And now here I am, trying to be with you, while you're still going home to her every time. And I'm just... oh, I don't even know what to say. I still can't believe you snooped through my things when I specifically asked you not to. I trusted you."

"Yeah, well, I trusted you, too."

"I think maybe it's best you leave. Right now. Doesn't Elizabeth have dinner waiting for you? Please. Just go. And get the hell out of my chair."

But he doesn't. He stays the night. Why I don't just kick him out, I don't know.

Leo drinks some more, then stumbles into bed after he thinks I am asleep. I'm not. I can't sleep. I suppose I should be paying closer attention.

I ask God for signs, then conveniently choose to ignore the ones I don't like.

Chapter 35

Of course I forgive him. I always do. I've gotten what I wanted, sort of. I am in a committed, loving relationship. Except that it's with a married man who is not my husband. So I am his mistress. I wince at the sound of the word, but in truth it is who I am. And the role of mistress has unspoken rules to it, or at least it does for me. I want to be respectful. I don't want to do anything to cause this to blow up. It's bad enough I live in my own secret hell about it, but I don't want us to be discovered. Then I would be forced to deal with public shame.

I have only his office and cell phone numbers. I've asked for Elizabeth's cell number, just in case anything happens to him while I am with him. But he won't give it to me. He has his own paranoia.

He's already had heart attack number one. I worry about when number two might strike. I've asked him what I should do, should it happen when we are together. His only instructions to me are to call 911, anonymously, and leave him wherever he is. Just walk away.

Yeah. Right. I envision a crime scene investigation follows, like one of those things we see on television, where my fingerprints are found, and they track me down, and so now instead of just being found out to be the mistress I become someone who fled the scene of a horrible tragedy in a man's life. Though how do they even know the fingerprints are mine? Does Big Brother have me on file and I don't know it? But I've strayed. Um, I mean I've strayed from my point. There was a point.

The rules. The mistress rules. I never call him at home. Most mornings he is in his car by nine, on his way to work, so before that time, if I need to talk to him, I am simply not allowed. He assures me his email is private, instructs me I can use it anytime, but it's the museum's email, so I don't trust it. From nine-thirty until a little after five I can call his cell, but preferably not the office line, because even though his secretary now knows who I am, and fairly likely has figured out who I am in his life, I have to be careful to not over use it. *I'm glad she has me figured out because I'm not sure I do.* I have the phone number for his direct line, but she answers if he's not in, so now I'm back to the overuse thing. From five-thirty until seven-thirty I have the most access. I can call without any worry of someone else picking up, though occasionally someone does, and then I'm back to the previous rule. Oh, how I hate the rules.

Seven o'clock. That's magic time, the time when he calls me, Monday through Friday nights. Grace and I are finished with dinner. She's in her room doing homework, I'm cleaning up the kitchen, and he's wrapping up his day in the office. For about half an hour he's mine, and I get to pretend those other parts of his life, the ones where I don't exist, can't exist, I get to pretend they don't exist.

Except once in a while when he calls me at seven o'clock, most often on a Friday, it's from his cell phone and he's in the car on his way home. Those calls are okay, except for the moment when he pulls into his driveway, their driveway, and needs to hang up abruptly. Those are the nights when his phone call leaves me wishing he just hadn't called at all. I picture him as he walks into his beautiful house, Elizabeth's house, the one I've never seen and don't want to see but I'm certain looks like something out of *Architectural Digest*, and he says, "Hi honey, I'm home." She has dinner ready for him. They get to share the idle chit chat of domestic life, the part I do not. Instead I get to feel awful, because I am reminded of my role in his life. The mistress.

He tries to assure me it's not like that. He tells me their marriage has become more of a business relationship, not a romantic endeavor. He says he eats his dinner alone, then retires to his den, to do more work on his laptop, watch TV, drink a tall dose of whiskey, and head to bed. Sometimes I get an email from him, when he's there in his den, but I don't look for it, or expect it. At least not every night.

Waiting. I spend far too much time waiting. Waiting patiently, or as patiently as I can, for this married man with whom I have fallen in love. *What a ridiculous mess you have become, Lily.* Sometimes I wonder how I live with myself.

Christmas Day. Hands down the single worst day in the year in the life of a mistress. Because if he's still married, which obviously he is or one would be a girlfriend not a mistress, and if he has family – children, and possibly grandchildren if he is the cliché older man – then forget about it. He will be with her, and with them, every time. A mistress will absolutely always be alone on Christmas Day.

I have Grace, so I'm not necessarily alone, I just don't have Leo with me. And this year, I don't have Grace. She's with her dad.

Christmas morning. I wake up feeling more alone than I can ever remember. And as I sit here with my tea, in front of my tree with lights and ornaments and vestiges of previous Christmas mornings when Grace, Eddie, and I were together as a family, I am struck with a horrible thought. WHAT IF everything I think, feel, and believe about my life is incorrect?

What if Leo is never going to leave Elizabeth to be with me? What if he's just using me, because I'm stupid and gullible enough to believe he might? What if my prayers, and asking for signs, and hearing words in my head that I think are the voice of intuition coming from God - what if it is all just wishful thinking on my part? What if I'm only hearing what I want to hear? And what if, oh horrible what if of what ifs, what if I blew my one shot at marriage by expecting too much of Eddie? Maybe he was a good husband. And maybe I should have been more patient with his depression. And maybe I should have stuck by him through that time and stayed true to my vows of "through sickness and health." Did we even say that? I don't remember, and it doesn't matter now because it was his anger that drove me away but now I look back and wonder if I destroyed my own family, only to move on to destroy another family?

So goes the inner monologue in my head this Christmas morning. Families everywhere are gathered together in their pajamas, celebrating the joy of being together, including Leo and Elizabeth, together in their designer home. I'm the one sitting here alone, wallowing in more self pity and remorse than I ever thought possible.

And in a flash, I think I know how he felt.

Is this the pit of loneliness that drives someone to do what my father did? I contemplate the possibility. Have I brought down too many people, caused too much damage, that maybe I should just exit myself from their lives? What would it be like, to do as he did? A quick end to my pain. A disappearance into the dark abyss of death. And more practically speaking, how would I do it?

He tied a sailor's knot. One final, perfectly executed turn of the rope that for so many years was part of his joy, to become on that day his final act. Only to yield a violent end, and a horrible discovery for Brian. I do not wish to leave that sort of final vision of my body in the mind of anyone.

I consider something less gruesome. And indulgently peaceful. An easy way out. I go to the linen closet, and rummage through the odds and ends in the back. Yes, here it is. A bottle of leftovers, prescribed for me when my marriage was falling apart, just a little helper during the nights when sleep eluded me. They're surely expired by now, but does it matter? I'm surprised by how many are here.

I was so scared to take them at the time. Afraid I would become addicted. I dump them out on the bed. Count to twenty five. Surely that should be enough. Maybe I should grind them up. Mix them with some ice cream. Enjoy a big old hot fudge sundae before I sleep through eternity. The heck with a last supper. I'll end with dessert, thank you.

But wait. It's Christmas Day. There's a church service at eleven o'clock that my friend Celia invited me to attend with her. If I don't show up she'll come looking for me, and I don't want my plan to ruin her day, so my hot fudge sundae will have to wait. I put the pills back into the bottle, then throw it under the blanket to hide it from the cat.

So much for my master plan. Singing "Joy to the World" and "Oh Come all Ye Faithful" in church with a hundred other voices does not leave one in the mood to end it all.

And there's Grace. My dear Grace. What was I thinking? I'm appalled that I even considered doing to her what my father did to me. She deserves better. And so do I.

When I get home from church, there is a surprise Christmas gift waiting for me in my driveway. *What the...?*

"Leo? What are you doing here? It's Christmas Day." I'm a master of the obvious today.

"Yes, well. Surprise. Elizabeth and her sister got caught up in the kitchen making dinner and all but kicked me out of the house for a while, so I decided to sneak down here. I've only got an hour."

"Well then stop talking and come on inside." I unlock the front door, and he follows me. It takes us all of about two minutes to find our way into the bedroom, strip down, and find our way into, well, you know. No time to waste. It's frenzied, hot, and lovely. Until he rolls over.

"What's this?" His hand reaches under his back, and comes out with a pill bottle in hand.

"Uh, that's mine. I was cleaning out the linen closet earlier and I guess I forgot to throw that one away." *Nice save.*

"You were cleaning out the linen closet on Christmas morning?"

"Never mind, Leo. You wouldn't understand. Just hold me, please." And he does, for about five minutes. Then gets up, dresses, and is out the door.

But I'm grateful for it. Because that's another thing we mistresses do. We settle for crumbs. Just a few minutes, sandwiched in where he can make it fit without anyone finding out, and we're happy. Really we are.

I eat the hot fudge sundae for dessert, minus the extra garnish.

But it doesn't satisfy me. It never does.

Chapter 36

Is it possible for a man to have an affair like ours without his wife knowing something's not right? He tells me their sex life died years ago. He claims he's not cheating on me with her. Now, how ironic is that statement? He tells me they sleep in a king sized bed, and explains it's possible for two people to sleep together night after night in a bed as big as theirs and never touch, and I believe him. I believe him because I want to believe him, have to believe him, because to imagine him in bed with her any other way is too painful.

I believe him, but wonder about her. Does she miss it? He tells me she isn't interested any more. Maybe she has her own man on the side, and so this works for both of them, unspoken, unacknowledged, but it works for them.

Though honestly it doesn't. Not for me. Not any more. I've grown impatient. He talks about the possibility of asking for a divorce. But this is huge. Because it's a 'can't go back' step. I know he would stay married if I wasn't in the picture. While not a happily ever after kind of marriage, it's still a commitment he would honor, until death do them part. Maybe he'd find someone else to be his mistress instead of me, but he'd stay married.

Then of course it's possible he's lying to me about all of it. After all, he lies to her about me, so who's to say he's not lying to me about her. Maybe they are quite happy, and everything he's told me about it, about their life together, maybe it is all a lie. Maybe the joke is on me.

Even if he does decide to leave her, there's no guarantee it will work any better for us. I suppose I should remind myself to be careful what I ask for. I think I would feel obligated to make our relationship work, even if it doesn't.

There'd be no "let's try this relationship on to see if it fits." No, it would be more like, "I left her for you. Now you've got me."

I only know what it's like to have him here in my cozy home as a guest for a night or two at a time. And what it's like to stay in a plush hotel with him, and a few less than plush ones, too. I don't know enough about how he lives, though I remember what the inside of his desk looked like, before I cleaned it out for him.

I imagine how wonderful it might be to create a home for him. To fix his breakfast in the morning, and pack his lunch. To kiss him goodbye as he heads out to work. To be the one he comes home to at the end of his day. To fall asleep in his arms every night. The great domestic fairy tale.

He tells me he's working on it, weighing the pros and cons to make his big decision. He does this with a series of lists, the same as he does at work. I would love to see those lists, to read what he's written about me. But then again, maybe I wouldn't. I might be appalled. And then I might make it easier for him, because I would be the one who walks away, and he wouldn't have to.

There is so much I don't know, but the one thing I do know is this has been going on far too long. It's time. Something must change.

Another winter has passed. He stored his boat in my yard, and plans to retrieve it to put it in the water this weekend. He has a mooring nearby. He's become familiar around here. Grace now thinks of him as mom's friend, rather than my former boss. She's developing her own relationship with him, which is kinda cool, since her dad lives five hundred miles away, so she benefits from a man in her life, too. She seems to accept the friend thing without question, maybe because she is young enough to not know to be suspicious, even though she knows he is married. We are ever so careful to show no physical signs of affection in her presence. I'm embarrassed to admit I've learned to lie so well to my daughter.

Another Saturday waited for and finally here. I've cleaned the house. Stocked the refrigerator with grapes, a fabulous blue cheese, and a bottle of champagne, our favorite bed snack, perfect for feeding each other after round one. Grace and I will be out all day, so I leave a key hidden under the mat in front of the side door. He promised me he will have his decision made by today. Grace will go to a friend's house for dinner, to create the space for us to share a romantic evening to celebrate what will surely be a pivotal moment in our relationship.

I'm with Grace, and I'll be seeing Leo in just a few hours, so I've left my phone in my car. No need to carry it with me.

We get back in the car around five o'clock. Yes, there it is. My phone shows a new voicemail awaits.

Chapter 37

I listen to the message he left on my phone an hour ago, and know immediately from the tone of his voice I'm not going to like this.

"Lily. It's Leo." There's a long pause. "I don't even know how to say this. I've left a note for you in the garage. Hate me if you want to, but please know, please, please always know how much I love you."

Grace comes bouncing over to the car. "I'm ready to go home now." She stops. "Mom! What's the matter? You okay?"

I must look ashen, like I just heard someone close to me died, which is not far from how this feels. I do my best to shake it off and muster a smile. "Yeah. Sorry. Just got some sad news from a friend. Let's get you home and off to Kylee's for the night." I want to race home to read the letter he's written. Or maybe I don't.

This can't be real. I can't possibly have invested all this time, waited for him, only to have him choose to stay with Elizabeth and abandon me. It strikes me how utterly backwards, upside down and truly wrong that sentence is. Because if he makes his choice to be with me, she would be the one left alone.

The ride home seems to take forever. When we reach the driveway, Grace notices immediately. "Hey, looks like Dr. Leo got his boat today. Cool! Do you think we'll get to go out with him sometime soon?"

I ignore her question. "Get your stuff together. I think you're being picked up in about five minutes, aren't you?"

The door from the house to the garage looms like the gates of hell. Much as I want to rush out there to read what he's left behind, I can't. Not until I'm alone.

My beautiful daughter gives me a big kiss and hug goodbye, then looks at me again through the eyes of one who knows me all too well. "Mom, you sure you're okay?"

"Yes, Grace. Well, no, but I will be. Don't worry about me. Just have fun tonight, please? I'll come get you around ten o'clock."

Kylee's mom has just pulled into the driveway. Another hug, and Grace bounces out the door, full of joyous anticipation for her evening. Much as I thought I would be right now. I never expected this.

It occurs to me that his voicemail might have been a fake. He loves a good practical joke. I allow myself to enjoy a brief moment of hope. Maybe, when I go into the garage, there will be a dozen roses next to an envelope, with instructions to call him so we can begin our celebration. Maybe he is waiting nearby in his car. Maybe...

I consider pouring a shot of whiskey for fortification, but decide against it. Best to deal with whatever it is in full control of my emotions. *Yeah. Right. Like that's possible now. Just breathe, Lily. Breathe.*

I reach for the door knob, hesitant to turn it, fearful that something on the other side might be ready to jump out and bite me, while still hoping for roses. One last deep breath, and I open the door. Peer inside.

My garage has never looked so empty. Not since moving day. The various floats, lines, and life jackets that he stored here along with his boat are all gone. As are his coolers, and oars to his dinghy. No visible evidence of him remains.

Except for a single white standard No.10 envelope, lying alone in the middle of the floor.

One word is written on the front. Just my name, written by his hand.

I take my time as I unfold the letter. I want to stay in this moment, to savor the last few seconds I have to live the illusion that maybe, just maybe, in spite of appearances, it will be good news.

My dearest Lily,

You know by now I love you deeply and forever. You also know by now I must set you free, so that this great treasure of our love does not erode away as result of my constant vacillation.

After all this time, even I cannot believe I have not yet decided what to do about my marriage. But it is true. I have not. And I can no longer deny the fact that my indecision IS a decision. I can also no longer offer you any reasonable hope that I can or will give you the care and support you deserve, and that my love for you so desperately wants you to have.

A big part of me wishes it were otherwise. But we both know I could not and cannot come fully to you without first deciding what to do about Elizabeth. Even if I could muster the courage to come to you now, I fear my guilt would eat away at our relationship.

The ONLY way I can get to you is to reinvest in my marriage and find it impossible. When I approach the brink of leaving her for you, I feel great pangs of guilt for not having chosen to do that first, before I began to commit to you in my own strange way. Even as I lack enthusiasm for this whenever I think of you, something deep within me knows it is my greater commitment and responsibility, and I must at least try. And to truly give it a chance, give her a chance, I know I must release you. You and I must assume that our relationship in its present form and potential is over.

I do also feel and expect to carry with me enormous guilt for turning away from you, and from us. It may even become the larger and more painful guilt for me, knowing the pain this will likely cause you. The thought of losing you moves me to tears, and you know I do not do that easily.

This is my decision for now and the foreseeable future. It may not be forever. I realize I may well come running back one day, likely of course only to find you long gone. An unselfish part of me, in fact, wants it to be so, because it will mean you have found with someone other than me the true, honest love you deserve. I cannot ask you to wait for me. To do so would be unfair to you, more unfair than what you have already endured.

Only you can decide whether our relationship can survive in some new, less intimate, less painful form. My great hope is that we will not become disconnected, but rather can find some mutually rewarding and acceptable way to remain fast friends and soul mates. We have given each other great love, trust, peace, respect, confidence, and even fidelity. You are now part of me.

I will gladly be there for you to the fullest extent I can. Our love will always live on.

Leo

I can barely read through my tears. Why did I not see this coming? How did I ever believe he would do otherwise? This is who he is, who he always has been. A man of responsibility.

I fold the letter. Return it to its envelope. A hush has fallen over me, over my house. I walk back into the kitchen. I'm not sure what I should feel, even if I could feel in this moment. I'm just... numb. I can't argue with his logic, even as my heart is ready to explode, or maybe just stop beating.

When in doubt, my typical response is to find something to eat, preferably something sweet to dull the pain. So I go to my refrigerator. Open the door. And there it is. The bottle of champagne. Evidence of what I thought tonight would be, staring me in the face. My mood flashes from pain to anger. I slam the refrigerator door shut.

"Nooooooooo." A primal scream escapes my body. I can't breathe. I collapse to the floor. Start to yell obscenities, insults, accusations all aimed at him. So loud he might just be able to hear me from a few miles away. "You fucking idiot! This is bullshit. Absolute, utter bullshit. I actually believed you loved me. Sure, stay with her. I'll find someone   else.   Someone   younger. Someone...someone...single! I gave you how many years of my life and this is how you thank me? You probably planned this all along. Gaaaawwd. What an idiot I am." I shriek. I yell. I sob. I scare the cats and the dog. Then, I stop.

Out of the corner of my eye, I see my phone. I reach for it, knowing full well it is a bad idea right now. An extremely bad idea. And speed dial makes it all too easy to make the call. I'm surprised he picks up.

"Lily? Are you okay?"

Chapter 38

"How dare you ask me if I'm okay?! I got your fucking letter. How could you do this to me?" I unleash full force on him. Must sound like a madwoman just escaped from someplace with lots of locks on the door. *Why didn't I think first before I dialed?*

"Now, Lily, calm down."

"Don't 'now Lily' me. Screw you. Reinvest in your marriage? More like you're reinvesting in her trust fund. Why didn't you think of that before you screwed me?"

"Lily, please don't say things like that."

"Oh, excuse me. Made love to me. Made me fall in love with you. Gawd, I can't believe what a stupid fool I was."

"Lily, please don't do this."

"Please don't ME do this? Screw you. Better yet, go screw her." I punch the end button and throw the phone across the room.

I cry some more. The phone lies on the floor, just out of reach, and mocks me with its silence. It had been my lifeline to him. But he just pulled the proverbial plug. Our relationship is dead. Flatlined.

Sitting here, eyes closed, I breathe, slowly, and try to regain my composure. No man is worth this amount of pain. I'm stronger than this, aren't I? I should not allow him to have this effect on me. And just as my breathing settles into a relatively normal pattern, I am startled back to life by his ring tone. A fake sound of kissing, so I would always know when it was him. Even my phone is mocking me now. What a stupid sap I was.

I pick it up, not sure whether to answer or let it go to voicemail. Thankfully I am wise enough this time to know I can't talk to him. Not right now. Not yet. So I let it go.

Will he leave a message? I wait. Yes, there it is. I guess it's safe enough to listen, as long as it doesn't tempt me to call back.

Cue the voicemail. "Lily. It's me. I understand why you're upset. You have every right to hate me. Just please, please, don't call yourself stupid. You're not to blame in this. I am. And I'm trying, really trying, to do the right thing." *Good grief he's crying now.* "I'll be on Cape tonight. Gonna sleep in my car at the marina. Call me if you need to talk, Lily. I want you to be okay. And if you decide not to call me, that's okay, too. Just please know that my love for you is real. I simply can't do this to you anymore, or to her."

And there it is. Couldn't he have stopped before those last three words? I know he's doing the right thing. Might even be able to applaud him for it, with time. Just not yet. Not right now. My heart hurts too much. There's no room in it tonight for compassion. The pain, the loss, is too deep. I've gone numb.

No, I can't call him back. Not yet. Maybe never. I need time. Time for what, I'm not sure, but time.

I busy myself with cleaning up the kitchen. I turn on the radio, but all the lyrics point to my pain. Maybe silence is better. I take a shower. I know I should probably eat something, but I have no appetite. Not now. I consider opening the bottle of champagne, just for me, to celebrate my independence. It occurs to me I just lost the title of mistress. Now that's a good thing, isn't it?

I indulge in a glass of wine instead. The first sip feels warm and round sliding down my throat. Then the rim of the glass comes into focus, and my mind wanders back to his finger, circling the rim that first night at Gill's. No, can't go there anymore. Damn him. Even the wine glass mocks me. *Time, Lily. You just need time. Time to heal.*

I sit on the couch, phone in hand. I listen again to his last voicemail, but stop just short of the part where he brings her into it. Against my better judgement, I touch the "call back" button. He answers on the first ring. "Hi, Lily. How are you?"

"I don't think you have the right to ask me that question right now." It's a snarly reply on my part, but it's real.

"I understand," he says, "but I can still be concerned about you. I want to know how you are."

"Honestly, Leo? I don't think you get to want anything from me right now. This sucks. Big time. I had a celebration planned for us tonight. Thought for sure you would decide in favor of me. But I was wrong. Oh, so wrong. And you win no matter what. You have someone else's arms to go back to. But I'm left sitting here alone, all by myself."

He's slow to respond. Cautious. Tries to be gentle, in the face of my anger. "Lily, you know it's not like that."

"Do I? Seriously? I'm not sure what I know right now."

"You know this is what I need to do, don't you?"

He's right. I know he's right. There's just no way I can admit it. Not yet. I want to punish him first. I start to cry again. I don't want him to hear me like this, don't want to give him the satisfaction of knowing how weak I feel right now, but it pops out of me before I can filter. "This hurts so damn much. I miss you already."

"I know, Lily. It hurts me, too."

I let that one pass. "Where are you, Leo?"

"I'm in my car. Like I said I would be. At the boatyard."

"Can you come over? Here?"

"I don't think that's a good idea, do you?"

"I don't know. But you didn't even give me a chance to say goodbye, you just pulled the rug out from under me without warning." There's silence. A long silence.

"Lily, I want to do nothing more right now than to take you in my arms, hold you close, and tell you it's all going to be okay. But we both know what will happen if I come over."

I know he's right. He's trying to be strong for both of us, and I love him and hate him for it in the same instant. Besides, I'm supposed to bring Grace home in about an hour. How did it get to be this late already? I'm exhausted.

"Yes, Leo. You're right. I'm sorry. Forgive me, but I can't do this. I can't talk to you, it's just making it worse. I'm going to hang up now." And I do.

It's quiet.

Until the phone rings. Again.

Chapter 39

"Hey Mom, I know we were gonna hang out together tonight, bake cookies and stuff, but Kylee wants me to stay here. Can I, please?"

Oh no. I was just thinking maybe an evening with her would be a good distraction, but I know I'm a mess, and I don't want to have to explain to her why. Besides, maybe God's just gifted Leo and me another night. *No, don't go there, Lily.* I give in to her anyway. "Sure, honey. Call me in the morning when you get up, please?"

"Thanks. And hey, I'm sorry you had a sad day today. I love you, Mom. We'll play tomorrow." Her words hit the mark.

"Thank you, Grace. I love you, too. You're a dear, wonderful daughter. Have fun tonight, okay? And don't worry about me. I'll be fine."

"Thanks, Mom." She hangs up.

Without a moment's thought, I call him again. He answers on the first ring. "What's up? Are you okay?"

"Leo, please stop asking me that. I'm calling because Grace just called, and she's not coming home tonight, and so I thought, well, no actually I didn't think, I just had the phone in my hand and I hit speed dial and, well, would you come over here, please? Can't we share one last night together?" Oh crap, I'm whining. *You're stronger than this, Lily. Don't sound so needy.* "I promise I'll let go of you tomorrow. But tonight, I want you here with me. You owe me one more night."

The truth is, he doesn't owe me a thing. And I am, in fact, needy. I need to be in his arms tonight, one last time. My body craves it. Who knows how long it will be until I get to make love again. Might be a lifetime. Right now I can't imagine it with anyone other than Leo.

Fifteen minutes later he knocks. I open the door. Our eyes meet. We share a few seconds of pain. I try to be stoic, to punish him for my anguish. But in spite of my best efforts, I start to smile. He reaches out. I'm back in his arms. Home.

"C'mon, let's go inside before your neighbors start to wonder," he says.

We walk in through the kitchen to the living room. Sit on the couch. Look at each other. No words. I think he may be slightly afraid of me. He probably should be, given that it was less than half an hour ago I hurled those insults at him, shrieking like a madwoman.

I reach out, touch his cheek with my hand. I can't believe he's here, right here, with me. I lean in to kiss him. It's gentle. Tentative. I'm afraid to open the flood gates. But it is oh so sweet. A taste of something I might never have again. Like an alcoholic having one last drink on the way to rehab.

We pull apart. He takes my hand with both of his. "Lily, are you sure you want me here tonight? You know this doesn't change anything. I still need to follow through with what I said I'm going to do."

"I know. I know. And you're right. But can't we share just one more night together? Make love with me, please, just one more time?"

His eyes search my face, as he tries to discern if it will help, or deepen my wound. "You know I love you. I just don't want to do anything to cause you more pain. You sounded so awful on the phone earlier."

Now it's my turn to take his hand. I place it on my cheek. Look at him with tears in the corners of my eyes. "Please?"

Without another word we get up from the couch. I start toward the bedroom, reach my hand behind me for his. The same as I did that night at the beach. He takes it, as he did then. Except this time, we both know where we're headed.

The dance of our lovemaking begins. Slow and tender at first, until the emotions of the day take over. It becomes frenzied, wild, just shy of angry. Then moves to that higher place where two souls meld together. Of course we finish together. We always do. Then lay quietly. My mind rushes in. *This can't be the last time.* I roll away, my back to him, and tears start to fall. He reaches his arms around me. "Lily," he whispers, "please don't cry. Not now. We don't have to say goodbye. Not right now."

"I know, Leo. I just can't bear the thought of never sharing this again with you."

He's quiet. Then surprises me with his next words. "Somehow I have a feeling we will do this again. A love like ours doesn't end."

My pain fueled anger returns. I spin around to face him. "How dare you say that? You can't leave the door open on my heart. I have to be able to close it up tight after tonight and assume it's over."

"Shhh. Please don't do this. Not now. Don't spoil what time we have left. Just let me hold you."

I want to argue more, but he's right. Again. I settle back into his arms. And we fall asleep.

The phone startles us both awake. Its Grace. "Hey, Mom, can you come get me now?"

There's no time for another time. He's already out of bed, half dressed, buckling his belt. I look at him, open my mouth to speak, utter just one word. "Leo." Part question. Part pleading.

He comes over to my side of the bed. Sits down next to me. "We have to do this now, Lily. And it's probably best that we do it quickly. Your daughter needs you, and I need to move on to do what I said I was going to do. You told me you have to assume this is over. So you have to let me go now. Because if there is any glimmer of hope for us to ever have a future together, it can only be if I cleanly resolve the other thing. Just like I said in my letter."

Oh, how I hate it when he's right. But I don't know how to do this. Every fiber of my being wants it to be otherwise, even as I know on another level how right he is. I hate it, but I know it.

"So, Lily, I want you to remember three things. However angry you choose to become with me, and I understand if you need to be, honest I do, just please remember these three things."

Our eyes remain locked, even as our bodies have already begun the disconnect.

"Okay, Leo, I'm listening."

"Pay attention. There will be a quiz at the end."

He's attempting humor, but I'm in too much pain to smile. "Get on with it, Leo. You obviously don't understand how hard this is for me right now."

"I do, Lily. Just pay attention. Maybe it will help. Number one. We don't have to say goodbye. Not like it's forever. I'm still at the other end of the phone if you ever need me. I'm still here for you. You know that, don't you?"

I'm not sure what to say, so I just nod my head.

"Number two. I don't know how, and I don't know when, but this wasn't the last time. We will make love again."

I open my mouth to argue. He puts a finger to my lips to silence me.

"And number three. And this is the most important one, so pay attention. Just because I'm about to do what I'm about to do, our love doesn't end here. This love, our love, will last forever. You know that. How can it not? You've become a part of me."

And he's done. Still naked, I wrap myself up in his fully clothed arms one last time. I think this must be how an infant feels, swaddled in a parent's arms. Safe. Secure.

But the moment is fleeting. He says, "I need to go now. Just remember those three things, please?"

I nod yes.

"Oh, and there's one more thing."

"Seriously, Leo? You think I have any brain capacity right now to remember a list?"

"This is the easy one. And I mean it with every bone in my body. Whatever the outcome of what I'm about to do, this WILL turn out wonderfully for you, Lily. Please know that."

There's one last gentle kiss to the tip of my nose, then he leaves the room. I wonder if he expects me to follow him. I do not.

I sit on the bed, still naked. I hear him close the door. The car engine starts. Then I listen to Angel fly off down the road, just like our first night. Except this time, it is not the beginning. This time, it is the end.

It is finished.

Thank God for daylight. I don't cry. Just get up, pull the bed together, go through the motions of getting dressed. I'm on auto pilot now. It's time to go get Grace. To start my next new life, without him. Time to start over. Again.

Until the next day, when yet one more email arrives. In the subject line he has typed "The First Day of the Rest..."

Seriously, Leo? Like you didn't already hurt me enough? I should probably just delete, but you know me well enough by now to know I can't. I will read whatever it is he has to say.

Good morning, Lily,

I am mindful that we need to establish some thoughtful rules of engagement lest I backslide instead of progress with this. And that would be a pretty awful thing given all the time that has passed and growing stress and disappointment that you have endured.

But just a couple of things to insure that I left you with the right message yesterday.

To be sure you were listening (though this can be a self-test if you'd rather not report your answers), here is the quiz I told you I would give:

1) We do not have to say _____.

2) We will _____ _____ again.

3) This love will last _____.

4) You ARE a _____ of me.

And by the way, this test is worth 100 points with the first four questions each worth only 10. For the remaining 60 points:

5) Whatever the outcome, this will turn out _____ for you.

Whatever your total score now, you must memorize and remember these answers, forever.

Leo

I've surprised myself. Been okay, for the most part. Thought this would be a lot harder than it has been. I've told myself all sorts of stories to get me through. Ugly ones. Sad ones. Even happy and bright ones, about a future that might await me, with an appropriate, emotionally available man. I hold on to hope for the future to help let go of the past.

Being out of touch has been surprisingly easy. Going cold turkey is proving to be the best way. I was super proud of myself for not responding to his "day after" email. Took it on as the first test of my new resolve to be stronger, to be okay all by myself. There were two days of intense withdrawal, and then it got easier. I no longer dream we'll make love again someday, or he'll decide his marriage is not viable, leave her, and come back to me. I think his guilt will quite likely keep him there. And it probably should. I just hope she loves him, and they are happy together. Honest, I do.

Yeah, right. What a crock of horse manure that is. You didn't believe me, did you? My "strong all by myself" lasted about three days. Then reality set in. It's been hell.

Every night at seven o'clock I wait for the phone to ring. It doesn't.

Every night around eleven o'clock I experience a wave of nausea and mild panic when I wonder if the great divide of their king size bed has come back together. We didn't talk about new rules. If he's going to truly reinvest in that relationship, does it mean he might try to make love with her? Of course it should, but I can't bear the thought.

Occasionally I think I should go on a sexual conquest of my own. Find someone to "do" as guy speak would say, but that's not my style. Besides, how will I explain the tears that most certainly will fall from my eyes when someone holds me like he used to? There is only one man in whose arms I want to be, and he's back with his wife. We miraculously dodged the bullet and she never knew. All is as it should be.

I learn I'm a miserable failure at the waiting game. I'm angry. Out of sorts. Feel stuck. I am supposed to assume he's not coming back, but my heart is not ready to say goodbye. It wants to hold on to the possibility that we are not done. That in fact he will be back someday. That his damn list of three is correct.

My anger grows. I wonder, was it ever a reality that he might decide to be with me? I mean, why would he leave her? He had it all. Elizabeth in the perfect house, and me for easy sex whenever he could fit it into his schedule. He held the cards. He was in control. I was at his mercy.

I think I should use my anger as fuel. Get mad, seriously mad at him. "You did this to me. And now my life is in ruins." But Leo doesn't deserve all the blame. I was complicit. I knew what I was getting into from the beginning.

Instead I turn the anger in on myself. My intuition appears to have failed me. It's always been an accurate guide for my life. I made the mistake of believing he was the one. Was I so caught up in my love for him, my lust for him, that I misread the signs?

Mourning. That's what this is. I am mourning the loss of a significant man in my life who refused to feel the depth of my love for him, and made a choice to exit himself out of my life. I had no voice in the decision. And it occurs to me the awful parallel of what I've just said to the loss of my father. Maybe it's not just the loss of Leo that I'm grieving.

My therapist, Rose, tells me that grief has a long tail, and on it rides the remains of any previous losses not properly grieved. Makes sense, but man, oh man, it feels awful.

I tried to love him. Truly I did. But apparently it wasn't enough. I remember that in the week just before my father died, I did not reach out to him. More specifically, I remember thinking several times that week that I should pick up the phone, call him, and ask how he was, but I did not. It was as if something held me back from doing so. And now, in hindsight, it becomes far too easy to blame myself. What if I had called, maybe the night before, and expressed my love and support for him. Might he have changed his mind, and not done what he did? Do I carry some of the responsibility for his final choice on my shoulders?

Oh, what a tragic thought. Is this why I have chosen to love a man who I thought needed to be saved? Am I trying to make up for what I think I didn't do well enough with my father?

Leo isn't my responsibility. Never was, and certainly is not now. He presented himself to me as a man unhappy in his marriage, that one comment he made when we had lunch right before he left for Boston, and I took it as an open invitation to cross all boundaries of what was appropriate and ethical and moral in order to try to save him. Only to have him leave me, and go back to her.

Five minutes ago, I was a ball of emotion on the floor of my bedroom, curled up in a fetal position, sobbing, pleading for God to help me. I know God hears me. But I'm not sure I'm listening properly, if there are answers in response to my cries. I thought all along that I was being led back to Leo. But if that's true, why would it end up putting me into a place of such pain? Again. And again. And again. I either need a new set of ears, or a new God. *No, that's not right, Lily.*

God is God. Period. Okay. Then I need to fine tune my hearing.

This isn't new for me, going back to a man who has hurt me only to set myself up to be hurt again. Remember Ray? I wanted so desperately to feel his love that I allowed him to do things I knew weren't right. You'd think I would be wiser by now.

Maybe I think deep down in the midst of all of this there is some sort of answer for me in how to process my pain. Too much loss in my days. I need to find the key that will unlock it and allow me to release it. *Yeah, good luck with that one, Lily. This is a lifetime scar. It's never going to heal. Haven't you figured that out yet?*

So I sit here alone in my grief. I can't make him love me. Oh, I could whine and carry on and throw myself at him, and I suppose some, no, many, would say that I already have, way beyond what should be considered enough.

I need to let him go, to take better care of my own emotions, and to stop falling into a bundle of raw pain when I think of him. I need to find a way to be angry at him, so that I can move on with my own life, and to allow God to put a better man in my path, one who wants to love me as deeply as I want to love him. No more rejection, thank you. Bring on someone available, please.

I just spent the past hour trying to find his note. No, not Leo's. My father's. His cliché suicide note. I know he left one. And I know that I have the original hidden away somewhere, because my mother did not want it. It is an odd relic of one of the most tragic days of my life that I have turned into a sort of holy day, for it is the day he was released from his pain.

I'm not sure why today of all days it has become so important for me to find it. Maybe because Leo's birthday looms on the calendar, which of course is also the anniversary of the other Friday the thirteenth. Maybe I simply feel in need of a distraction.

I don't find his note, but I do find the coroner's report. My mother gave me that, too. Provides more information than I really care to have, but it's here. He died at approximately two o'clock in the afternoon. It states specifically *by means of asphyxia due to hanging. Manner of death is regarded as suicide.*

It goes on. *The deceased, a 58-year-old male, was found by a neighbor who broke into the house after being called by the daughter who indicated that she had been unable to reach him. She had contacted his place of employment midday and they said that he had called in this morning, indicating he would be late, but that he never appeared. He was found inside a locked bedroom in his residence, hanging by a rope. There was a note found indicating his intent to take his own life. The deceased was in the process of a divorce brought on apparently by an alcohol abuse problem on his part, and was due to vacate the premises on the day that he was found. There is no evidence to indicate that any other person was involved in this death. Postmortem toxicology showed no significant findings and a blood alcohol level of 0.00.*

Well now, that just seems like way more personal information and speculation than needs to be there. First of all, it's not even correct. I didn't call Brian. My mother did. And the truly ironic statement? *There is no evidence to indicate that any other person was involved in this death.* Seriously? I know the point is to deny the existence of any foul play, but, well, never mind.

He did get the last word though, didn't he? A blood alcohol level of 0.00. The alcoholic left this earth 100% sober. I'm not sure if that's good news or bad news.

A week later, Leo's birthday dawns as a gorgeous, blue sky and sunshine day on Cape Cod. I'm good. I don't call. I don't email. I don't text. Until around three o'clock, the phone is in my hand and his cell number is ringing. *What was I thinking?*

Before I can hang up, he answers. "Leo Stocker." There it is. The voice that has the capacity to melt my resolve. Surely he knows it's me by his phone's caller ID, though he doesn't sound the least surprised. But why the formality?

I attempt cute and coy. "Hello, Dr. Stocker. This is a voice from your past."

"Hey, I'm in a meeting. May I call you back in a few?" So abrupt. *Is he angry I called?*

"Sure. You've got my number."

He hangs up. I smack myself on the forehead. I should have waited. Shouldn't have called at all. Now I'm stuck, waiting again for the damn phone to ring. What's wrong with me? Why do I do this to myself?

The wait is, blessedly, only a few excruciating long minutes. I answer in the middle of the first ring. "Hi."

"Well, Lily. How good to hear your voice. Sorry I couldn't talk when you called. Work thing."

"I know. Look, Leo, I shouldn't have called. I apologize. It's just that it's your birthday, and you know what a sap I am about..."

He cuts me off. "I know." Now his voice softens. "How are you?"

"Pretty good, actually. I've surprised myself with how good I've been." I suppose I should be polite and ask how he is, but I'm afraid of the answer. So instead, with my heart on my sleeve, I say, "I'm probably not allowed to tell you this, but I miss you."

"Of course you're allowed to tell me. I miss you, too. Do you remember those three things I told you?"

I ignore his question. Can't risk going there right now. "I'm sorry, Leo. I shouldn't have called you. I don't know what I was thinking. I can't do this. I do wish you a happy birthday. And I hope you are well. But I hope you understand if I don't ask you more about your life. I need to go now."

"I know. And I understand. But I do still love you."

"I know, Leo. I know." I hang up without saying I love you back to him. In the short span of about one minute I've just unraveled far too much of my work of trying to walk away.

The rest of the day creeps by. I decide to write to him, to say those things I intended to say over the phone, but did not. Could not.

Dear Leo,

I probably shouldn't have called. But I did. It's your birthday. And I needed you to know I'm thinking of you. Oh, bullshit to that. I wanted to hear your voice, and your birthday was as good an excuse as any. Profuse apologies. Please forgive me.

I've just re-read the letter you left in my garage. And the one you emailed to me the day after. When I can see clear to put my selfish ego aside, I can hear the love that is within your words. Sad as I am to not have you in my life in the way I had dreamed of for far too long, I must agree you are doing the 'right thing.' You must be where you are. You MUST investigate your life with Elizabeth, and give it its chance. And I must, somehow, let go of you, and set you free to do that.

I love you, more than I can tell you. Probably too much. Some say in every relationship one person loves the other more. Well, I believe in this case I am the one who loves you more. Sometimes it surprises me you disagree. You say or do things that paint a picture of me being able to move on all too easily and 'get over this.' Not so, Dr. Stocker. Simply not so.

You are married. You have been since this began. And I should have known, long ago, to respect that. Should have known someday it would come around to bite me, as it has now. God's slapped my proverbial hand.

I do understand why you are doing this. I see in you a man who simply can't leave his marriage, who still in his soul believes that to be his larger obligation, and a commitment to be honored, in spite of what we've shared during our time together.

And so, IF I TRULY LOVE YOU, I must find a way to walk away. To stay in touch, call you, reach out - only makes this more difficult for both of us.

I've said this before, and I'll say it again. If you can be happy in that relationship - if you can make it truly worthwhile and the right place for you to spend the rest of your life, then please do so. Just please promise me you won't stay there simply out of guilt. I want you to be loved, just as you want the same for me.

It's my turn to walk away now, for you. I need to give you more room, to not yank you back to me. Just please don't ever forget the good that we shared. And know that down here on Cape there is a woman who loves you dearly, who cherishes her memories of time spent with you, and who will always think of you when she looks out over the blue waters of Buzzards Bay. How could I not?

> *Love,*
> *Lily*

Chapter 41

I didn't send the email. I worried that if I did he would feel obligated to write back, and we would get caught up in each other again. Better to just let him go. It got easier, a little bit, after the birthday mess I created. Maybe I needed to call him, to remind myself of how wrong it was on so many levels for me to do so. *Boy, look at that sentence. That speaks volumes, doesn't it?*

In spite of my fears about being without Leo, life has gone on. I've had a few dates, but my heart isn't in it, hasn't healed yet, so I've chosen to focus instead on my work. I've been painting a lot more, and found a few new galleries to represent me, selling enough to stay afloat financially. I'm developing a reputation for myself, on my own, without his help. I even sent an application to the Copley Society for professional artist membership. It was rejected, but at least I tried. *Good girl, Lily. Keep trying.*

Summer was tough. I drove past the boatyard numerous times. His mooring sat empty. Yet another sign of his reinvestment in his other life, boating closer to home, not near me. I think back to when his old boat sat under my window at the lake apartment, and how it comforted me. Now I sit alone.

Autumn is easier. I'm okay, or so I keep telling myself. Except when the wind turns a certain way, and the scent reminds me of our first day. The enchanted one.

We've had no contact since the phone call on his birthday. I want to show him I am willing to let him go. To surrender it all. To trust God to bring someone new and wonderful in his place. If only I can make it through this day, the first passing of our anniversary without him, I think I'll be okay.

It's mid-morning. I've been at my desk for the past two hours. The phone rings, but it's in the other room, so I choose to ignore it, and feel quite proud of myself for doing so. It's not his ring tone. I haven't changed it yet, so I would recognize it if it was him. Besides, he's not going to call. He's with Elizabeth now. I must accept it as fact.

An hour later I walk into the kitchen and see the phone on the counter. The caller ID shows a number I don't recognize. Probably a telephone solicitor. I consider deleting it, but decide I should listen, just in case it might be a new client. So I cue up the voicemail message, and let it play through speakerphone while I pour a glass of water from the fridge.

"Good morning, Lily. It's me. I'm on Cape, about three miles away from you. Can you please call me when you get this? Oh, and by the way, I have a new cell. Call me back at this number."

Holy crap. No wonder I hadn't recognized it. More to the point, why is he calling today of all days? Just when I've finally gotten over him. Sort of.

I'm not sure what to do. I've worked too hard to get to where I am. I don't want to unravel all of my work again. But he sounded urgent. And he's only three miles away. Where is he? Is he in trouble? I dial his number.

"Leo Stocker," he says.

"Hey. It's me."

"Thanks for calling back."

"Of course, Leo."

"So can you meet me at the beach? I don't want to do this over the phone."

"Do what?"

"Please don't ask any questions. Just meet me. Can you do that?"

"Uh, sure. Give me about twenty minutes?"

"That's fine. See you there."

Old habits resurface quickly. I do as he says. I don't dare ask more. Just say yes. Like always. And then try not to panic when I hang up. Question after question rolls through my brain. *Why today? Why now? Why did I say yes? How could I have possibly said no?*

I attempt to change my focus to a more practical concern. The recurring question of what to wear.

I decide to just go as I am today. Minimal makeup. He hates makeup anyway. Unintentionally, I end up wearing exactly what I used to say I would if I were ever to marry again. It would be a beach wedding, and I would be the bride in blue jeans, and a white T-shirt, topped with a stunningly graceful sweep of a veil. I'm all ready, except for the veil. *Oh my goodness, Lily, how have you let yourself race back there so fast?*

Leo always runs late, so I figure I have a few extra minutes to relax before I need to head out. I brew a cup of tea. Choose chamomile again. Some honey. It's all too familiar. I've done this before, to calm myself before we meet. At the same beach. At the same time. When I said I'd meet him in twenty minutes I hadn't looked at the clock. Turns out we agreed to meet at eleven o'clock, just like the first time. Grace is in school. I'm alone.

This time, however, I choose to drive, not walk. This time, I want to be sure I have a quick exit strategy, just in case. In case of what, I'm not sure, I just know I don't want to be trapped if he says or does something to upset me.

Fear overrides excitement. I wasn't prepared to see him today. Fantasized about it, maybe. But never expected it to be a reality.   °

His car is already in the parking lot when I arrive. He's standing at the shoreline, looking out to sea. I stay in my car and watch him for a few minutes. There he is. The man of my dreams. The star of my nightmares. He turns around, sees me, and smiles.

I take my time, all too aware of how much this feels like a scene from a movie, but unsure yet whether it's going to be a romance, a comedy, or a tragedy.

I walk across the parking lot. Stand beside him, with both hands in my pockets, so I can resist any urge to touch him. He speaks first. "You look...fantastic."

"Yeah, well, I've lost ten pounds since you last saw me."

"Wow. Good for you. It becomes you. Been working out?"

"No. Just didn't eat for a month. Weight melted right off."

"Oh." He's quieted by my passive aggressive jab.

My hands are still in my pockets. I stare out at the water. I can't look at him. "So, why'd you call me? And why today of all days? Are you even aware of what the date is?" I realize I sound more annoyed than I might intend. Or maybe I do intend.

"Of course I am. It's not a coincidence. Lily, please look at me."

"No. I can't." I am speaking slowly, each word deliberate. "You have no idea how hard this has been for me. Please say what you have to say so I can get back to my life." In my head the sentence continues. *You know, the one without you in it. The one I created after you dumped me.*

"I understand. You don't trust me. But I have news, Lily. Big news. Will you please look at me? This is important."

I take my hands out of my pockets, wrap my arms across my chest as if for self protection.

He continues, "I did it. I did what I said I was going to do. I tried the best I could to make my marriage work."

Did he call me here to rub salt into my wounds?

"We went to counseling. Tried it all."

I look at him. My eyes plead for him to not inflict any more pain. Then I look away. He puts a hand on my shoulder and turns me back around to face him. "It didn't work. It turns out she was as unhappy as I was. We'd both grown distant. It wasn't just me."

I stare at him as I let the words sink in. I'm afraid to believe what I think I just heard.

"It's over, Lily. We've filed for divorce."

I still don't say anything.

"Did you hear what I just said? I'm going to be a free man. We're not quite there yet, but it's in process. And I'm not sure I should ask this at this point - for all I know, you might be dating someone else by now - but I still love you, possibly more than I did before. I've missed you more than I knew I could miss someone. Do we have a chance, Lily? Not to go back, but to try again?"

What's wrong with me? Why can't I speak? Do I still need to punish him, or am I just stunned? My mind cannot believe this is real. My heart is afraid to believe it is.

He asks me, more directly this time, "Do you still love me?"

I look into his eyes. "Of course I do. I never stopped."

Now he's the one who reaches out his hand first. I push it aside. Instead offer my arms. He takes me into his, and lifts me off the ground.

When he lets go, I step back, cautious again. I say, "But can you understand why I'm afraid to believe you? I refuse to open my heart to you until I know without a doubt this is the real thing. I don't think I could survive the pain of losing you again."

"I do understand."

"So, tell me again. Slowly, please. What's really happening here?"

"I'd be happy to, but can we go sit somewhere? Preferably at a table where I can sit across from you and look into your eyes while we talk. I've so missed looking at you."

"I know just the place. Let's go."

I suppose the truly romantic movie scene would have us drive away together in one car, but I'm not ready yet to abandon my escape plan. Or to believe I'm going to get my happy ending. Not here. Not today. It's too soon. This was too easy.

Did I say easy? Allow me to correct myself. Letting go of this man was one of the most difficult things I've ever tried to do. Am I really willing to throw that away, and let him back into my heart?

Chapter 42

We're back in our favorite booth at Gill's. It's lunchtime, so I don't have to ponder the wine question of should I or shouldn't I. Enough other reasons to ask myself that question right now.

I start. "So, you said you want to talk. And I'm going to do my best to listen without interrupting you. I just need you to please promise me one thing."

"What's that?"

"Please don't hurt me again."

"Lily."

His look says the rest. I can see his pain. I can stop beating him up now about the past five months. It occurs to me for the first time today that's all it's been. Just five months, though it felt like five years. Or maybe decades.

"I'm going to spare you the details," he says. "I'll tell you what you need to know, what I think you'll want to know. Then you can ask me whatever questions you want. We filed for divorce a week ago, which means it's going to take a little while for our attorneys to figure out the details, and for the courts to do their part. You know our finances are complicated."

I wince.

"And...Lizzy and I are still living together."

My wince turns to a cringe.

"But we're in separate bedrooms."

Back to the wince. There's a question that begs to be asked. "Does she know about us? About me?" He pauses, as if uncertain how to respond. *Uh oh.* This can't be good.

"She doesn't know, though she certainly suspects. That's why I have the new cell phone. It's free and clear of our history. Doesn't show any traces of the old us."

Ouch. Does he know how harsh that sounds?

"Lily, do you understand me? I'm trying to protect you. If she finds out about you, about us, what is so far a relatively amicable divorce could turn ugly. Real ugly. And that wouldn't be good for anyone."

"But Leo, need I remind you there isn't an 'us' right now? You broke up with me last June."

"You and I both know what went on before. And it's a dangerous history."

So my gut feeling has been correct during the past hour. I do need to remain cautiously optimistic. This isn't going to be easy for me.

"So, Leo, what's the bottom line here?" I ask. I'm not planning to make it easy for him, either. Guess I don't feel like I have to, after what he's put me through.

"The bottom line is I am working my way back to you. Back to us. But it's going to take a little while. Hopefully no more than a few months. In the meantime, we need to be even more careful than before. She knows you. And she's always been suspicious of you. Remember the day she found us out at the lake?"

"Yes, of course I remember."

"If she finds out about us before it's final, I know her well enough to know this will turn seriously nasty. And expensive."

"So what exactly is it you want from me, Leo?"

"Will you wait for me? Please? Can you find a way to be patient just a little longer?"

I sigh. If he hadn't said please, I would probably respond with a smart assed retort. Yet the way he said it, the tone of his voice, the look in his eye, well, I can feel the walls I've built around my heart beginning to crumble.

"Do you even need to ask, Leo?"

I reach out my hand across the table, but he doesn't take it. "We still have to be careful," he says.

"What exactly do you mean by careful?"

"I know this is going to sound rough, but it means minimal contact, and certainly extra caution in public. It's going to be worth it in the long run, though. I promise."

My food has grown cold. Untouched. Just like me. I'm not sure what to say. It's possible I've just been served my fairy tale happy ending, but it's accompanied by a huge helping of delayed gratification I have to swallow first.

"I don't know, Leo. I'm not sure. I mean, you know I want to be with you. I'm just not sure how to do this part. You're asking me to undo all I've worked so hard on these past five months, and I'm not sure I trust it yet."

"I know. I'm asking a lot of you. But if it helps to take the pressure off, you should know I'm going through with the divorce no matter what."

"Well, I guess that's a good thing. But I still need a little time to process this."

"Take as much time as you need. Though I still haven't heard you say yes."

I say, "I'm sorry. What was the question?" I'm not being coy. Just confused, and a bit overwhelmed.

"The question is... will you wait for me? Do you want to give us another try?"

"I don't know, Leo. I mean, I know I still love you. I never stopped, even when I should have given up all hope. And now you're back here, well, sort of, and I just, well, like I said before, I just need some time to process this before I can answer you. I'm sorry."

"No, don't say you're sorry. I understand. I'm guessing you didn't expect to hear from me today, and now I've sprung this on you. Is there someone else? I didn't even ask you if you were available."

"No, that's not it, Leo. I'm just afraid. Give me a little time. I'll let you know. Soon. I promise."

"Take whatever time you need, Lily. You've waited long enough for me. Guess it's my turn now to wait for you."

He pays the check. We walk out to our cars. I lean back against the door of mine, grateful it's here for me. I ask, "So, what are the rules now? Am I allowed to call you?"

"Yes, though probably best not on my cell. Call the office, around seven, any day. I'm there alone then."

And just like that, I'm cast back into the role of secret hidden mistress. Except this time around I'm a mistress who isn't allowed to touch my man, and I'm still not even sure if he is my man.

"I don't know, Leo. This already feels much too much like before."

"I assure you, it's not. It's going to be different this time. You just have to trust me. Oh, and Lily, there's one more thing."

"What, Leo?" Again I sound more annoyed than I intend to.

"Remember those three things I told you, back in May? The three things I wanted you to never forget?"

"Of course I do. How could I possibly not?" He doesn't know about how I clung to them for the first month, then wrote them on a piece of paper and ceremoniously burned it in my fireplace.

He says, "I think the answer to your 'I don't know' lies in those three things. Spend some time thinking about them. Then call me. When you're ready. I'm not assuming anything. It's totally up to you now to say yes or no. I'm simply asking if you still want to be with me." He lifts my hand to his lips. Kisses it. "I'll be waiting for your call."

He walks to his car. Gets in. Smiles, then winks at me as he pulls away. Smug son of a bitch. I do still love him so.

I drive back to the beach, our beach, on my way home. To consider, as he suggested, what he told me last May.

Number one. We didn't have to say goodbye. Looks like he was right, because here we are, back in touch again.

Number two. We would make love again. We haven't yet, but the option exists, or at least the potential for it does, more than it has in the past five months. So I guess I can say he was almost correct there, too.

Number three, our love would last forever. I am part of him. I'm not sure how much I still believe this one. I've just spent the past five months questioning how he could walk away from us. Am I ready to take the risk?

It's three o'clock. Time for Grace to come home from school. I'm not allowed to call him until seven. A good thing, because there's a lot to consider. What about my dream of someone new, someone without the baggage this relationship carries? Saying yes to Leo means letting go of new possibilities. It means instead I go forward dragging along the old suitcase full of guilt. Am I willing to put all of my hopes on this man, again, in spite of what has been? Might it be possible, if we wait until after his divorce is final, to start clean and fresh and leave the baggage behind? Damn him for opening the door to my heart again. I worked so hard to close it.

So many questions roll around in my head while I drive Grace to ballet. Then bring her back home. Fix dinner. Pass the time until I can call him. I'm still undecided what I will say. He didn't say I had to call him tonight. But I know I can't wait. I need to get on with my life.

Grace heads up to her room to do her homework. Seven o'clock. The time I dreaded for so many weeks this summer. Even rearranged our evening routine so I'd be distracted away from it. I take a deep breath. Reach for the phone. I'm ready now. I'm resolved to do the right thing. It's time to stand up for me.

He answers, as usual, on the first ring. "Leo Stocker."

And that's all it takes. Just the sound of his voice. I'm like a bee to his honey. "Yes," I say.

"Yes?"

"Yes. I'll wait for you."

And just that easily, I'm back in the game. Did I say easily? *Good Lord, what have I done?*

Chapter 43

He's back in my life. Except he isn't. It's more like the potential of him is back.

And there are rules, again, more strict this time than before. I may not call his cell phone unless it's an emergency. And I can't call the office until, well, you know by now what time. We are on heightened alert to avoid discovery until after his divorce is final.

Winter is slow. We manage to see each other only about once a month. The good news is he will not spend Christmas with Elizabeth and the kids this year. She opts instead to spend the week with their grandchildren. Poppa, that's his grandfather name. Poppa is left out this year.

Grace is also with her father this year for the holidays. So for the first time Leo and I get to share both Christmas and New Year's together, but only the day parts. No overnights. He needs to be home in the evening in case she tries to call him there. I know he's doing his best to keep it clean, but it hurts. During the day he can claim to be at work. And he probably would be, if it wasn't for me. No, more likely he'd be with her and with the kids. The switchboard is closed for the holidays, so the office phone can't ring through. Fortunately his cell phone doesn't disclose his location.

My patience wears thin. Leo reminds me it will be better on the other side. "Stay focused on the long game," he tells me. The other side of his divorce will be our time.

Again I grow impatient. I'm guarded, afraid to fully re-open my heart to him. What's the saying? Hurt me once, shame on you. Hurt me twice, shame on me. Well, I've had enough shame. I don't need any more, thank you.

We spend New Year's Eve day together, then he drives home. And I drive to the airport to get Grace. She and I ring in the new year together. I feel tired. My throat is scratchy. A ticklish cough that starts in the afternoon is lodged deep in my chest by midnight. Probably just the stress of it all. Nothing a good night's sleep won't cure.

I wake up alone in my bed on New Year's Day. Add to my symptoms a now raging fever. And when I cough it feels like razor blades are scraping my lungs from within. So I spend the first morning of the new year in the hospital emergency room. They send me home with massive antibiotics and a narcotic cough syrup to help me sleep through the night. That's a blessing. Sleep has been a myth lately.

It doesn't make me feel any better to have to do this without him. You know how people talk abut being sick and tired of a situation? Obviously my state of health, or lack thereof, now reflects my emotional condition. I'm literally sick and tired of waiting for him.

Three days later, Grace joins me with a fever and cough of her own, though I'm thankful it's not as bad as mine. We're quite the pair, as we try our best to take care of each other. When we run out of juice and munchies, we time our doses of acetaminophen to bring our fevers down simultaneously and make a dash to the grocery store before the fevers surge again. Stock up on juice, juice, and more juice. Our taste buds are confused, dulled by the fever and congestion, but we remember what feels good, so add to the list a box of Lucky Charms. And Oreos. Comfort food for the uncomfortable.

Grace recovers more quickly than I do. Fever gone, she's ready to head back to school after a week at home. My fever remains, as do the razor blades. After another trip to the doctor, and a chest x-ray, and I'm told it's bronchitis. It probably was pneumonia at some point, but then the drugs worked their magic. Still, I can't remember the last time I felt this sick and miserable.

My emotional exhaustion doesn't help. It's a bitch doing this alone. I have far too much time on my hands to think. I worry he might change his mind and not follow through with the divorce. He tries his best to reassure me during the few minutes we have to talk at the end of each day. "All is well. Be patient, my princess." I want to trust what he says, but find it difficult.

Going to my studio is difficult. It's far too cold a place to be when I don't feel well. I set up an easel in my bedroom, just the basics of what I need, to work on a commission that came to me a couple of months ago, back before my world fell apart. Did I say fell apart? An odd choice of words, since it should be that it came together, with Leo doing his part to complete his divorce and make his way back to me, but it feels so lonely without him. In any case, the rent must be paid, and the bills keep coming in, oblivious to the fact that I'm sick, so I cannot afford the luxury of not working.

To my great surprise and delight, my painting is flourishing. Perhaps it's my pent up emotion unleashing itself on the canvas. I'm working on a portrait of a man with his dog, and it is as if the muse has rushed in to take care of me. I love lying in bed staring at the piece on the easel. The painting almost paints itself. I wonder if there is a message in this for me, about my creative process. *Don't try so hard, Lily. Trust it. Trust it all.* After I finish the portrait, I move on to some larger seascapes. Skies, mostly, over calm water. I think I want to dive into them and swim away.

The deeper meaning through art thing? I'm still skeptical of it. And I think there's a lot of bull that is tossed around in the name of higher thinking. Now, please don't get me wrong. I'm all for a good liberal arts education. Got one myself. I love the idea of searching for meaning in life. But it might be another reason why I shied away from being an art major, in spite of my love of paint, or an English major, though I love to write.

I remember hearing a professor talk about her desire to push students to seek not just first level or second level meaning from a paragraph of Hemingway, but third, fourth, and sometimes even fifth levels of meaning. And pardon me for being so pedestrian, but I thought to myself, *how does she even know those meanings were intended?* MAYBE he was simply writing a cool story about fishing because he loved going out in boats. A frustrated fisherman with a drinking problem, living in Key West. Does she know both he AND his father committed suicide? And she wants to attribute fifth level meaning to individual words within a sentence? Please. Don't be ridiculous.

I'm starting to dabble in writing down my thoughts about my paintings. I write stories, or sometimes just short paragraphs, to go with them. It's as if the pieces are beginning to speak to me. They take on a life of their own. Perhaps I should blame it on codeine in my cough syrup. Whatever it is, I like it. Though I haven't told anyone about it yet. I've become all too adept at keeping secrets.

January, February, March, finally April. With the passage of time, my strength is restored, and my optimism is renewed. Spring beckons, flowers bloom, and it's time to think about the beach. Boats start to appear in the harbors. My life feels like one of those old black and white movies where the passage of time is marked by the ripping of calendar pages off the wall. I'm ready for the drab to go Technicolor. Leo and I only get to see each other about once a month, but he assures me our time is near.

I'm weary of being home alone, facing my demons. I'm ready for a trip to Oz, where wishes are granted and fantasies fulfilled.

Though today is one of my less patient days.

Seven pm. Magic time. The phone rings. Here we go again.

Chapter 44

"Hello, Leo, how are you tonight?" My voice betrays my impatience.

"Leo who? I'm calling for Liliana Daniels."

Oh crap. I didn't look before I answered. It's not him. I removed his ringtone several months ago, when the fake kiss became an annoying reminder. And in my current state of caution I have not yet replaced it.

"Yes, this is Liliana. I'm sorry. Who's this?"

"It's Jack."

I pause. There's only one man who ever called me by my full name. I should have known it was him. "Pardon me. I was expecting somebody else." There's an understatement. My voice softens. "How are you, Jack? It's been a long time." The sound of his voice takes me back. Why is he calling? And why now of all times?

"I'm good. More importantly, how are you? You didn't sound too happy when you answered the phone just now. Did I catch you at a bad time?"

"No. Sorry about that. I was just...distracted." The call waiting signal interrupts our conversation. It's Leo. *Of course it is.*

"Are you getting another call?" he asks.

"It's not important. My voicemail will pick up." Tonight I'll let Leo feel what it's like to not be able to get a hold of me when he wants to. *Passive aggressive much?* Yup. So be it.

"I'm surprised to hear from you, Jack. Happy, but surprised."

"Yeah, it's been a long time, hasn't it? I don't remember when. But hey, listen, let me cut right to the chase. I'm in Boston for a few days on business. Heard through the old grapevine that you were living on the Cape. Thought maybe since I was so close I might offer to drive down and buy you dinner. You know, for old times' sake."

Why now, of all times, has my college sweetheart decided to show up? I should rephrase that. He was my college crush. Unrequited love. Best of friends, but we never dated. Though there was a time I was so lost in my starry eyed affection for him I would have immediately dumped anybody else, in a heartbeat, to be with him. But he was always dating somebody else, or I was, and our single times never aligned.

I do have quite a knack for falling for the unattainable, don't I? I just don't understand what bizarre sense of humor God must have to make him show up in my life while I'm in the midst of waiting for Leo.

"Liliana? You still there?"

His voice snaps me back to the present moment. The phone shows a new voicemail from Leo. I'm stuck in between. *Boy am I ever.*

"Yes. Sure. I mean, yes, I'm here. And yes. Dinner sounds great. Come on down and I'll show you my new world." The same words I spoke to Leo not so long ago. Here I go again. Or not. I have the presence of mind to ask Jack the most important question. "And will your wife be joining us?" I'm not going down that road again.

"Nope. It's just me."

"Oh?"

"Yeah, there's a story to tell you, but not now. We split up about a year ago."

"Oh. Well, I'm sorry to hear that."

"You are?"

"Well, of course I am. I never like to see someone go through that. So how about if you tell me more over dinner?" I give him my address. We agree to a time. He gives me his cell number.

He says, "By the way, I answer it twenty-four/seven. If you need to change anything tomorrow, just call me. Otherwise, I'll be in your driveway at five-thirty."

Imagine that. An unmarried man, and I have permission to call anytime I want to, no rules. What a concept.

I wonder if I need to tell Leo about this. Then I remember his voicemail is waiting for me. It's almost seven thirty. He'll be in his driveway in a few minutes. Should I listen first, or just go ahead and call? I dial his cell number. Whatever he said in his message he can certainly tell me again in real time.

"Hi. It's me. What's up?"

"Did you listen to my message?" He sounds annoyed. Or maybe I do.

"Nope. Sorry. I was on another call." *Yeah, with my old crush, who is now available, and oh, by the way we're having dinner tomorrow night.* Filter in place, I keep that piece of information to myself.

He says, "Well, here's the thing."

"Oh, great, now there's a thing?"

"C'mon, Lily. Why so grumpy tonight?"

"Not grumpy. Just tired of all this."

"Yeah, well, I thought you'd be happy to know we have a final divorce date in sight. Sixty days from now, I'll be a free man."

Woo hoo. He's right. I should be thrilled. Only two more months to wait. In the meantime, temptation is luring me to dinner. Legal temptation. Open, honest, single, don't have to hide from anyone temptation.

"Gee, Leo, I guess that's good."

"You guess? I thought you'd be overjoyed. I'm doing this for you, remember?"

A knot forms in my stomach. "You what?"

"I said I'm doing this for you. The divorce. I thought you'd be ecstatic. You're finally going to get what you've wanted all along."

Oh my. We shouldn't talk about this now. Not on the phone, when we have only a few minutes.

I do anyway. So much for my filter. "But I never asked you to leave her for me. I thought you did this because you decided you needed to for your own good reasons. Remember you said you were going to get the divorce whether I was here or not?"

"C'mon, Lily. We both know it isn't quite that simple. Listen, we don't have time for this now. She's expecting me home for dinner and I don't risk being late or this could all blow up in our faces. We're so close to the end. Let's not do anything stupid. Can we talk about this another time? I can call you a little earlier tomorrow night, say around six?"

"No, Leo. I can't. I have other plans." There's something he's never heard from me. He's used to me dropping everything for him.

"Oh," he says. "This weekend, then? I can call you sometime on Saturday."

"Yeah. Whatever."

"Whatever? What's up, Lily? Are you okay?"

"No, frankly, I'm not. My patience is about run out. And now you just dumped your divorce on me, like it's my fault. Go home, Leo. Go home to Queen Elizabeth. She's got dinner waiting for you, remember? God forbid you do anything to upset her. Don't give another thought to how I feel. Same as usual." I can't help myself from dripping sarcasm all over him. "Call me on Saturday if you want to, but right now I have to go."

"I love you, Lily. Remember that. You're part of me."

"Yeah. Whatever. Goodbye." I hang up.

Well, that wasn't good. And the timing couldn't have been much worse. Now not only do I have a date tomorrow night, but I will go into it with things unsettled and ugly with Leo. Am I a master at setting myself up or what?

Chapter 45

Friday. I'm still stunned. Last night in the span of about an hour I transitioned from girl alone, to girl about to go on a date with an old flame while another man is about to divorce his wife to be with her. How did I get from there to here? And isn't the question usually about getting from here to there? It appears I often address life backwards.

He was supposed to determine the future of his marriage on its own merits. I never asked him to leave her for me. Or maybe I did without knowing I did. I just don't know. Sure, it was an unrealistic expectation for him to decide it without any influence from what we had shared, but to say he's leaving her for me drags along all sorts of guilt in its net.

Then there's this so called date of mine tonight. If Jack had called several weeks ago I'd be excited. Might be thinking he could be the one, or at least the next one, or that maybe he is the reason Leo and I didn't work out. It would have been easy. Clean. Uncomplicated. I could unleash the college fantasy and give it free rein to see where it wants to go.

Instead, I feel like I'm about to cheat on Leo by seeing Jack tonight.

Now, how ridiculous is this? I'm a single woman, worried I might be cheating on my married boyfriend by going out to dinner with a single man.

Then there's the timing to consider. For this girl who believes deeply in divine order and looks for signs, why is this happening now? I ignored Leo's phone call while I was on the phone with Jack. Then when I did call him, what should have been a joyous conversation turned sour. There's no time to talk further tonight, unless I do something stupid like excuse myself to the ladies' room and sneak out to call Leo. But that wouldn't be right. I'd be cheating on Jack, and who knows, someday we might consider this our first real date. I wouldn't want a secret phone call with Leo to be a part of the memory of the night.

Oh my. It's like I'm praying to God asking for a sign, and now I'm saying the neon one isn't bright enough, I need something more obvious, please. Something impossible to misinterpret. Maybe skywriting? Like in the *Wizard of Oz,* when the Wicked Witch writes *surrender Dorothy* in the clouds. Maybe that's what I need. *Surrender Lily.* But surrender to what? Or to whom?

I suppose I could call Jack and cancel, and make time instead for Leo. But no, I'm going to go on my date with Jack. Why shouldn't I? Jack is the man I dreamed about before I even knew Leo. Worst case, I discover he still has the capacity to sweep me away, and I create more drama and confusion in my already messed up life. Best case, I learn it's all in the past, and I can go on with Leo, and never have reason to look back or wonder what if. Maybe that's why this is happening now, so I can be free to move forward without regret.

Time again to decide what to wear. I've done this before. The similarities are striking. The differences far more remarkable.

It's Friday night dinner, so I can dress up this time. Black knit tank dress, with a floral cardigan. Always the black tank top in some form. I guess it's my thing. Sandals. Silver jewelry. Happy makeup. More than I usually wear with Leo, since he doesn't like it. But I do, so I allow myself to indulge.

Next decision. Where to go for dinner. I know it won't be Gill's. That's our place, Leo's and mine. It would be far too strange, and disrespectful.

I'm still struggling with the irony of my situation. Jack is the man who I always wanted to date but never did. He's single. And I'm single. Tonight we finally get to explore our potential. Only I will do so with my fingers crossed behind my back. Crossed not for good luck, but in the way we do to make something not really count. Like I'm lying, and I know I'm lying, and I want to protect myself from whatever evil forces might be out to get me because I'm lying.

Well, honestly, it's more like I'm living a lie. And if that isn't enough, I'm about to go out on a date with one of the most honest men I have ever known in my life. I certainly can't tell him I am on the verge of starting a new life with a man who is about to divorce his wife to be with me. Good Lord, how did I get myself into this one? What bizarre, sick sense of humor does God have to time it this way? Is this a test of my love for Leo, or maybe a test of respect for myself?

All great heavy questions to ponder, if I didn't have less than half an hour until Jack is going to show up to sweep me away. I mean pick me up. In his car.

I'm dressed. Makeup is on. Purse is packed. It's five-fifteen. He's due here in fifteen minutes. I pour a short glass of wine to take the edge off my nerves.

My phone vibrates. *Oh Leo, not now, please.* I know I shouldn't but I pick up anyway. I'm deadpan in my greeting. "Hi."

"Hello, princess."

"I thought we agreed to talk tomorrow, Leo?"

"I know. We did. But the office cleared out early, and I'm here alone, so I thought I'd surprise you." Thank God at least he's in Boston and not about to show up at my door. Wouldn't that be a lovely mess if they both showed up in my driveway at the same time? He says, "Aren't you happy to hear from me?"

I hesitate, about four seconds too long. Hope he doesn't notice. "Of course I am, Leo. I just can't talk. Not right now." I've got my eye on my driveway. Silent prayer. *Please, God, get me out of this gracefully.*

"What's more important than us? You got a date or something?"

Now I can either say yes, or I can lie. Lie to this man with whom honesty has become so important to me.

"Well, since you asked, yeah, I kinda do." *Damn.* It jumped out of my mouth ahead of my brain.

He says, "Oh." Then there's dead silence. Is he waiting for me to say something else? I look out the window again. There's a car in my driveway. *Oh crap.*

I say, "Look, it's not actually a date, it's just an old friend. That's all. You know my heart belongs to you. But he called, and it's Friday night, and well, shit, Leo, how many nights have I sat here alone while you continued to share a house, hell, a bed, with your wife? Gimme a break. It's just dinner. I've had to trust you for how long? Don't you trust me?"

I see Jack is walking to my door. Oh my. The years have been quite good to him.

"Leo, I'm so sorry about this. I know it's awful timing, but I have to go, right now. Can you call me tomorrow, please? I do love you. You know I do."

"Yeah. Sure. Whatever. Have a nice date." Now he's the one dripping the sarcasm. We hang up. The doorbell rings. No time to think. I swig the last drops of wine from my glass, pin on my best fake smile, and answer the door.

"Liliana! Are you okay?"

How bad must I look that those are his first words?

"Yes. I'm fine. Just had a weird phone call, that's all. But hey, it's so great to see you!" He reaches out his arms, I think to hug me, but no, he's handing me flowers.

"Oh, Jack, they're beautiful. And so thoughtful. Thank you." Even better, or maybe worse, he's remembered my favorite. A spray of white daisies with a single peach colored rose in the center.

I look up from the flowers, and our eyes catch for the first time in such a long time.

Oh my. I'm in trouble now. Big trouble.

Chapter 46

I pull myself together. Leo. My heart belongs to Leo.

Jack drives one of those smaller suv's. Good on mileage. Highly functional yet comfortable. Just like him. The quiet, sensible type. No loud flashy sports car for him.

I suggest a waterfront restaurant called The Chart Room. It's a place where I'm always likely to run into others I know. The kind of place where I don't dare to go with Leo.

Our conversation flows easily. We have a lot of years to catch up on.

He orders a bottle of wine for us. A deep dark Malbec, my favorite. How does he know? Leo drinks that awful Chardonnay. Canal water to my taste buds.

Stop making comparisons, Lily. It's not fair to anyone. I deserve this evening. It's about time I let go a little.

We finish the first bottle. Move on to a second. I'm amazed at how easy it is to be with this man. I don't do a head jerk every time the door opens, afraid of who might come in and see us.

We laugh. A lot. Thoughts of Leo fade far into the distance. This feels so good. Much too good.

Our dinner finished, we linger over dessert. Dark chocolate ganache torte. Perfect pairing to the Malbec. My hands are on the table in front of me. *How long has his been on top of mine? And how did I miss it landing there?* Blame it on the wine.

"So, why didn't we do this years ago?"

His question pierces through our small talk. His tone has changed. Almost a little too serious.

"I don't know, Jack, I guess maybe because you didn't like me in 'that way' back then."

"Excuse me? What do you mean I didn't like you? I adored you. Just never thought you'd be interested in a simple guy like me."

"Are you serious? I had the biggest crush on you, but you kept fixing me up with your friends so I assumed you weren't into me."

We stare at each other. The corners of his mouth begin to turn up into a smile, and it's just enough to allow me to return the grin.

Maybe it's the wine. All I know is that a door just opened and I must decide whether to close it, or walk through it with him. This feels all too familiar, and in the same breath, totally new and different.

There is no wife.

My brain tries to capture my attention over the protests of my heart who would prefer to keep it quiet. *Lily, you have to tell him. You can't lead him on.* It's like the annoying voice of conscience. No. Correct that. It IS the annoying voice of conscience.

Quite frankly, I don't want to tell him. Not now. This feels much too good. Why should I have to ruin it? For what? The potential of a relationship with a man who is still married to someone else? His phone call earlier this evening comes back to me. But I can't think about him right now. I don't want to think about him right now.

"Jack, this has been, well, I can't even find the right words for it. Wow. But I think you need to take me home now."

He looks puzzled. "What did I do wrong?"

"Oh, you've done everything right. Trust me. Absolutely, perfectly right. It's just that my life is, well, let's just say it's complicated."

"Is there someone else?"

What is it with these men and their uncannily perfect spot on questions tonight? I don't answer him.

He continues, "I thought you said your divorce was final years ago and you're single?"

"Yes, I am. But there's..." *Oh Jack, why didn't you call me a month ago?* Luckily that question stays in my head and away from my mouth. The wine is wearing off just enough to allow me to think again. My filter is back in place.

"Jack, you are an absolutely lovely, wonderful man. And this evening has been amazing. I'll try to explain it all to you later. Just not right now. I can't." *Because I don't know the whole story myself.*

"Okay."

I can see the hurt on his face. Confusion, too. And I can't fault him for any of it.

The thirteen minute drive back to my house is quiet. Too quiet. I search for more words. For the right words. But they don't come.

We arrive in my driveway. I ask, "Do you want to come in?"

He says, "I don't know if I should. What happened back there?"

"Just call this bad timing. My life is complicated." I'm afraid to make eye contact. I reach for his hand.

He pulls it away. "Yeah. You said that. But why? Is it me?"

"No, Jack, you are as wonderful as you've always been. Maybe even more so. It's my own junk." *I should tell him the truth. I know I should. I just can't. Not right now.* "I need a little time to straighten some things out." I reach my left hand up to his cheek. What a dear, gentle soul. So unlike... *No more comparisons. Get yourself together here, Lily.* "I've thought about you for so many years, and now you're here, and I'm ..."

"You're what? What is it?" A hint of anger creeps into his eyes. Or maybe it's pain. This man doesn't get angry. Not easily. He's patient as the day is long. It's one of the things I've always loved about him. If that's anger I see in his eyes, I'm the one who has put it there. Why can't I just take this man into the house with me and allow it to go wherever it wants? *Damn you, Leo. Look what you've done to me.*

"Jack, it has been absolutely wonderful to reconnect with you tonight. I hope you know that."

"Yeah, it felt that way to me, too. But then it was like you flipped a switch. What's up?"

"There's someone else." It jumps out of my mouth. Yes, that's definitely anger now in his eyes. And rightfully so. I led him on.

"Damn it, Liliana, why didn't you tell me this hours ago? Were you just playing with me, to see if you could get my attention?"

"No, I wasn't. I promise." *See, I knew I shouldn't have told him.* I've backed myself into a corner. "So, here's the thing."

"Oh, great, now there's a thing?" The same words I used earlier with Leo, now turned around on me. He's not making this easy on me, and I can't blame him. I'd be angry, too. Seriously angry.

"I don't want to hurt you, Jack, I really don't. I just have to give this other thing a chance. I'm too far into it."

"Who is he? Anyone I know?" There's the question I've been dreading. Because they do know each other. Far too well.

I lie. Too easily. "No."

It's a gorgeous starlit night, but I start looking for lightning bolts. Surely God's going to strike me down. I had conveniently forgotten the connection. Forgotten what I learned when working with Leo, one time when he was musing to me about Elizabeth. I'd thought she looked familiar when we met, but wasn't sure from where, and given how she'd dismissed me, I hadn't asked.

Elizabeth had dated Jack, briefly, fresh out of college. Leo stole her away and married her. He always had a thing for younger women. It was quite complicated. Jack and I had lost touch by then, and I hadn't met Leo yet, but I heard about it through our college friends. How could I have forgotten? Now Leo is divorcing her, to be with me.

What perfect punishment this will be for me. She'll be available again. Probably reunite with Jack. They'll walk off into the sunset together, and I'll be stuck with Leo.

Ouch. *Stuck with Leo?* How dare I think of it that way?

Meanwhile, Jack's waiting for me to say more. So I do, uncertain when I open my mouth what might come out. "I need some time. I know I can't ask you to wait for me. You need to move on with your life. Assume me not in it." Double ouch. That's what Leo told me to do, not so long ago. Was this karma coming back to haunt me? I look into Jack's eyes. His anger has softened to pain. I think I preferred the former. His pain is just too awful to witness, knowing I'm the one who put it there.

I say, "If anything changes for me, you'll be the first one I'll call. You do know that, don't you?" I know far too well how meaningless those words are to hear at a time like this. And infuriating.

"I don't know anything right now, Liliana." He keeps using my name, my full name, in that beautiful, lyrical way he has of saying it.

I put both hands to his face. Lean in to kiss him goodnight. Oh my, he smells good. He turns at the last second so I get only his cheek to kiss. Guess I deserved that. "Good night, Jack. Thank you for a beautiful evening."

"Yeah. Whatever. You take care now." Take care? Is there anything less personal he could have said? Take care is one of those phrases we use to get out of a long conversation with someone we'd prefer not to be talking to. It's a polite way to sound like we're interested in their well being, but only in the most casual of ways.

I walk to my front door. Open it. Turn the light on inside. Wave goodbye. Force a smile. He does the same. Just a nod. Then he's backing his car out of the driveway. No engine roar. This isn't Angel.

I'm home, alone. Just me and my guilt. Hurting too many people with my selfish behavior. Longings of my heart all fucked up. Apologies if I offend with that language, but there's no clearer way to say it. What's the old military slang term? SNAFU. That's what I've got here. Situation Normal All Fucked Up. Welcome to my love life.

I've just totally screwed up what might well have been a fantastic next first date. For what? A married man who may or may not be leaving his wife, so maybe we can start a life together, mired deep in guilt and lies. He told me he had news, but I have no idea if it's good or bad.

The wine glass calls to me from the counter. The one I used earlier to calm my pre-date jitters is now mocking me. What's one more glass? I pour it, nice and full. I don't think this evening can get any worse.

Into the bedroom. I take off my bra. Who created these damn underwires anyway? Must have been some cruel man's joke. Strip down everything else except for my panties, then throw on a comfortable oversized not so sexy but oh so comfortable sweatshirt. I grab my laptop, carry it out to the living room with me.

I settle into my big comfy couch, my one new indulgence since moving here. It takes me in, no questions. My computer is on my lap. What was the word that came to mind earlier? Oh yeah. SNAFU. Probably not a real word. Google it for a definition. There it is. Exactly as I thought. *Situation Normal, All Fucked Up.* Describes my life all too well. *Normal my ass.*

Another sip of wine, well, more like a gulp. There's more. I mean in the dictionary. Though there's also more wine. Not a bad idea. Who the hell cares right now anyway.

TARFUN. The second variation after SNAFU. *Things Are Really Fucked Up Now.* Yes. That's it for sure. Maybe that's the word I need to describe my situation. TARFUN.

There's one more. FUBAR. *Fucked Up Beyond All Recognition.* Burn it to the ground and start from scratch kinda bad. Well, thankfully it's not quite that bad. Leo still loves me. Maybe Jack, too.

Leo. Oh, yeah, remember Leo? I wonder what his news is.

I look up another word. Philanthropist. That's what Leo is. The privilege that comes with being married to Elizabeth. Look what's just above it. Oh, this is priceless. Just above philanthropist in the dictionary is philanderer.

That's what he is! A philandering philanthropist! In one evening, I've wooed and then stomped on the heart of a good honest man who had been the fantasy love of my life for years, and for what? A philandering philanthropist. I swig another gulp of wine, turn out the light next to the couch, and pull a quilt over my head. There's another one for the dictionary search - quilt and guilt - just flip the squiggly at the bottom of the first letter and one becomes the other. *Ahhh. The wine does so inspire my thinking.* I settle in comfortably under my quilt, with my guilt tucked in next to me. I fall asleep. No, to be honest, I pass out. *Sweet dreams, Lily.* Hopefully tonight I will dream of...nothing. My dreams only get me in trouble.

Morning light wakes me up, or perhaps more accurately it tries to. The cat is laying across my hips, light in comparison to what feels like it must be a mountain lion draped across my head. Even before I open my eyes, I start to count last night's drinks. There was a glass while I waited for Jack, to calm my nerves. *Oh, my dear precious Jack.* Then the first bottle we shared. Then another half bottle. Thankfully we didn't finish that one. *See, Lily, it wasn't much.*

Then I see the glass on the coffee table. The oversized one meant for swirling reds at wine tastings but I think I filled it pretty full last night, after I got home, maybe two or three times. Forgot about those. The ones I would've been just fine without, but thought to myself *oh, one more won't hurt* and here, this morning, it does hurt. Like I need more pain in my life.

The coffee table starts to vibrate. No, it's my phone. *Oh crap.* I forgot to turn it back on after we left the restaurant. It's coming back to me now. Such a horrible end to a perfect evening. The phone continues to buzz, annoying as hell. I don't even want to look at it. Could be Leo, or Jack, but frankly I don't think I could talk to either of them this morning. Not until I have some time to figure out what I'm going to do next.

The phone finally stops. I look at the caller ID. It was Grace. *Oh my. Grace!* What time am I to pick her up? I have no idea what time it is now. *Get a grip, Lily.*

Nine o'clock. Need to pull myself together. I consider locking the phone away for the day so I can ignore both of my men. *My men.* Yeah, I wish. Probably lost both of them in one evening. *Way to go, Lily.* I decide to take a quick shower to wake me up and wash away my sins. *Good luck with that.* My conscience, or whatever is left of it, is mocking me.

Saturday drags on. The hangover dissipates. The phone stays silent. I probably should call Jack to apologize, but there's not much more I can say.

Then there's Leo. If I wait one more day to hear his big news it won't be the end of the world. Unless his news is that he's changed his mind about the divorce. In which case it will be the end, but then I'll be free to pursue Jack, who probably will never want to speak to me again.

Evening. Ten o'clock. Finally late enough to go to bed, grateful to have made it through this day. Leo didn't call me, and I didn't call him. Grace is already asleep. Normally I'd pour a glass of wine right about now, but not tonight. Not going there again any time soon.

My phone rings. I take a quick look. It's Leo. But there's no way he'd call me at this hour on a Saturday night. I answer with a question. "What's wrong?"

"Well, hello to you, too." *Damn. He's been drinking. This can't be good.* "What could possibly be wrong?" he continues. "My marriage is over, and you went out on a date last night. My life is perfect."

"Leo?" It's part question, part sigh. "I don't understand. How is it you're calling me at this hour? Where's Elizabeth?"

"Lizzy's gone to her sister's for a few days. Says she can't stand the sight of me. Pretty, huh?" I hear the ice cubes swirling in his glass. "Yup, just me and Mr. Jack sitting here together."

Jack? Did he just say Jack? He's with him? This is far worse than I expected. How did he find out? Then it occurs to me. He's referring to his whiskey of choice, a very different Jack. Whew. There was a freaky three second ride in my brain.

"So, how was it?" he asks.

"Leo, you've been drinking. Let's not have this conversation right now."

"Or should I ask how was he?"

Does he really expect me to answer?

"C'mon, big girl. You can tell your buddy Dr. Stocker anything."

Obviously he does.

"We had dinner, Leo. Just two old friends sharing a meal. He didn't come into my house, and he didn't even kiss me goodnight." *Even though I tried to kiss him, and he turned his cheek.* I decide to keep that to myself.

"Yeah, right. I know you better than that."

Someday I'm going to learn to stop when I'm ahead, but obviously today isn't the day. "Well, if I played by your rules I guess it would've been okay to sleep in the same bed with him as long as we didn't touch, right?"

It's a verbal tennis match. Lob to Lily. Who smashes it back into his court. He falls silent. Guess I aced it.

I try again. Quieter this time. My brain may not have decided what I'm going to do with my dilemma, but my heart knows, and steps forward to speak. "Leo, I love you. It's you I want to be with. You know that. But you're scaring the crap out of me with this 'big news' thing."

He responds, his tone softened in response to mine. "It's a good thing, Lily. A really good thing. Can I come see you tomorrow?"

"But I thought we weren't allowed to until..."

"You're right. But it's okay now."

I'm stopped in my tracks. Is this real? Did he just suggest what I think he did?

I'm not sure whether to laugh or cry. Maybe some of both. Again I answer with a question. "What time can you be here?"

Chapter 47

Sunday afternoon. Grace has gone to a friend's house. Seems to just always work out, every time Leo and I are facing a crucial time together. I don't have to look for places for her to be, they just show up. Like there's some sort of grand plan that allows us to come together. Or maybe she's simply a popular girl who gets invited out a lot.

Two o'clock. He called this morning to confirm. The phone lines are open again.

I'm not sure I'm ready for this. Ready to do it. Or ready to believe it.

My nerves are a mess. I sense there's a huge turning point about to happen in my life. If it wasn't the middle of the afternoon, a Sunday afternoon, no less, I'd have a glass of wine. But no. I need to stay clear headed. Grounded. Normal. Whatever the hell that is. Thank God I had the wisdom to buy a bag of Oreos yesterday. One vice I can still allow.

Two fifteen. I hear Angel in the driveway. I've positioned myself in my favorite lawn chair in the back yard. There may be fresh air required to get through this. *Why am I so nervous?* This is supposed to be a good thing. I'm just not sure what to expect.

I hear the front screen door open, then slap shut. Need to fix that. Another time. *Stay focused, Lily.* I hear him call my name.

"I'm out back," I yell in return.

What's taking him so long? Did he not hear me? Is he looking for me in the house? Then he walks out the back door, wearing khaki pants and a dress shirt. I thought he'd be more casual but he does look great this way. Still catches my eye and makes me smile, especially when I haven't seen him in a while.

I want to rush into his arms, but I know I don't dare. Not yet.

He says, "What's a guy gotta do to get a hug hello?"

I rise out of my chair, cautiously. Then he holds me, and I loosen up, though only a little.

He feels it. "What's the matter? You okay?"

"Yeah, just kinda nervous."

"Why?"

"I don't know. You said you have big news. I'm scared."

He smiles. His voice softens. "It's all good, Lily. All good."

I do so want to believe him.

He asks, "Do you have anything cold to drink?"

"Sure. Follow me. Iced tea okay?"

"Perfect."

We head into the house. I walk into the kitchen, then stop.

"How did I do?" he asks from behind me. There on the counter is a vase filled with roses. Red ones. Romantic ones. Now I understand his delay in getting from the front door to the back.

"They're gorgeous." I put my face to them, inhale deeply. "Thank you." Roses, just as I had hoped I would find in the garage a year ago. They're here today. A reward for my patience? A kiss is in order, followed by a longer, less cautious hug.

I pour two iced teas. Hand one to him.

"Shall we go back outside?"

"Sure."

We settle into lawn chairs.

"So," I say.

"So," he replies. I think he is truly enjoying drawing it out like this. "How's it feel to be sitting here with a single man for a change?"

I was with a single man two nights ago and it felt damn good, says the sarcastic voice in my head. Then his words sink in.

"Single?" I ask. One word. Huge question. I search his face for clues.

"Yep." Grin spreads on his face.

"Seriously?"

We seem to be big on the one word sentences. I try to string together a few words, challenged to do so as my mind is racing ahead. "I thought it was going to be weeks longer?"

"Yeah. Sorry about that. Kinda lied to you. Was hoping to be able to surprise you. Like this." He winks at me. Just like he used to, what feels like a million years ago, in staff meetings. Long before it meant anything, or at least before I knew it did.

"Are you saying what I think you are?" I ask.

"Yes." He leans in, taking my hands in his. "The final word came in on Thursday. She moved out on Friday. She's gone to live with her sister. So I wasn't lying to you when I told you she'd left."

We take a moment for another hug. This is starting to feel good. Much too good.

"Things are moving quickly," he says. "We've got a contract on the house. We close in a month. So I've need to be out by then. It's over, Lily. I'm yours now. If you still want me."

Oh my. It dawns on me this is likely why he called me, on Thursday, when I was on the phone setting up my date with Jack. This was the reason for his phone call I didn't have time to listen to. And it explains why he was able to call last night from home.

"I can't believe this. Are you sure?" What a stupid question, but the words are all jumbled in my head, let alone what makes it out of my mouth.

He says, "I've got papers to prove it." I can tell by his smile he's telling the truth. I wrap my arms around him, straddle his lap right there in the chair. I feel genuinely happy, like a little kid. Quite possibly look like one, too.

"There's one more thing," he says.

"Oh no. What now?"

"Did you catch the part about how I'll be homeless in a month? We need to start looking for a house. Today."

This is fast. Too fast. I haven't had a chance to get used to the idea that he's single.

Words fail me, but he's still talking. "Why aren't you more excited about this? Isn't this what you've been wanting?"

"Yes. But all at once? Give me some time to process this, Leo."

We've been so focused on his divorce, I'm not sure we ever talked about what would happen next. *Pay attention, Lily.*

He says, "I've already talked with a realtor, and she's lined up several places for us to look at this afternoon. We're meeting her at her office in about half an hour. Do you want to change your clothes first?" I now understand why he's dressed as he is.

"Um, of course. I'm sorry, Leo, this is just all so fast. Please give me a little time to catch up with you."

"Whatever you need." The right words, though his tone betrays his disappointment.

"Want to come in and talk to me while I change?" My mind continues to race. *A house? A move? What about Grace?* She doesn't know about us yet, thinks of us as friends, knows he's my old boss, but not someone to live with.

We walk inside, through the kitchen, past the roses. I love my cozy home. It's my safe haven. My single girl making it on her own house. I'm not sure I'm ready to leave here. Not yet.

He plops down on the couch in the living room. "You go change your clothes. I'll wait here."

I head into the bedroom. Need to pull myself together. Changing clothes is easy. My head and my heart, not so much. Then I hear him ask me a question, but I have to ask him to repeat it. He hates that, even though I have to repeat things all the time for him, hard of hearing as he is, and stubborn enough to not admit to it.

He sounds annoyed. Louder this time. "I said nice daisies. Where'd you get them?"

Oh, no. Jack's flowers. You'd think by now I'd be better at covering my tracks. Was there a card? *Oh please let there not have been a card.* "I bought those for myself last week. Just a treat to cheer myself up." That's my second lie to him today. I wonder if a rooster will crow somewhere if I tell a third.

"Nice." That's all he says. Guess my answer placated him.

I'm dressed. Never thought of dressing up to look at real estate, but I need to look like I belong with him. And I wonder, do I? Belong with him? I don't know. A question that will need to wait.

I love to look at houses. Dreamed for so long of creating a home for him, for us. So why do I now feel the need to dig in my heels like a mule and yell, "Stop! Don't push me!"

It doesn't matter. I have no choice. He's already set appointments for us. First, a condo. Does this man even know me? I'm an antique farmhouse kind of girl. He loves the condo. I find it far too bland, too cookie cutter.

Next on the tour, a brand new home in a development of other brand new homes. The whole place sounds hollow. Too sterile. Too Stepford Wives.

His disappointment in my reaction shows. He says, "Other women would be thrilled by a place like this."

"Yeah, I know. But I'm not like other women, remember?" I'm trying to be cute, to add some levity to what is becoming a stressed afternoon, but how ironic is that statement? Because have no doubt about it, I WAS the other woman.

Thank goodness we agree on the next two, but not in a good way. Beautiful on the outside, they're poorly built on the inside. The afternoon grows long. We both weary of it. Our frustration builds, with the process and with each other. The first afternoon of the rest of our life together, and it's not going well.

"I've saved the best for last." He sounds vaguely triumphant.

"Oh great. I can't wait," I mumble, grateful in this moment for his hearing loss.

I want to get excited about one of these, honest I do. But I've learned all too well from our time together to be guarded. No more hopes dashed on the rocks.

He tells me about it. "I know you like older places. This one was built around 1945, I think. Sits right in the middle of an acre." *I'd prefer 1845, but an acre is good. Maybe I can have a garden.* "No neighbors. Conservation land beside and behind. Realtor tells me it's got good bones, though it needs some redecorating." *I like to paint and wallpaper. Sounds promising.*

We turn into the driveway. "Leo, I saw this place a while back during an open house. It's a decorator's nightmare."

There was a time I spent Sunday afternoons going to open houses, dreaming of the day, which is now this day.

Leo parks the car. Turns it off. Looks at me. Not a good look. "What's up, Lily? Why so negative? I thought you'd be thrilled to do this. Isn't this what you want?" Again, that question. Is he referring to the house, or to us?

I know I should be more appreciative, but in this moment I'm just too damn overwhelmed and confused. I say, "I don't know. I don't know what I want." It comes out snippy, followed by a heavy sigh.

He says, "I was just asking about the house. Did you have to take it there?"

By 'there' I assume he means the relationship talk.

"Damn it, Lily. I don't understand you. I've upended my life for you..."

"And I didn't ask you to."

"Yeah, you kinda did. And here I am. Every place I've shown you today is better than that crappy rental you're living in. And this is the thanks I get?"

Now he's gone too far. He didn't have to insult my home.

Wonderful. We're starting our history with this house by having a fight in the car in the driveway. And the realtor just arrived, so now we have to get out and pretend that everything is fine, which somehow we manage to do. We've learned all too well how to hide our feelings.

The realtor takes a phone call, giving us time to walk around on our own. I fake my best attempt at an apology, and hate myself for being so sheepish about it. "I'm sorry my reaction disappointed you. I know you just want to please me, and I sound like an ungrateful bitch. You're right. This place is more interesting than I remembered. Maybe it does have more potential than I thought. Forgive me, please?" Even as those words come out of my mouth, I know I don't mean them. And besides, why did I just apologize for how I feel?

"So, are you saying you like this one?"

How did he do that? I fell on my proverbial sword, and he flat out ignored it. "Maybe. It's been a long day, Leo. I need to pick up Grace soon, and figure out how I'm going to tell her about what's going on. Can we just let the house stuff go for now? Maybe we can have a second look after I've had some time to get used to the idea. Maybe even bring Grace with me to see it sometime this week."

I'd love for him to offer a hug right now, or one of those smiles that melts me. Have him tell me it's all okay, that he loves me. Instead he shrugs his shoulders and turns away. "Yeah. Whatever."

We are quiet during the drive back to my house. I stare out the window, not sure whether I want to yell at him or melt into tears. We're in my driveway. We hadn't discussed how long he could stay. I ask, "Want to come in for a few?"

"Sure. It's not like anyone's waiting for me at home."

Ouch. Reality laced with an ample dose of sarcasm.

As we walk inside, my cell rings. "Mom, they've invited me for dinner. I know it's a school night. But can I stay?"

"Of course. Call me when you're done and I'll come get you."

"Thanks, Mom." *Oh, my dear Grace, how I am going to spin this to you so you will understand, but not suspect?*

He stands at the front window, staring out to the street.

I walk up behind him. "That was Grace. She's not coming home for dinner. I made a lasagna earlier but now I'm going to be eating it by myself. Care to stay and join me?"

He turns toward me. Extends his arms. Voice is softer now. "Come here. Please."

And once again, I do as he asks. So obedient. And hopeful. I'm back in his arms.

"I'm sorry, Leo."

"No, it's my fault. I dropped all of this on you too fast. Will you let me try again?"

"Of course."

"Lily, I love you. You know that."

I hug him tighter, but I'm still afraid to look him in the eye.

"Look at me. Please?"

Again, I obey.

He puts his hand under my chin, in that way that I love. Tilts my face toward his so that he's looking into my eyes. "Will you accept me into your life now?"

I answer him with a kiss.

Without another word, he takes my hand, and leads me into the bedroom. His list of three rolls around in my mind. "We do not have to say goodbye. We will make love again. This love will last forever, you are a part of me." One, two, three. Turns out he was right on all counts. The lasagna will keep for another night. For now, I need to be fed by his touch. I need to be reminded of why I waited for him for so long. Of why he's done what he's done to be here with me. What type of house we live in shouldn't matter at all. As long as we're in it together, and there is a bed, we'll be just fine.

Just keep telling yourself that, Lily. Don't worry about how you're going to tell Grace. You'll find a way.

And whatever you do, don't you dare think about the other woman who is feeling hurt, rejected, and alone tonight, probably scared for her future, while you take delight in this man. Don't go there. You can't afford it.

Chapter 48

Be careful what you wish for. You just might get it.

I wish someone had said that to me when I needed to hear it. Or maybe someone did, and I wasn't paying attention. It's also possible I simply chose to ignore it, because I didn't want to hear it. I probably laughed in her face and tossed it aside, determined to achieve my goal no matter the cost.

We buy the decorator's nightmare after going back no less than seven times to look at it. I suppose more accurately he buys it. Which I guess means Elizabeth buys it, or at least her money does, which scares the hell out of me, because it means if anything happens to Leo, I'll be out on the street. It's not exactly my dream house, but it's a nice enough place. I mean, it has good bones. I can work with it. Tear off the splashy floral wallpapers. Replace them with fresh paint and murals to my heart's content.

I finally get to play house with the man of my dreams.

Until reality sets in. First week in the new house. We're establishing new patterns together.

I ask, "So, Leo, where should we put the laundry basket?"

"What do you mean?" He looks at me like I've just asked him the question in a foreign language.

"You know. The thing you put your dirty clothes in before they go to the washing machine."

"Yes, I know what a laundry basket is, but I don't understand your question."

"Okay, let me try this another way. When you and Elizabeth were together, where did you put your underwear when you took it off to take your shower?"

"I just dropped it on the floor."

"And?"

"And when I got out of the shower, it was gone."

Oh boy. The term "spoiled brat" come to mind.

So, I have some retraining to do. I tell myself it will be fun.

With Leo paying the mortgage, my financial burden is considerably lighter. I am responsible only for Grace and my personal expenses, and he takes care of the house. Not a bad arrangement. And while I'm not working a 'real job' now, I suppose in a manner of speaking you could say I'm still Leo's personal assistant. He goes off to the office every day while I take care of the house, prepare his meals, and do his laundry. Funny thing is he liked it when I worked for him, before. Now it seems not so much. Apparently I don't live up to his expectations, nor he to mine. It's not how I imagined playing house with him would be.

I envisioned we would become a real couple. I'd finally be able to share him with my friends, not have to hide him, or us, anymore. I pictured us living out our happily ever after part of the story as equal partners.

It works for a while. Until the judgement creeps in. Obviously Elizabeth was one heck of a housekeeper, or possibly she simply knew how to hire great help. All I know is I have great difficulty living up to his standards and expectations.

We've invited a few friends over for a dinner party. I'm thrilled to pull my old china out of the boxes it lived in while I went through all of my moves. I've cooked a scrumptious dinner. Set the dining room table with silver, flowers, and candlelight. The perfect hostess. Or so I think.

Leo offers to pour the wine. He reaches up into the cabinet and pulls out a glass. Then right there in front of our guests, he holds it up to the light, inspects it, makes a sound of disgust, and puts it back. I'll say it again. He puts it back. Doesn't wash it. Doesn't even put it in the sink to wash later. He simply registers his disappointment in me, in my housekeeping, and returns it to the cabinet. I watch him go through ten glasses before he finds six he considers clean enough. With each one he pulls out, I cringe. And our guests grow silent. Is he unaware of the judgement he is casting on me? The others see it. But nobody says a word. They never do.

It hasn't been all bad. That's what I tell myself. Grace and I have a beautiful home to live in, my expenses are minimal, and I get to sleep every night with the man of my dreams. Funny thing, though, how being together every night changes things.

Chapter 49

I don't get it. What do women expect of me? I try my best to love them. Work hard to pay the bills. Well, okay, Elizabeth paid her own, but not Lily. She allows me to take care of her. I put a roof over her head, and a pretty fine one at that. But it's not enough. She tells me, "I need you to love me. I need you to listen to me, to talk nicer to me, to respect me." Well, doesn't she understand I'm doing the best I can? I can't always predict what she wants me to say. It's like she has this script set in her mind of exactly what is supposed to come out of my mouth, and if I don't say it right, then I'm just wrong. Or a stupid idiot. And trust me, I'm neither.

Then she says, "You still care more about her than you do about me." Like she thinks Elizabeth is more important to me. Well, now, I don't care how much you fall in love with someone else, you don't just flush away so many years of marriage, do you? And besides, Elizabeth still holds the purse strings over me. Lily would freak out if she knew. She thinks I'm heading off to work every day to provide for her, but really it's just to provide for me. There is stuff Elizabeth doesn't pay for anymore. Like my boat. And my fishing trips. So yeah, if I am an idiot, it's not about Lily. It's the ties I haven't cut yet from Elizabeth. I just haven't told Lily. Ironic, isn't it? I kept Lily a secret from my wife all that time, and now I'm keeping Elizabeth a secret from Lily.

It's Elizabeth's Daddy's money keeping this roof over our heads. He owns the house. Well, his trust does. The one Lily thinks I set up to protect her from my family. Won't Lily be shocked if something happens to me and the trust requires her to move out in thirty days. It's her biggest fear. But if I die, and that happens, I won't be here to see it, so what do I care? It's all okay. It's just a financial arrangement. If it keeps everyone happy, then what's the harm in it? For now, Lily is happy. Or at least happy enough. I think. She's got me. And she's got a house. That's what she wanted. So why shouldn't she be happy?

Chapter 50

The phone rings. "Hey baby, it's me."

I do love the sound of her voice on the phone. "Hi, Sarah. Been a while. What's up?"

"I have an opportunity for you."

"Oh, good." My sarcasm is obvious. Whenever I hear the word "opportunity" I think I'm about to be solicited to join some pyramid get rich quick scheme or scam. But from Sarah?

"Sarah, you know I don't do that sort of thing."

"Oh, I know a lot of things you do that people think you don't. But that's not what I'm talking about. You haven't heard what I have to say yet."

She's right. I have a terrible habit of interrupting people. "Sorry, you just caught me at a bad moment. Talk to me."

"How would you like to have a few of your paintings exposed to the rich uppity-ups of Boston?"

"Well, hello, why wouldn't I?"

"Exactly what I thought."

"So, please tell me more."

"I've gotten myself involved with a charity auction, and it includes a sealed bid art component. It works like this. You donate a piece or two, preferably something fairly large that can garner a high price. Potential donors will be able to view the pieces online and at a private location in Boston, and place their bids in advance. And then the night of the gala, you get to be introduced to the buyer and share dinner together. Who knows, if you hit it off, you might find a great new collector or benefactor. Pretty cool, eh?"

"I'll say. I know just the pieces, too. Two of my skyscapes I just finished. Paint's still wet on the canvas."

Sarah says, "There's one extra thing you need to do with the paintings, though."

"Oh, what's that?"

"They want to include a couple of paragraphs with each piece, you know, words from the artist about why you painted what you did. What's your meaning behind the painting? That sort of thing."

"You mean the thing I've always said I hate?"

"C'mon, Lily, hate's a strong word. Just tell a little bit about how the painting moves you, why it called you to create it."

"Alright, Sarah. Just for you. I'll try."

"Trust me on this, Lily. I have a feeling you're going to love it. Might even expand your artistic horizon a bit."

"Like I said, I'll try. You know I'd do anything for you."

"Anything?"

"Within reason, Sarah, within reason." Gotta love that she always finds a way to remind me of her love for me. Can't say I don't enjoy it. "So, anything else I need to know? Like when you need all of this?"

"Sometime next week would be great."

"Next week?"

"Yes. The paintings will be placed on exhibit for the bidders, then the gala itself is in mid-May. You can do it. Oh, and by the way, you're welcome to bring a date if you'd like."

"Sounds great, Sarah. Count me in. Please. And thank you. I'll ask Leo if he can come. Is that okay with you?"

"Of course. But only if you promise me you're going to go shopping with his credit card for something new to wear. Preferably slinky and black and elegant, and maybe cut down to..."

"Now, Sarah! He's going to be my date, not you!"

"I know. But a girl can dream, can't she?"

"Yes, you know you can. Me, too. I assume you'll be there?"

"Wouldn't miss it for the world. Something tells me it's going to be an unforgettable night."

"One more thing, Sarah. You didn't say where it is?"

"Oops. I forgot that part. Since it's mid-May, the Bostonians are willing to make their first trek down to the Cape. It's in Chatham. A spectacular place on the water called the Chatham Bars Inn. Have you ever been there?"

"Oh, once upon a time."

I should have known, the morning I spent on Newbury Street. It was right there in front of me, and I missed it. My future. No, I don't mean him. He wasn't there. I'm talking about the combination of painting and writing. Walking out of Trident Booksellers into Johnson Paints. I felt so deliciously happy in both.

I came home that morning with new brushes and a small pile of books to keep me company. I've never been a particularly fast reader, so I don't finish a whole lot of them, but I enjoy bits and pieces of as many as possible. I flip through the first few pages, then open randomly to somewhere in the middle, and allow the book to speak to me, trusting that I will magically turn to the right spot, to hear whatever it is I am supposed to from each. Novels, nonfiction, and home decorating books - they all entice me. Nothing like going to sleep with visions of beautiful rooms dancing through my head all night. Maybe it's why I always enjoyed dreaming of a home, a real home, that I could make my own. Painting out of oil tubes onto canvas is one thing, but having an entire wall to use as my canvas on a far grander scale, well, that's the thing that dreams are made of.

Sarah's project has challenged me, but I'm surprised with how much I enjoyed putting words on paper to go with my paintings. Can't figure out for the life of me why I avoided it as long as I did, answering the question "what is it you are trying to say with this piece?" Well, rather than making them ask, I get to tell them now, in my own words. And I'm stunned to find out how much I have to say. Why have I kept so much to myself through the years, afraid to give voice to my thoughts, to my emotions? I'm still not certain that my art has the capacity to change the world, though maybe through my words combined with images, I might suggest a more serene, loving way of looking at the world.

Chapter 51

"C'mon, Leo. We're going to be late."

"I'm trying to find my blue tie. You know. The one with the fish on it?" Good grief. He sounds just like Grace did the morning we met him at the lake.

"And why do you need that one tonight, Leo?"

"Because a lot of this crowd is my work crowd. They know me. So I have to look like me."

"They know you, but this is my night, remember?"

"Yes, I know. So let me have a little fun, won't you?"

"Sure. Just tell me how do I..."

"Wow." He looks up at just the right moment, as I enter our walk-in closet, already fully dressed. Guess the new dress hit the mark. Sarah was right. "You've come a long way from that first show back in Pennsylvania. Remember, the night we met?"

"Of course I remember, Leo. Do you honestly think I'd forget something like that?"

"No. But here. I have a gift for you. Thought you might like to have something new to remember your special night, but I seem to have dropped it." He's fumbling around on the floor in the closet. Then he gets up on one knee, holding a little black box. With a big grin on his face. "Lily Daniels, I love you, and I'm so proud of you. Tonight I want the world to know you're mine. Will you marry me, and wear my ring?"

He's caught me totally by surprise. "Oh, Leo. Of course I will."

"Is that a yes?"

"YES! But please stand up so I can hug you. This dress is far too tight for me to bend down to where you are." He does as I ask. I'm trembling. The ring is stunning. A simple gold band, with diamonds channeled the entire way around the circle. It's perfect. Elegant. The princess now has jewels. "Shall we go?"

He says, "Allow me to fetch your carriage."

I'm on cloud nine. Prince Charming just proposed to me. In a closet. Not exactly what I pictured, but he proposed, and I said yes. And now we're off to the ball.

We pull up in front of the hotel. I'm embarrassed as I am flooded with memories of the last time. But we're legal now. We don't have to hide from anyone, not even Elizabeth. She still doesn't know it's me, though she knows he's moved on. Claims she doesn't want to know the details. Doesn't make sense to me, but right now it doesn't matter, does it?

Leo tosses Angel's keys to the valet. Opens my door. Helps me out. I still haven't figured out how to do this gracefully, but it helps when he extends his hand to me and pulls me up. I remember the time I took his hand getting onto his boat, out at the lake.

The weather is picture perfect. The crowd is dressed in the usual black tie finery, women brilliantly colored, in contrast to the men in their black tie penguin garb.

I'm Cinderella walking into the ball on the arm of my handsome prince. My adolescent dream come true. And my paintings, they're here somewhere, too. Real magic.

There. Across the room. I see them. And there's a woman standing in front of one of them, admiring it. Leo offers to get us champagne. Says he'll join me in a moment. Tells me to head on over and start my schmoozing. He's taught me well.

I follow his command. Move in behind the woman standing there. She turns to face me. *Oh my.*

Chapter 52

"I was wondering when you'd show up." Her first words to me.

I try not to stammer as I reach for something to say. "Goodness, it's been a long time. How are you?" I'm hoping Leo got lost in conversation with someone else. But no. I see out of the corner of my eye he's headed our way. He's walking with another man, and not paying attention, so I can't signal him away. *Breathe, Lily, breathe. Keep talking to her. Maybe he'll see before it's too late.* "I'm surprised you recognize me. It's been a long time, since the exhibit at the college."

"Oh, my darling, there was also the horrible day at the lake. But that was long ago and far away in another lifetime, now wasn't it?"

"Yes, you're right." I try to match my laugh to hers, but it comes out forced, closer to a gerbil squeak. "So what brings you here today?"

Leo has stopped to look at a painting. Thank goodness.

She says, "You've come a long way in the past few years, Ms. Daniels. I trashed your sunsets that night at the college, but absolutely love these newer ones you're doing. There's more passion in your work. If I didn't know better, I'd say you paint like a woman in love."

Oh my, she's digging my hole even deeper. And now Leo is walking toward us.

"Well, um, sort of. More importantly, I get to paint on location now instead of from photographs, now that I'm living..."

"Why, Leo! Fancy meeting you here. Look who I found!"

Leo gives her a peck on the cheek. I've never before seen him at a loss for words.

I do my best to save the moment. "Elizabeth, thank you for the compliments. I do appreciate them, more than you know."

Leo still hasn't moved. He's trying to catch my eye for a clue of what to do next, but there's no time. And Elizabeth just noticed my left hand. "Why, I was right! Look at this gorgeous ring. So who's the lucky guy?" Then she stops. Looks at him, back at me, and at him again. It's her turn to fall silent.

I guess there's no way around this. Leo has found his composure. He moves to my side, puts his arm around my waist, smiles, and says, "I am."

Elizabeth's smile turns to red hot anger, for just an instant, then to an odd look of satisfaction and triumph. "You lousy cheating bastard. I KNEW it was her."

"Now, Lizzy, let's not create a scene. There are people here."

"I have no need to create a scene. We will deal with this privately, later. Meanwhile, the show must go on. You miserable prick."

How is it southern women have the ability to deliver a line so snide and at the same time dripping with honey?

Now it's my turn to fall quiet. My perfect, romantic evening with Prince Charming has just turned into my unveiling. And not in the artistic sense. We're saved by a clinking of glasses.

"Ladies and gentlemen, if I might have your attention, please. We'd like you to move to the parlor, where we will present the pairings of artists with their benefactors."

Oh, thank goodness. A distraction. We all receive the news as an opportunity to exit gracefully from our awkward moment. Lizzy throws one last verbal jab. "Not to worry, Leo darling. I'll have the last laugh tonight. Just you wait."

I'll spare you the blow by blow and cut to the chase. It's taken years, but it turns out Elizabeth Browning, formerly Stocker, has in fact become my next best collector. She remembered me from the college show, and was truly impressed by my growth. She purchased my paintings in the auction. But she had no idea I was Leo's, oh, how shall I say, next best acquisition?

So the three of us ate dinner together, there at the Chatham Bars Inn, with my new ring on my finger. Talk about awkward. My life has always been stranger than fiction. Just can't make this stuff up.

Chapter 53

He left her, for me. But only sort of. He divorced Elizabeth, yet his commitment to her lingers. As does his guilt over what his choice meant to his family. Honesty may not be his strong suit, but responsibility is. He still spares her pain whenever he has the chance.

Time passes when you're having, well, sure, let's call it fun. Though it hasn't been. Not like I hoped it would be.

Fast forward several years.

We got engaged, but haven't married yet. The public reason is that his financial situation would totally ruin any chance I have for financial aid, so we can't, until Grace is out of college. That's what we tell others when asked. We've set a tentative date, but don't discuss the details. I got the jewels, and the title, but I'm not sure I'll ever make it to the altar. At least not sure I will with this man.

Living together has definitely not brought the domestic bliss I had hoped. Maybe it was better to be the other woman. *Did I really just say that?*

Maybe I should paint him as the evil one, so you'll take my side. But I can't. It wouldn't be fair. I contribute more to the ugly than I care to admit.

Oh, I've read the books, and seen the movies, where the husband who cheats on his wife is cast as the villain, but we all know it's never that simple. Because for every man who is unfaithful in his marriage, there is a woman, the complicit accomplice to the crime.

I was that woman. Am that woman. Yet I yell at him and argue with him, about how her needs still come before mine, how certain emotional decisions are made to decrease her pain, rather than mine. Deep down, as I beg for more from him, I wonder if he still loves her. And I worry he might be with her those nights when he stays in the city instead of commuting home.

Talk about divine retribution. She was the victim. She made a commitment to him, and him to her, and he broke it by being with me. She was the one who bore the largest share of the pain of their fractured relationship. He tries to convince me their decision to break up was a mutual one, but I know deep down in my heart it isn't the full truth. What if he is unfaithful to me with her? Is this a case of paranoia, or intuition?

Perhaps we've been doomed from the start. How can a relationship begin in secret, endure an ongoing series of lies, and find a happy ending? All I ever wanted was my prince, who would whisk me away to his castle, so we could live there together, happily ever after. I got the first part, but as for the happily ever after, well, it's just not working out that way.

Think about it. We fought in the car in the driveway the first time we looked at the house. The memory haunts me every time things get rough between us.

Generous as Leo has been, I continue to ask for more. My insecurity begs for more. He says "whatever I do, it's not enough" and I yell back "that's not true" but it is. I need constant assurance of his love for me. I need to know he values my needs more than hers. I want to hang my head in shame to think that let alone say it out loud.

Why do I allow my own doubts and fears to get in the way? Maybe if I could forgive myself I wouldn't need his assurances quite so much.

It isn't all bad. There's been a lot of love shared, too. Except over time, it has eroded.

I'd like to blame it on his work. The pressure it puts on him. I try to be good, whatever that means. But a good girl wouldn't have done what I did. She wouldn't have stolen another woman's husband.

I try to change, thinking it might help. Maybe if I do this instead of that, he'll love me more. Maybe if I say it this way instead of that way, he'll understand me. Maybe if I rearrange the furniture properly in the house, the feng shui will heal us. Yeah, right. What's the saying? Like rearranging the deck chairs on the Titanic.

Sure, I can tell you about our fights, and you can take sides, but I'm afraid you might choose him over me. Some already have.

I remember a comment his cousin made to me. It still makes me wince. It was during one of the few family gatherings I'd been invited to. Not with his children. I was never invited to any of those. But several cousins were there with their spouses, and a few nieces and nephews. It was later in the evening, with just a few of us sitting around. I don't remember what Leo said, or what I said, but I remember what Leo's cousin said about what I said.

He looked at me and said, "Why do you talk so nasty about him?"

I cringed. Leo used to tell me about how critical Elizabeth was of him. And I felt sorry for him. Until I became her. Now I empathize with what it was like to be her, with him. And the man who I loved so deeply, wanted in my life for so long, how dare I now speak in such resentful tones about him?

My self-worth has plummeted. I've gained twenty pounds. And sought counseling. I should go back to the gym. I've begun to question whether we should take some time apart, but I'm not sure how we can, since we live together here in the house he bought for us.

My guilt has became a pair of handcuffs holding me here. We broke up a marriage to be together. How could we possibly end this relationship? We have to stay in it, we have an obligation to make it work, or all of Elizabeth's pain and loss will turn out to have been in vain.

We get a small break this month. Leo's headed south for his annual two weeks in Florida. The wealthier collectors spend their winters in Florida, mostly Palm Beach and Miami, to escape the harsher elements of New England, so Leo follows them there for a week of work, then a week of fishing. We went together, twice, back in the early days. But not this year. I get two weeks at home by myself. Maybe we'll miss each other. Maybe...

Chapter 54

"I can't believe you booked your flight to leave ON my birthday. You know how sentimental I am. And you'll miss Valentine's Day, too." I'm fully aware that I'm whining, but I don't care. I'm not happy, and see no reason to hide it.

"What difference does it make? We can celebrate your birthday the day before I leave, and Valentine's Day is just a day on the calendar. I'd probably work all day anyway."

I acquiesce, as I have grown accustomed to doing all too often with him.

As soon as he is out of the house I settle into, dare I admit it, a joyful exhilaration at having the place to myself for two weeks. I can eat what I want to, when I want to. Come and go by my own schedule without thought to when he'll be home or available to join me for dinner, or what time he needs lights out at the end of the night. The place is mine. All mine.

Even the animals settle into the relaxed pace. By now we have two dogs and two cats. Fur bodies of unconditional love I call my family, with Grace away at college.

The first thing I do after he leaves is clean. Because Leo, for all of his judgement about my housekeeping, is more on the slob end of the scale. I clean so there are no more piles of mail scattered around the kitchen table, or coffee rings on the counter from where he leaves his spoon, or dirty underwear on the floor of the closet. I clean out a clear runway for my two weeks of time alone.

He may be leaving me on my birthday, but I refuse to sit home alone and feel sorry for myself. So I send an email to twenty of my woman friends, an invitation to celebrate an impromptu pot luck birthday dinner with me in my home. I'll provide the place, and a main course, if they will provide everything else. Absolutely no gifts allowed, just food, wine, and lots of laughter. And love.

Twelve respond yes. It is a great success, all of us together in my dining room. While most of them know only one or two of the others, they bond quickly, and trust one another immediately. Each one is offered a chance to share whatever she wants of herself. There's a thirty year age span from youngest to oldest, and a wide range of incomes and life experiences. The house is filled with laughter instead of argument. It is agreed we will continue to get together every month, on the first Sunday night of the month, at the home of whoever's birthday occurs in the month.

My week is off to a beautiful start. My home is filled with the love of female friendships. And I just helped to create even more of them. I've proven to myself I am still good at building relationships, even if my one with Leo might suggest otherwise.

This year his fishing week comes first, which means he is living at a campground. Frugality rules. No tent or trailer, instead he rents an Econoline cargo van, the type contractors use. Gutted out to empty on the inside, he throws down a twin size air mattress, and calls the van his home for the week. He's invited me to join him, but seriously? Gives me the shivers to imagine what it must look like after he's lived in it several days. He calls me every evening. The seven o'clock phone call is a habit by now.

He left on Sunday. It's now Friday. I stayed up way past midnight last night, reading in bed, just because I could. Leo requires me to turn off the light every night at eleven-twenty-six p.m. The same time, every night. He takes great pride in accusing me of being a control freak, though I wish once in a while he'd look in the mirror at his own actions.

The phone wakes me up out of a sound sleep. It's seven o'clock. Who could possibly be calling at this hour? Wait. That's Leo's ringtone.

I answer. "Hello?"

"Hey, it's me."

"Yes, I know. What's up?"

"I'm sick."

"What's the matter?"

"I think I got food poisoning or something. Anyway, I was sick last night in all sorts of ways you don't want to know about."

Yuck. In the van without a bathroom? He's right. I don't want to know.

"Are you okay?" Seems like a dumb question to ask, but fresh out of a sound sleep it's the best I can do.

"No, thank you for asking, I'm not. There's more."

Uh oh.

"I sort of got hit by lightning last night."

"What?" I think it comes out more squawk than question. "What do you mean?"

"My AICD went off last night."

Leo suffered his first heart attack years ago, but his cardiologist considers him at significant risk for heart failure, so recently recommended an implantable cardioverter defibrillator, known more simply as an AICD. It's like the thing in television shows, when someone's heart stops beating and they bring out the electric paddles, yell "clear" and shock the guy back to life. Well, Leo has a tiny one of those inside his heart to monitor his heartbeat and deliver a shock to his heart if it detects too low or too high a rhythm, hopefully bringing it back to normal. That's right. Eight hundred volts in a tenth of a second, by surprise, from inside the chest.

"I thought you said you had food poisoning?"

"I know. I do. Or I did. But last night when I was walking to the bathroom I got shocked. I jumped straight up in the air, about a foot off the ground. I looked around for the storm. I was sure it was lightning. But it wasn't."

"Have you called your doctor?"

"No, it just happened the one time. I'm not going to be the guy who cried wolf."

I'm stunned. If it went off, it means this isn't just about his stomach. "Don't be stupid, Leo. What if it gets worse? Please promise me you'll call your doctor as soon as we get off the phone?"

"Stop overreacting, Lily. If it happens again, then maybe I'll call."

"Maybe? But Leo..."

"Just let me do it my way. I'll be fine."

I can't do a thing. He's seventeen hundred miles away. "Okay, but call me back, soon, please? I'm worried about you."

"Why, Lily? I'm bullet proof, remember?"

Yeah, until the one time you aren't.

I do my best to go about my morning. Feed and walk the dogs. Check email. An hour later, he calls back, as I asked him to. Good boy.

"Hi Leo. How are you?"

"Well, they say lightening doesn't strike twice. But I'm now living proof it does."

"What?" I heard him. I just don't want to believe him. Think maybe if he says it again it will have different meaning.

He says, "It just went off again."

"So, I assume you called your doctor. What did he say?"

"I told you I don't want to bother him."

"Seriously, Leo?" Part question, part disbelief. I know I should be compassionate, but this is ridiculous. "Get yourself to a hospital."

"I can't."

"What do you mean you can't?"

"The nearest one is about half an hour away, and I don't want to risk this happening again while I'm driving. Especially since I have to deal with the Seven Mile Bridge. I don't want to end up in the water. And honestly, I'm not that worried about me, but I don't want to be responsible for killing someone else on the road."

How altruistic of him. "Leo, I have some more information for you about this. I called my friend who is a physician's assistant, and..."

"Why would you do such a thing?"

I think *because I'm worried about you, you asshole* but I keep it to myself, ignore his question, and continue to talk. "She thinks you're probably dehydrated from the stomach thing, which can throw your body chemistry off, and cause heart rhythm issues."

"Great. So I'll drink a bunch of water, and buy some Gatorade and bananas, and I should be just fine."

"No, that's not enough, Leo. Please, PLEASE call your doctor? Ask him what you should do. Maybe you need to call an ambulance to take you to the hospital, get hooked up to an IV or something."

"Why? Because your friend said so? She's not a doctor, and she doesn't even know me. Besides, you're overreacting, like usual. I'll be fine. Let's get off the phone now so I can go to the grocery store. There's a Winn Dixie just a few blocks away. I'll let you know what happens."

Let me know? There's no talking to this man when he's this stubborn. "Leo, I love you. But I feel helpless so many miles away. What can I do for you?"

"Just stop worrying, and get on with your day. I'll check in later."

I have no choice but to do what he's asked. I can't force him to call his doctor. And if I make the call myself, he'll be infuriated.

So I obey *(note to self: do not include the word obey in our vows if and when we ever get married.)* I go on with my day. Can't say I'm not worried. This is huge. What would I do if... no, can't go there. To be happy to have the house to myself for two weeks is one thing, but to consider the possibility of losing him forever is just too much. We've worked too hard to get to where we are. I want his unwashed dishes back in the sink, and his dirty underwear on the floor of the closet. Even a coffee ring or two on the counter might be comforting.

An hour later I decide to go for a swim. The indoor lap pool exercise type. My therapy. It means I'll be out of touch with him for about an hour, but he's told me not to worry. I call him before I head in.

"How are you doing?"

"Fine. I and my bananas are quite happy here at the library doing some computer work. I figure at least if something happens I'll be around people who can call 911."

"And what did your doctor tell you to do?"

"I haven't called him yet. I told you I don't want to waste his time. I've been fine for the past hour."

"Leo, you can't just ignore two shocks."

"Don't tell me what I can and can't do. Let me do this my way."

"No. You're not bulletproof. Do you have any idea how upsetting this is to me?"

"But this isn't about you, Lily. Just leave me alone."

"Fine. Goodbye." I hang up. Can't believe we just fought about this. I'm only trying to love him. To show him

I care. Doesn't he understand? He's behaving, well, let's just say he's behaving badly. And I didn't even say I love you. What if something happens, and our last words were ugly ones? I press redial.

"What?" He's clearly annoyed.

"I love you, Leo. I just wanted to remind you."

His voice softens. "I know, Lily. I'm just scared."

"Well, then..."

"I will. I promise I'll call. Right now, okay?"

"Yes, thank you."

"Go enjoy your swim. I'll be fine. And one more thing..."

"What?"

"I love you, too."

"I know you do."

We both hang up, in a much better place now.

Time to stick my head under water for a mile or so. He's calling his doctor. It's all going to be fine.

Chapter 55

The pool is my happy place. It's where I go to escape from stress and worry. The initial entry into the water is always a bit shocking. Bad choice of words today. Let's just say the water feels cold, but within a lap or two I'm unaware of the temperature. I settle into the rhythmic breathing required by the swim. It's good for me, like a moving meditation. I manage to forget about what's going on in Florida, what I might be missing on my cell phone.

Inhale. *I trust you, God.* Exhale. *Thank you.* The water works its magic, and a mile later I'm ready to deal with life again. I take a quick shower, then head back to my car. My cell phone shows only one missed call. It was Leo. Probably to report in after he talked with his cardiologist. Good. He'll have the opportunity to say I told you so, he's fine, and all my worry was for nothing. He'll be delighted to prove me wrong, and truthfully, I'd love to be wrong right now.

I dial into the voicemail. "Lily, call me as soon as you can. I'm in an ambulance on the way to the hospital. I love you." I've never heard such fear in his voice. He's left me hanging, again, with too little information. The swim's magic aura of calm instantly vacates my body. I need to talk with him, but when I call back it goes straight to voicemail. So I have no choice but to leave one of my own. "Hey, it's me. Where are you? You said you were in an ambulance, but what happened? Call me, please, as soon as you get this. I love you, too, Leo." I feel so helpless.

For the first time today I realize I may have to travel to Florida. Soon. Like tonight or tomorrow. I should probably start to prepare, just in case. The dogs will have to go to the kennel, but I don't know for sure yet, so it doesn't make sense to take them now. I guess I'll not be able to leave until tomorrow morning at the earliest. I'm in hurry up and wait mode. And I don't even know where he is, or what's happening.

Is there someone else I should call? Like Elizabeth? I realize I don't have enough information to know what to tell her, and a call from me would only serve to alarm her, so probably it is best to wait.

The phone rings. His ringtone. I jump at it. "Are you okay?"

"Yeah, well, I'm alive, anyway."

"Not funny, Leo. Where are you?"

"I'm in the hospital. The emergency room."

"But you said something about an ambulance?"

"Yes. It went off, again."

"Oh, no..."

"About a dozen times."

Maybe he is bullet proof. I ask the obvious question. "Are you okay?" *Stupid question.*

"Well, like I said, I'm alive."

"Okay, that's a start. So tell me what happened."

"I can only talk for a minute or two, until the doctor comes back in. Anyway, I was at the library, working away quite happily at my computer, when the damn thing went off again. And again. And it wouldn't stop. The librarian called 911. I think I scared the hell out of her." *Yeah, join the club.* "She probably thought I was having seizures or something. One of the times it went off I had my keys in one hand, and a banana in the other, and when the shock hit, the keys flew in one direction, and the banana in the other. I think I may have yelled, too, or maybe yelped like a wounded dog. Pretty comic scene."

Comic? I'd call it terrifying. I later learned the shock causes not only a correction of the heart rhythm, but also contraction of the chest wall muscles, vocal cords, and diaphragm. Which can cause an involuntary brief yelp from the patient. I can't imagine what it must have been like for an uninformed stranger to witness.

It occurs to me if he had called his doctor last night, or this morning, all of this could have been avoided, but I'm just wise enough to know this is not the time, not yet, to say I told you so. I need to be caring, compassionate, and supportive, not judgmental.

"Leo, is it still happening? When was the last one?"

"They got me hooked up to an IV and that seems to have stopped it." I bite back another I told you so. "Now they're trying to figure out what to do with me."

"What do you mean? Do you need me to fly down? I hate you having to go through this alone."

"Not yet. I'm going to be fine. Why don't you believe me?"

"I don't know. Maybe because you've just been taken away by ambulance after a dozen shocks to your heart? Leo, do you want me to call anyone?"

"No. But thanks. I already called the office."

Of course he did. Just like the day the towers fell, and he was in New York City. I was in a panic, unable to find him. He called his secretary first. Left me alone to wait and worry.

I ask, "Are you sure I can't do anything?"

"Nope. We just have to wait. You know I hate this."

"Yes, I do." I pause, then say, "I love you. But you scared the hell out of me with your message from the ambulance."

"Yeah, well, it wasn't exactly my finest hour."

"Just keep me posted, please? My phone isn't going to leave my side. And please call me first next time, not your secretary."

"Yeah. Sure. Whatever. Here comes the doc. Gotta go."

And just like that, I'm alone again. Just me and my worry.

I try to do some mindless paperwork, but I'm far too distracted to focus. An hour later, the phone rings. I look at the caller ID. Great. Just what I need.

I answer, cautiously. "Hello, Elizabeth." By now I have her cell number in my phone.

"Why the hell aren't you on a plane on your way to Florida right now?"

"Because Leo doesn't want me to come yet."

"Who cares what he says. One of us needs to go there, right now."

"I agree, but I'm thinking we should wait to hear what the doctors say first. If I do need to fly down, I'll need to take my dogs to the kennel first. So probably the best I can do is catch a flight tomorrow morning. But only if Leo wants me to."

"The hell with the dogs. Let them loose out the front door and just go. This is Leo we're talking about. Isn't he more important than your damn dogs?"

I try a more logical approach.

"Elizabeth, you didn't hear what I said. Leo doesn't want me to come yet. I asked him. I can go tomorrow, but not tonight. And please don't be ridiculous. I'm not going to put my dogs out in the street. Even if I fly into Miami now, there's still a three hour drive to the hospital from there, and a chance they might be moving him, so it just doesn't make any sense to go yet. And the last thing I need right now is to show up and have Leo be angry with me. Let's wait to hear what the doctors say. He may have just been dehydrated from the stomach flu. Did he tell you that part?"

"Yeah. Whatever. So listen, I'll buy your plane ticket if it helps."

"Sure. Thank you. It's generous of you to offer." Good. My logic appears to have worked. She gives me her credit card numbers. We agree to call each other when we have updates. Say polite goodbyes. Isn't this cozy, his ex-wife and I fighting over who should go save the idiot. I mean, the man we love. Or loved. Does she still love him? This isn't exactly the right time for me to ponder this question.

Time to think clearly, Lily. Time to work on a plan. Florida in winter. What do I need to take? First thought is my bathing suit. Still wet from earlier today, but it will be dry by morning. I hang it up in the bathroom, somewhere obvious so I'll see it and not forget it. Sandals? Probably in the back of my closet. Sunscreen? Who knows where. Though I doubt I'll get much leisure time at the beach. Unless he is pronounced well, and we can share it together. See? I'm always on the lookout for the happy ending.

I wait again for the phone to ring, for Leo's ringtone. The story of my life with this man.

I consider calling him first, but there's no point. Finally around seven o'clock he calls. What a shock. I mean surprise.

He says, "Hey, you."

"Hey."

"It's me."

"Yeah, I know. And?"

"Well, I've learned a few things today."

"Me, too. Like how stubborn you can be." It slips out.

He surprises me with a chuckle. Must be feeling better. "Thought that's one of the things you find more endearing about me?" I swear he must have winked when he said it.

"Okay, Leo, so tell me please. What have you learned?"

"Not to get sick in a small town in Florida with big city technology implanted in my chest." *So, now he's the master of the obvious?* "There isn't even a cardiologist available on a

239

Friday evening, and the emergency room folks haven't a clue what to do about my AICD. Their only solution so far is to want to move me to a hospital with the defibrillator technology."

"Is that a good thing by you?"

"I guess. But the nearest place is in Miami."

"Is that a bad thing?"

"No, except they don't want to risk putting me in an ambulance for three hours. So they're talking about a helicopter ride."

"Wow, that's crazy."

"Yes, and damn expensive."

"I assume your insurance will pay for it?"

"Probably, but you know how I hate to spend other people's money."

Yeah, well, it's the price you pay for ignoring the first two shocks. Blessedly I don't say it out loud. "So when's all this going to happen?"

"I don't know. It's already dark here. So I guess not until morning. Just wish I could get the hell out of here."

Ah, the impatience thing. Totally understandable in this case. And maybe a good sign.

I say, "You know, Elizabeth called me. She was all over me for not coming down tonight. I told her you didn't want me to, but I don't think she believed me. And I know she didn't agree with me. She got all freaked out about it. Told me to just set the dogs loose in the street and get on the first plane I could."

"So I heard. She called me after you talked. Said the two of you didn't exactly see eye to eye."

How sweet. Leo and Elizabeth commiserating about me. I decide to let it go for now. I say, "She offered to buy my ticket."

"I know. She told me. I think it's unnecessary. And inappropriate."

"But if it makes her feel better..."

"Look, can we not argue this right now, Lily? We'll figure it out tomorrow. The good news is there have been no more shocks. But the doctors in Boston need one of those computer reports from the AICD to figure out if it was truly a cardiac event or just dehydration." He has a portable monitor he uses at home to send in remote readings. It's supposed to travel with him. I glance over to his bedside table. There it sits. At home with me.

"Leo, why didn't you take it with you? Isn't that part of why you have it?"

"Yeah, well, it seemed too bulky to pack."

Great. He can pack three suitcases full of fishing gear, but no room for his health? One more crisis we could have avoided if he didn't consider himself bulletproof.

"Lily, you know how much I hate all of this, don't you?"

"Yes, you already said so. Believe me, I'm not exactly enjoying it either." *Still not the right time to say I told you so.* "Okay. So let's make a tentative plan for tomorrow, depending on where you are. I can drop off the dogs at the kennel at eight-thirty, catch an eleven o'clock flight with a layover in Baltimore, will put me in Fort Lauderdale by about five. I'll have to drive to Miami from there. Not ideal, but it's the best available on short notice, and we can let Elizabeth pay if it makes her happy. Otherwise it costs a fortune."

"I still don't like the idea. Let's give it the night. Who knows, maybe they'll ship my body home tomorrow and you won't have to come at all."

I don't appreciate his gallows humor. "Call me in the morning, please? You know it's making me crazy to not be there with you. I feel pretty helpless up here."

"I know."

"Oh, and this is awkward, but do you need me to call your kids?"

"No, thanks. Elizabeth already has." *Of course. Appropriately so. What was I thinking?*

I sigh. "I love you, Leo. You scared the hell out of me today." I'm repeating myself, but it bears being said again.

"I know. Me, too. And yes, of course I love you. You know I do."

"Of course. Call me if you have anything new, or even just to say hi. Please? No matter what time it is? My phone will be on your pillow beside me in our bed."

"I will. Get some sleep. Looks like a long day ahead tomorrow."

Understatement of the year. My two weeks to stretch out and enjoy the house to myself are now officially on hold. Looks like I'm going to Florida tomorrow. And it's not to visit Mickey Mouse.

Chapter 56

Saturday. I'm at the airport in Baltimore. My connecting flight doesn't leave for another hour. I call to check in with Leo.

"I've got good news and bad news," he says.

"The bad news first, Leo. What's up?"

"They want to do a stress test before they'll release me."

"And that's bad news because...?"

"Because they can't do it until Monday. Which is when the guys will get here to check out my device."

"You're in a posh hospital in Miami and you have to wait two days to be seen?"

"Yeah, crazy, huh?"

"So then what's the good news?"

"I figure they must not be too worried about me if they are okay to let me sit here and wait until Monday."

I guess there's a certain logic in his thinking. Though it seemed much more urgent this morning when they put him on a helicopter instead of in an ambulance.

"Oh, and there's more good news. The labs they ran on me showed I didn't have a heart attack, so now they just want to figure out why I got shocked so many times."

Great. I'm rushing to Florida, possibly for no good reason other than his ex-wife's panic. And I'm only halfway there. Stuck in the middle. Just like always.

Leo reads my mind. "Maybe you should fly back home. Nothing exciting happening here."

I ponder the possibility for a moment. "No, I've come this far. I'll see you in a few hours. You shouldn't have to go through this alone."

Wings up. Then down. Rental car. Drive from Ft. Lauderdale to Miami Beach. Find the hospital. It's been a long day.

I walk into his room. He's at work on his laptop, which sits on his hospital tray table, in the middle of all the wires going to monitors for his heart, IV, and oxygen line. He appears to have not noticed my entrance. I say, "Hellooo? It's me."

He barely looks up. "Be with you in a second."

"Seriously? Don't I get a kiss hello or something?"

"I said just a minute."

Wow. This isn't starting well. I've dropped everything to be by his side and this is the greeting I get? I sit down by his bed. I'm not one to hide my emotions, or at least not to do it well. Especially when I'm tired. Surely he can tell I'm annoyed.

An awkward minute or so later he closes the computer. Looks up. Forced, fake grin. "Hi."

"Hi." I return the smile. Sort of.

"So, here I am," he says.

"Yes, you are."

"What's up?"

"Well, I'm here, and you're still in the hospital. Now what?"

"I told you, you didn't need to come."

Oh, my. Maybe he's right. Maybe I shouldn't have. Apparently my expectation of a joyful reunion, complete with emotional hugs of relief to be together, I guess it was just another one of my imaginary scenes.

I try to save the moment. "Can a weary traveler get a kiss and a hug from her bionic fiancee?"

"In a minute."

I've just flown seventeen hundred miles to be by his side, and he's still got the computer on his lap instead of me. "Leo, please put that damn thing away. I'm here."

"Don't tell me what to do."

I'm tempted to make an escape of my own and head straight back to the airport.

But he closes the computer, and hands it to me so I can put it somewhere out of reach. Then he pats the bed beside him. I slide in. Put my arm around him.

I say, "So you got to ride in a helicopter. Fun, huh?"

"Yeah. Real fun. Tell you about it sometime. But not right now. Just sit here with me."

We fall silent, together. The good type of silence, feeling our closeness. No need to fill the space with noise. I exhale, deeply. After a few minutes, say, "So, what happens next?"

"Well, we wait. And you know what a patient guy I am. This is such a huge waste of time and money. Maybe I should just unplug all of this stuff, get dressed, and drive us out of here."

You might think he's joking, but I know him well enough to know he's not. Oh boy, here we go. "Don't be ridiculous. You know you can't do that."

"Of course I can. They're practically ignoring me until Monday. And the food here is awful. Then there's the van I left behind and need to retrieve. We could drive down tomorrow to get it, and I'll come back in on Monday and let them do their tests."

What he's suggesting almost makes sense, but my fear and logic intercede. "It's too big a risk, Leo. What if something happens while we're driving?" His family would never forgive me. But I know he's feeling trapped, and his next sentence proves it.

"This is bullshit, Lily. I never should've let them implant this thing in in the first place. I'm considering a lawsuit."

"What? Why?"

"It misfired. Way too many times."

"Don't you think you should wait until you know more?"

"Well, we still have the van issue to figure out."

"Look, my flight isn't until Tuesday. If you're fine, they'll discharge you Monday after the tests are done. We can drive down together in the afternoon, spend the night, and come back on Tuesday morning. I'll change my flight to a little later in the day." I'm ad libbing, hoping it makes sense as I continue to look for an opportunity to turn this Florida mess into a romantic adventure.

"No. That won't work," he says.

"Why not?"

"Because I have a work event on Tuesday. Lunch. And I can't miss it. I'm the organizer."

"You're in the hospital, Leo. You could've died. Let someone else deal with Tuesday."

"Lily, it doesn't work that way and you know it. I have to be there."

I open my mouth to argue, then stop. There's no point. "Well, then, how else do you propose we get the van?"

"Like I just said, we should drive down tomorrow. I'll even let you drive. They want me to sit here in this bed all day. I'll just sit in the rental car with you instead, then drive the van back while you drive your car."

"No, I won't, and you can't."

"Fine. Then I'll do it myself."

"No."

I try some new logic. "Let's plan on Monday. Even if it means Monday evening, we'll get up early on Tuesday morning to drive back. What is it, about three hours? You can make your lunch, and I'll keep my same flight."

"Okay, but what if they don't discharge me until Tuesday morning? Then what?"

"Well, then there's probably a reason they're keeping you, and it would just prove the point of not going on Sunday. You don't even know if it's safe for you to drive right now. What if it goes off again?"

"Then you'll be behind me in your rental car."

"You've got to be kidding."

I know he's not. I also know I'm fighting with the part of him that needs to believe he's invincible and wants to walk out of here tomorrow and do it himself. "Look, Leo, we've both had a long day. I need to get some rest before I can think clearly again. You should probably do the same. I'll come back in the morning, and we can have breakfast together, figure it all out after a good night's sleep."

He's quiet for a moment as he lets it sink in, but only for a moment.

"Bring salt."

"What?" I ask.

"I said bring salt. This is the cardiology floor, and they have me on some damn heart healthy diet and it's the most bland thing I've ever tasted. Find a Wendy's or McDonald's and steal a bunch of those little packets for me."

"Yeah, whatever."

This is a man who requires so much salt in his diet he puts it on his Chinese chicken wings. Small wonder his heart has issues. Now he wants me to be an accomplice to his bad habits.

I give him a kiss and head out. It's time to drive around Miami Beach after dark in my rental car and attempt to find my hotel. The cataract in my right eye, scheduled for surgery in a few months, clouds my night vision so I can't read the street signs. Thankfully Elizabeth offered to put me up in a five star hotel. Ironic, isn't it? All those nights Leo and I stayed in posh hotels when she didn't know about me. Tonight I'll sleep in a beautiful beachfront Marriot, because she does know about me.

Yes, tonight I sleep alone in luxury at his ex-wife's expense. Though I suppose on some level it was always at her expense.

I wake early the next morning. Too early to go to the hospital, so I explore where I am. Discover I am indeed oceanfront. There is just enough time for a short beach walk and a quick swim. I'm thankful I thought to bring my bathing suit. It's February, and the Atlantic Ocean is deliciously warm and calm today. It isn't all bad. I can think of better circumstances for being here, but I'll accept the gift in this.

A quick shower. Get cleaned up. Pull myself together. Drive back to the hospital. Walk into Leo's room. His breakfast tray has just been delivered. *Good timing, Lily*. Except I forgot one little thing.

Chapter 57

"Where's my salt?"

His first words to me this morning. Not I love you. Not I'm so glad you're here, thank you for coming to take care of me. Just where's my salt. So much for the serenity of my swim. Twice ruined by him in the course of three days.

I lie. "I don't have any. I didn't pass any fast food places on the way." Well, not actually a lie, I simply didn't notice if there were any. I totally forgot about his request. Honestly I did. Though even if I had remembered, it wouldn't be my choice to help poison the man I love.

"I can't eat eggs like this. Go down to the cafeteria and steal a salt shaker for me."

"Leo..."

"Just do it. Don't argue with me."

Obedient little idiot I seem to have become, I do as he tells me. Go downstairs to the cafeteria. No salt shakers sitting around on the tables for me to pocket, so I have to ask for them, those tiny packets with the red writing on them. I say thank you, and tuck them away like contraband in the back pocket of my jeans.

Back to his room. He says thank you. The grumpy bear is happier now, while he eats his salty eggs. Until he speaks again. "Won't let me have real coffee, either. Just decaf."

Oh, great. Does he plan to send me back downstairs for coffee, too? I say, "They just want you to be healthy." He frowns at me. I try again. "So, what's next?"

"I've decided to concede on not getting the van today." *Well, thank God.* "But I think maybe you should get it tomorrow."

"What? I can't exactly drive down there alone, then drive my car and the van both back here. Won't it take two of us?"

"No. I have it all figured out. You drive your car to the airport. Park it there for the day. Then take the shuttle from the airport down into the Keys. Get the van and drive it back to the airport. Return it to the rental place, and get back into your own rental car. See? Easy."

"Shuttle bus? To the Keys? You mean like one of those things you see in the movies where the chickens run loose up and down the aisles?"

"I'm sure it's more civilized than that."

"Why can't we just stick to the other plan and do it together tomorrow after they discharge you?"

"Because what if they don't? I have my lunch commitment on Tuesday. Then more meetings on Wednesday. And the van is costing me fifty dollars a day to sit in the parking lot down there."

"Well, I suppose you chalk that up to the cost of ignoring the first two shocks." *Oh, crap. Why did I say that out loud?* Must've left my filter back in the hotel room.

"Great. Now it's my fault this happened?"

Inside my head a loud chorus shouts YES! but I say nothing. *Good girl.*

Instead I cave and agree to his plan. "Whatever you want, Leo. I'll go get the damn van for you. What else do I have to do tomorrow?" Images of the beach float through my brain. Me, in a bathing suit, with an umbrella drink in hand. But never mind. I've come all the way to Miami and apparently I only get ten minutes of beach time. No, make it past tense. I only *got* ten minutes.

He's still talking. "There's one more thing."

Great. I can't wait to hear this. "Oh, do tell."

"You need to clean out the van when you get there. My camping stuff is in it, and some fishing gear. Quite frankly, I don't even remember how I left it. The night before was pretty rough, sick as I was."

Oh, it's just getting better. I mean worse. A lot worse.

I'm a mom. I've cleaned up all sorts of bodily messes. But this? Now I not only have to ride the chicken express shuttle, but when I get there, I get to clean out the inside of his messy camping van, with the bedding and clothing in and on which he was sick, that has now been baking inside the van with ninety plus degrees and sun and no ventilation for the past three days.

I can't wait.

First, there is the rest of today to get through. We do manage to enjoy some of our time together. We talk the nurse into unhooking him from his monitors and IV long enough to go outside together for a while, after I promise to bring him back.

Leo's in a wheelchair, and I'm pushing him around the outer perimeters of the parking lot. He basks in the sun. I sit in the shade. South Florida afternoon sun is too darn hot for me. He loves it.

We walk past the landing pad for the med-flight helicopter. He shares the blow by blow of his flight adventure, like the mother of a newborn telling her birthing story. He was terrified. Cramped in a tight space with two nurses, worried he might be shocked again. He'd been through hell and back that day.

I find renewed compassion for this man. Open my heart and allow myself to feel the depth of my love for him. We each have a great capacity to anger and frustrate one another. Yet deep down, I love him more than I can put into words. Sure, he doesn't always talk the kindest to me. Orders me around like I'm still his employee. But honestly, I'd do just about anything for this man. I smuggled salt for him. How bad can it be to clean out his van?

Chapter 58

Another sunny Monday dawns on Miami Beach.

I'm in yet another hotel room this morning. Checked out of the other one yesterday, as we thought I'd be staying in Leo's room at the hospital last night. He's still trying to save pennies where he can on what is already a far too expensive trip. There was an empty second bed in his room and no roommate. The nurses told us it would be okay. Then just after dinner, a new admission. He moved into Leo's room. So back I went to the hotel for another night, in a different room. I wonder what the night crew thinks of me. Do they wonder if I'm a high end escort? Except I'm dressed in flip flops and blue jeans. *Sorry to disappoint you guys. I'm just a displaced once upon a time mistress.*

This morning's time at the beach will be short. A long day stretches ahead. I go for a walk, barefoot in the sand, and as I walk, a new potential obstacle occurs to me.

When I return to my room, I call Leo. "Hey, I have a question. If you are the one who rented the van, and it's in your name, then do you think maybe you need to call and ask them to put my name on as a driver, too? Otherwise, I don't think I'll be insured if something happens."

"Of course you will be. Don't worry about it. If we don't say anything, they won't know."

"But what if something does happen?"

"Stop worrying, Lily, it'll be fine."

"Leo, I don't like this. But I'm not going to argue about it with you. Not now. I'll see you in a little while. I need to stop by your room to get the key to the van."

Still not convinced, I call my insurance agent back home and explain the situation. Turns out I'm right. I'm not covered unless I'm named on the rental papers.

I call Leo. Tell him what I just learned.

He takes great delight this time in telling me I'm wrong. "I just called the rental agency and they said you're fine."

"Are you sure? Was it really that easy?"

"Lily, I told you it's fine. Don't you trust me?"

And there it is. The million dollar question. Unfortunately, my honest answer to his question is no. The man who lied to his wife for how long? No, I don't trust him. But I can't admit it. Not out loud.

I feel trapped. "Fine. Whatever. I'll see you soon." We hang up, the issue still unresolved. I guess I'm going to have to do it his way. Put myself at risk, so I can save his ass. If only he'd paid attention to the first lightning bolt, or the second, and gotten himself to a hospital sooner, none of this would be necessary. I'd still be at home, enjoying my quiet retreat, instead of spending the day retrieving his stinky van full of germs.

I wonder if I have ignored a few lightning strikes of my own. Has God been trying to get my attention about this man, and I keep choosing to look the other way? I can't marry a man I don't trust, can I?

Chapter 59

Time to put Leo's plan into action. I'm in my rental car, on my way to the megalopolis known as Miami International Airport. Too many steps need to happen today before I can call it a success.

Step one. Fight with Leo. Wasn't part of the plan, and certainly not how I would have wanted today to start. I stopped by his room to get the key. Hoped maybe we could heal over the earlier phone call. We didn't. We were polite. Matter of fact. Nothing more.

Step two. Drive to the airport in my comfortable rental car. This isn't so bad. Directional signage is clear. Traffic moves along at a reasonable pace. Tune in some upbeat music on the radio, not hard to find in Miami. It's like a Zumba class on wheels.

Step three. Drop my car off in the daily parking lot. Write down the location so I can remember it when I return.

Step four. Find the Key West Shuttle. Board the bus. No chickens in sight. Though I do overhear the driver tell one of the other passengers about a horrible stomach flu that's run rampant. So much for Leo's food poisoning theory. More likely it was viral, so my date today with the van might expose me.

I have few phobias, but one of my worst is an aversion to anything that might involve, sorry, there's no dainty way to say it, vomiting. More specifically, vomiting in a hotel room, alone, far from home, or on a three hour plane ride. Oh my, what have I gotten myself into?

Step five. I'm in the parking lot of the Winn-Dixie supermarket in the town of Big Pine Key. I find the van, and think how convenient it is that he parked it here, rather than somewhere remote. *Try to be grateful for the little things, Lily.* Open the windows. Let the heat and stench vent while I go into the store to buy cleaning supplies. Disinfectant spray. Air freshener. Paper towels. Hand sanitizer. Ginger ale, to settle an already queasy stomach. *Just anxious. Not sick, I hope.* Rubber gloves. Trash bags. I think I'm all set. A six pack of Oreos is an afterthought. Comfort carbs.

Step six. Clean the van. I open every possible door and window as wide as I can. Start in the front, driver's side. There are little pieces of paper and trash everywhere. Fast food bags with food wrappers and scraps inside. Soda cups, some with flat soda still in them. All obvious trash to discard. There's some loose change in the dashboard cup holder. Put it in my pocket. Business papers on the passenger seat and floor. Gather those together and stuff into a canvas bag found on the floor. Ten minutes to clean up the front. Not so bad. I discover rubber gloves grow sticky on my hands in this heat and humidity. But there's no way I'm going to risk exposure of bare skin to virus germs.

On to the back of the van. Oh, my. He warned me the bedding should go directly into the trash. He was correct. I hate throwing things away with useful life in them, but these towels, and the pillow, and the sheet, are all history. Bad history. There are more empty fast food bags. I fill an entire large black plastic trash bag with the obvious offenders. Try not to think about the smell. Try not to judge the man for being such a slob. He was sick. I can forgive him this, can't I?

I take a break to call, to check in on his progress with his own agenda for the day. The stress test was scheduled for ten o'clock. Hopefully they'll let him leave the hospital when I get back tonight, and we can stay somewhere in a lovely hotel room, together, just like old times. I checked out of mine this morning. Again.

He answers the phone on the first ring. "I hate this place."

"What? Why? What now?"

"I'm still waiting for the damn test." It's two o'clock.

"I'm sorry." *Why did I just apologize for his wait? It's not like it's my fault.*

He says, "Yeah, well, how's the van?"

"Pretty awful. But I'm working through it." I make sure to sound more cheerful than I feel. I'm hot, tired, and a little angry around the edges, but I know better than to vent my irritation to him. Not now.

"Yeah, sorry about that. But hey, thanks for doing this." First nice thing he's said to me today.

"It's okay." I lie, again. "I just hate to throw away so much."

"Throw it all away. I don't care if I never see any of it again."

Well, I guess it's good to have his permission. "I need to get back to work now. Got a long drive ahead of me when I'm done."

"Okay. I'll call you when I hear something from the docs."

Oh, yeah, the docs. Seems like Leo's health has gotten pushed aside by other events of today. I guess during this weekend's long wait we've forgotten about the potential severity of his heart condition. Good to be reminded why I'm here doing this. His heart failed him. Whatever the cause, the truth is he could have died. What if he'd been alone instead of at the library? What if he'd been driving? How dare I grumble about his mess, when it's possible I could be doing this under far more dire circumstances, without him at the other end of the phone? I need to be grateful he's just a four hour drive away, and that tonight I will return to him, and feel the warmth of his arms in bed beside me. At least I hope so. I need to use the energy of those thoughts as motivation to finish this job and get back to him.

By three o'clock, step six is completed. Three full garbage bags have been stuffed into various parking lot trash cans. Five other bags of things, plus a stack of fishing poles, have been piled neatly in the back of the disinfected van, ready to be off loaded into my rental car back at the airport. I'm sure Leo will discard more of it, but I'll leave the detail decisions up to him. Right now my priority is to drive this beast of a van back to Miami and get to the other end of this day.

Step seven. Return trip. Brain engages enough to remember to take advantage of the grocery store here and buy some food for the road. I've barely eaten today. No appetite. Not after what I've just seen and smelled.

I'm finally back on the highway. The van's shocks are built to assume a fully loaded vehicle, but empty as it is, it drives like an oversized tin can on springs. The rear end floats, and feels like a feather in the wind. Can't wait for the infamous Seven Mile Bridge. Enter phobia number two. Driving off a bridge.

Oreos and ginger ale. Dinner of champions. The drive's not too bad so far. I see the bridge looming in the distance. Turn on the radio. Maybe some music will comfort me, or at least distract me away from my fear. Jimmy Buffet. Of course. This is the Keys. Big Pine Key is at mile twenty-two on US Route 1. I made this trip all the way from Massachusetts, got within twenty-two miles of Margaritaville and turned around headed back north. I must be crazy. Should have spent tonight in Key West. My thoughts distract me enough so that before I know it I'm across the bridge, and I didn't drive off into the water. Progress. *Thank you, God.*

Traffic jam. Construction. Five o'clock. The phone rings. It's Leo. "Hey there. You in Miami yet? Wanna bring me some dinner from the outside world?"

"Nope. I'm stuck in traffic somewhere in Key Largo."

"That's all the further you are? What's taking you so long?"

I choose to ignore the criticism. I know I'm over sensitive when I'm tired. Maybe he didn't mean to be judgmental, though he always tells me I drive too slowly. I try a different approach. Fake cheerfulness. Change the subject. "So, what's the news from the docs? They gonna let you go soon? Maybe we can stay someplace nice together tonight."

"Good news and bad news. Which do you want first?"

Does this man not even know me? "Bad news, please."

"Well, the head doc, the one who says whether I stay or go, isn't coming back until tomorrow morning, so I'm stuck here another night."

Crap. So much for my vision of a romantic just like old times together somewhere lovely night. My motivation to hurry back just flew out the window. "Oh, I'm sorry to hear that. So what's the good news?"

"The stress test was fine. No new heart damage. I just got shocked twenty-one times for no good reason."

No good reason? Does he still not get it? For a reasonably intelligent man, he is still missing the obvious cause and effect behind this. He was dehydrated. He ignored the first two shocks. They stopped happening as soon as the paramedics got him hooked up with an IV. *Don't say anything, Lily. Don't risk making him angry again.* I say, "Okay. Well, that's good, I guess."

"I guess? Geez, Lily, this is great news. Except for the law suit I'm planning."

I decide I shouldn't talk to him any more, or I will say something I will regret.

"Hey, Leo, I need to hang up now. Traffic's starting to move and I want to get as much driving done in the daylight as I can. My cataract gets in the way of reading road signs at night and I don't know where I'm going." What I want to say is I can't talk with him anymore because of his stupidity. There have been too many people inconvenienced by his stubbornness, and I still have miles to go before I sleep. Literally.

Step eight. Miami airport. Again. It's dusk. Been a long day. There are halos around everything as I try to see past oncoming headlights. I drive the van into the parking garage to offload all of his stuff into my rental car. Sure hope I remember where I parked it. Ah, yes, I had the forethought to write it down. 4-D. But didn't write down in which garage. This place is huge, and the day's been too long. I think I'm in the right garage, but my car isn't where it should be. I'm on the edge of, well, pick one. Anger. Panic. Fear.

My cell phone rings again. I answer, annoyed, "What?"

"Is that any way to greet a sick man?"

"You're not sick." *Oops.*

"Well then why the hell won't they let me leave?"

Great. Just what I need. "I can't talk to you now. I can't even find my car."

"Where are you? I thought you'd be here an hour ago."

"I'm still at Miami airport, driving around the damn parking garage trying to find my car. I told you I was stuck in traffic."

"You're still at the airport?"

"Yes. Like I just said, I can't find my car."

"Why are you so freaked out?"

"Oh, I don't know. Cause I'm exhausted and dirty and can't see and just spent the afternoon packing up all your shit for you and almost drove off a bridge and this whole day has been fucked up."

"Don't overreact, Lily. What's the big deal?"

I hate being accused of overreacting. I react how I react. Nothing 'over' about it.

Then I see it. The sign. LOW CLEARANCE. Now I know how the guys in the moving van felt just before they hit the bridge.

"Oh my God. I don't know if I can do this!"

"What?"

"Drive the van through here." I panic. Shriek. Get through the tight passage intact. There's my car, waiting for me right where I left it, but I'm still on the phone, and now he's yelling at me.

"What the hell's wrong with you? It's just a day in Florida. You could've enjoyed it but all you've done is complain. I'm the one in the hospital. I'd happily trade places with you."

"Yeah, well, it's all your damn fault, Leo. This entire trip has been your fault." I'm too tired at this point to care whether or not I filter my words.

"Lily, you're crazy. Your shrink's got you so screwed up in the head you can't even see straight."

Yeah, he's right, but it's my eye doctor's problem, not hers. "I'm hanging up now, Leo. I can't do this anymore." And as I hear the words come out of my mouth, I wonder which 'this' I'm referring to.

How long have I lied to myself about this man? How many other times has he yelled at me when I've tried to help him? Not just to voice his frustration with a situation, but with personal assaults. He yells at me if I don't answer him the way he wants me to. When did the yelling start to outweigh the loving, and why haven't I noticed? Is it possible the road signs aren't the only ones I've been missing?

At least I've found my car. I unpack, caught between tears and anger. All this evidence of his messy week. And now I have to load it into my clean rental car.

But even after I do, I'm still not done yet. Step nine. Return the van to the rental place, which is somewhere a few miles away from the parking garage. So I'm back out onto strange roads, at night, with bad vision. Then I need to get the shuttle to bring me back here to my car. This whole thing is absurd. I should have let him do it. I should have let him clean up his own mess. How many times will it take for me to learn?

I'm still crying. Need to get a hold of myself, because the water in my eyes is making my vision worse. The phone rings again. Maybe I shouldn't answer it. Not now. But it's a normal ringtone, not Leo's. Who could possibly be calling me?

Curiosity gets the better of me. "Hello?"

"Hi, Lily. I heard you're in Florida."

"I'm sorry. But who is this?"

"It's Rose."

"Rose? Are you psychic or something?" It's my therapist. The one he just trashed.

She laughs. "Why would you ask that?"

The sound of her laughter helps me to relax. "Your timing is perfect. You have no idea how good it is to hear your voice right now."

"Well, your friend Celia was in this morning, and she told me Leo had a heart attack. Said you had to run off to Florida. Thought I'd check in to see how you're doing."

I don't think she's ever called just to check on me. Surely God has whispered in her ear this time. "Oh, Rose, you wouldn't believe. It's been, well, I just had a meltdown, and he screamed at me. Told me how screwed up I am. Even implicated you in it."

"Oh, Lily. So he's okay?"

"Yeah. Apparently. Just a royal pain in the ass. This weekend's been awful. No, correct that. Today's been awful."

"And what about you? When are you back home?"

"Not soon enough. But hey, I probably should get off the phone. I'm driving, and, well, I'll tell you more about it when I see you. Maybe sometime later this week?"

"Sure. How's Thursday at two?"

"Perfect. I should be back by then." I have a new goal.

"Hang in there, okay? You'll be fine."

"I know. Well, thank you for your call, Rose. You have no idea how incredible your timing is. It's a huge blessing to me you called just now. Like a reminder God's paying attention to me."

"It's just how it worked out. I'll see you Thursday. Take care."

What a stark contrast, how genuinely warm and personal the words 'take care' sound when spoken from the heart. Her phone call leaves me feeling like I've just had a refreshing shower. Back to the task at hand, I feel cleaner and lighter. I drop off the empty van at the rental place, then ride the airport shuttle back to the parking lot. The driver mutters, "Never had no one ask me to take them to another car before. That's a new one."

Yeah, right. Keep it to yourself, buddy. No more guff needed from anyone. Not tonight.

Step one hundred twenty seven. Um, I mean ten. It's nine o'clock. Back to the hospital. Twelve hours after I departed.

Leo is on the phone when I walk into his room. "She doesn't need your charity, Lizzy. I'll find her a place for tonight. Talk to you tomorrow." He hangs up. Glares at me. Then says, "You're finally here. What took so long?"

Oh, no. Not now, Leo. Please not now. I can't take any more.

I say, "It's done. I returned your stupid van. And the rest of your shit is in my car. Packed full."

"I thought I told you to just throw it all away."

Now he's second guessing how I did this? I choose to let it pass. "Was that Elizabeth on the phone?"

"Yeah. She offered to put you up for another night. I told her I'd take care of my girl tonight. I've found some cheaper places out by the airport."

"Leo, you can't be serious. After the day I've had, you want to send me back out there, back to the airport at this time of night, to try to find some cheap sleaze bag motel you found on your computer?" I'm on the edge of tears, again. Or collapse.

"Why such a princess today, Lily?"

"I can't see, Leo. My night vision sucks because of my cataract. You know that. And I'm exhausted. So Elizabeth wants to help. Why not let her?"

"She's done enough for us. Too much, in fact. I'll handle this. And why does it matter? Why do you need to be in some luxury hotel when I'm stuck here in this hospital bed?"

"Seriously, Leo, don't you even care about me anymore?"

Our eyes lock. Neither one of us says another word. He finally sees me. Sees the pain in my face. He reaches for his wallet. Pulls out his credit card and offers it to me. His voice softens, though only slightly. "Here. Take this. Go stay wherever you want. But I'm paying for this one."

I take his card, and realize I'm being tested. If I stay in the better place, where I was, then I prove him right. I am a princess. It doesn't matter if he's the one who turned me into one. *Good going, Lily. You got what you wanted.*

I give him a brief kiss. "Thank you. Let's both get a good night's sleep. I'll pick you up in the morning and drive you to the airport so you can get a car and go back to work."

"I just have to wait for the doctor to do morning rounds. They tell me I should be ready to leave by nine."

"Fine. Then I'll plan to be back by then. There's just enough time for us to get to Ft. Lauderdale for my noon flight."

He realizes his mistake in trying to send me back to Miami airport tonight. "Lily, I do love you."

"Yeah, whatever." I don't have the energy left to heal this over, not now, so I just say the words. "I love you, too. And I'm glad you're okay."

We've learned our lines well, what one of us needs to hear from the other. Though would it have hurt for him to offer a simple thank you?

"Goodbye, Leo." A new line, perhaps steeped with more meaning than I care to contemplate. Not tonight.

Step nine hundred seventy two. Check back into the Marriot. Again.

Once upon a time, Marriots were places of love. And lust. And romance. Tonight, it is my place to hide from the prince who somewhere along the story line has morphed into an ogre.

This lonely princess will spend her night alone, fighting off a terrible case of nausea she fears might be the stomach flu. Anxiety layered on top doesn't help. Nor does my deep dread of what lies ahead.

I will see him again in the morning. I hope it will all look better in the light of a new day. I should be grateful he's healthy. I remind myself this could be a lot worse. And tomorrow, I get to fly home, for five more days of retreat, to take some time to figure out what to do next.

It occurs to me it may not sound so awful, the day I spent in the Keys. It may in fact sound like I overreacted, like I was whining. After all, I got to spend three days in Florida in February, respite from the cold New England winter. It was my choice to not drive the extra twenty-two miles to Key West. Other women might have jumped at the chance. All expenses paid. Yet the personal cost was huge.

My last night in the hotel by the ocean I barely slept. I spent most of the night with a trash can next to the bed, certain I would hurl at any moment, grateful I did not.

The nausea continued throughout the next morning. I picked up Leo at the hospital, and drove us from Miami to Ft. Lauderdale. He didn't say a word about my driving. We moved his things from my rental car into his. He would drive to his lunch event, but first he saw me into the airport, ever the gentleman. I wondered to myself how this could be the same man who just the day before screamed at me and called me crazy.

The final word on his heart was it had sustained no further damage. Severe dehydration caused a rapid heartbeat which caused the AICD to do it's thing, twenty-one times. I called it his twenty-one gun salute. He didn't laugh.

The prognosis on my heart was far worse. Broken. Perhaps irreparably.

My nausea quiets as soon as I boarded the plane back to Massachusetts. My internal monologue did not. How could my fairy tale have turned so ugly? Was it a slow process of erosion, or did it happen overnight? And what could I possibly do next? I liked life in the castle. Couldn't bear the thought of another move. Or to have to start over, alone, again. Yet the way he talked to me was unacceptable. He'd been at it for a long time, but I chose to ignore it, to let it go. This time, for some reason, I could not. He called me crazy when I was exhausted. I suppose if he realized a few days later what he'd done, and apologized, it would have been fine, but when I referred back to it, his response was, "Oh, I think you're making things up. I would never talk to you like that." But I remember exactly what he said.

Leo came home at the end of his work week. And we tried. We did. We went through the motions. Even saw my therapist together. One time. There was supposed to be a second time, but he scheduled a conference call for the exact same time. He sat in his car in the parking lot and took the call, promised to come in if it ended quickly, but of course it didn't. Couples therapy, alone. How sadly ironic.

Florida happened in February.

How I refer to it now. Just one word. Florida.

Chapter 60

I'm back in Rose's office. Been trying to work on things with Leo, but I'm feeling stuck.

"So, are you making any progress with your decision?" she asks.

"No, you know me. I vacillate. I thought for sure on the plane ride home we were over, after how he talked to me, but then we got home, and, well, I still love him."

"Yes. That's clear."

"And I've been praying for direction, but don't seem to be getting any answers."

"Be patient. Maybe it's not time yet to make a decision."

"But there's this one odd thing that keeps happening."

"Oh, what's that?"

"My ring has been doing this weird thing."

Rose laughs. Then says, "I didn't know a ring could 'do' things."

"Well, mine apparently has a mind of its own. It's been spewing diamonds."

"Spewing diamonds? I don't understand."

"Yeah, well, see here how it has a bunch of small ones channeled all around?"

"Yes."

"And see how there's one missing?"

"Okay, now that you point it out I do. But they're small."

"I know. It's not about the size. It's like it keeps rejecting pieces of itself."

"Maybe you just need to have a jeweler take a look at it."

"I have. That's the thing. I had it inspected two months ago, when the first one came out, about a week before the whole Florida thing, and the jeweler tightened all of the others."

"So?"

"Well, it's lost two more in the past month. I'm telling you, it's like it doesn't like itself. I think it's a sign."

"Lily, listen to what you're saying. How does that sound to you?"

"I know, but I'm not making this up. See, every time it does this, I feel like I shouldn't wear the ring, because it has the sharp empty prongs that could snag on things. Ruined one of my favorite sweaters the first time it happened. So I end up not wearing it, until I can get to a jeweler and get it fixed. And then I have to pay for replacement diamonds. I mean, they aren't expensive, they're tiny, it's just the point of the whole thing."

"Which is?"

"I think it's a sign I'm not supposed to be wearing the ring. I seem to be spending more time without it than with it."

"So why would you not want to wear it? It's beautiful."

"It's not that I don't WANT to wear it, it's just, well, never mind. I don't think you understand."

"I'm trying to."

"It's like it's not my choice. The ring, it has a mind of its own, and appears to not want to stay on my hand."

"Is it possible you just need to find a different jeweler?"

Nobody understands me, or the way I interpret my world. Most of the time she does, but I'm pushing it with the ring thing. I've been asking for a sign. And I know it sounds ridiculous, but I think the ring is talking to me. No. Correction. Of course the ring isn't talking to me. But maybe the ring is being used by a great something or someone out there who is trying to send me a message. I need to take off the ring. It's time to get away from the spewing.

Baby steps. It's like courtship in reverse. First, a couple stops having sex. Then, they move into separate bedrooms, which makes it much easier to continue to not have sex.

How did I know when it was time to move out of our bedroom? An alarm went off.

We are both sound asleep. His cell phone alarm starts to beep. I give him a nudge.

"Huh?" He barely wakes. Doesn't move.

"Your alarm is beeping. Turn it off, please."

"I don't hear anything."

I repeat myself. "It's beeping. Please turn it off."

"If it's bothering you, then you turn it off."

"But it's on your side of the bed."

"Why did you have to wake me?"

"Because it's yours, and it's on your side of the bed."

"So you were already awake. Why did you have to wake me up, too?"

I try to understand his logic, but it won't compute. It's his alarm clock. It's on his side of the bed, and he's yelling at me because I woke him up to ask him to turn it off. I should know better by now.

Note to self: Love is supposed to be patient and kind. Love is not supposed to yell at me, or blame me at three o'clock in the morning for something I did not do. Love should not scare me with its anger, or place me in harm's way through it's selfishness. Love should be honest.

I suppose the alarm thing is a relatively small offense, but the last straw usually is, isn't it? I move into the guest room within a week. I allow myself to have fun with it, to create a room of my own. I take over a walk-in storage closet, clean it out and paint it with bright, clean, aqua and gold colors. Freshen up the bedroom walls, too. Colonial blue and sunshine yellow, with a pink ceiling. Color everywhere. A room to call my own. He'd hate it. He's a plain, white wall kind of guy. Offer him Baskin Robbins thirty-one ice cream flavors and he'll choose vanilla.

When I try to explain to him some of the things he's done, why I feel disrespected, he continues to claim to not remember. Or he will say, "I think you make this stuff up." Talk about feeling invalidated. He can take something I say and turn it around, in an instant, to make it my fault. He is a master at it. He should have been a lawyer. Or maybe a detective. He would have been good at the interrogation part.

And he has these conversation enders, things he will say to shut me down mid-sentence. Things I can't rebut. He makes it nearly impossible for me to speak my truth.

We continue on in separate bedrooms for the remainder of the year. Grace is away at college, so she isn't around to witness it, for which I'm grateful. I'm guessing she is, too.

Christmas I send him away, to share the holidays with his children, who I'm not allowed to be near. Even though he and Lizzy had done their best to resolve their marriage on its own merits, the suspicion was always there. They blame me, and shun me. Might as well make me wear a scarlet 'A' on my clothing.

I don't need their blame. I am quite capable of beating myself up at how much pain I inflicted on her, and on them. It remains the great sin of my life, my un-rightable wrong. I pray for forgiveness, but even if God forgives me, I still struggle with how to forgive myself. And maybe one day I should ask Elizabeth to forgive me, but I know that's asking her for far too much.

So he leaves on Christmas morning to spend several days with his kids. And yes, with her, too.

I share dinner with friends. Their happy, healthy nuclear family. Plus me.

"Where's Leo?" seems to be the question of the day.

"Oh, he's spending time with his grandchildren," I reply.

"Why didn't you go with him?"

"It was a last minute plan, and the kennels were full, so I stayed home to take care of the dogs."

When did I learn to lie so well? Years of practice, I suppose.

We've had sex only four times in the past year. Yes, I've kept track. I'm embarrassed now to admit it, though why should I be after all else I've admitted to?

It's not lovemaking, just two bodies rubbing against each other for physical gratification. Well placed friction. Then I retreat to my room, to sleep. He retires to his den, accompanied by his friend Mr. Jack, of course. To drink himself to sleep.

Oh, my dear Jack. Whatever became of him? Made a guest appearance one night, then disappeared. The good guy. The potentially clean, healthy relationship I tossed aside. For what?

I thought I had found my happy ending, living in the castle with my handsome prince. But the story went sour. The castle walls morphed into dungeon walls. I felt trapped.

It would be far too easy to call Jack now, in the midst of this, but there is no way I am going to repeat past mistakes. No overlap. No secrets. Been there, done that. Got the T-shirt. Got the scars.

Besides, Leo and I aren't done. Not quite. Not yet.

New Year's Eve afternoon. A man friend who knows my situation visits me in my studio with a bottle of champagne in hand, and some advice on what to do with it.

"Put this on ice. Call him at the office, and make some suggestions of how the evening might go. Make him want to come home to you. Make him want you all over again, the way he used to."

It sounds like a good idea. So I call Leo. Plant the seed. He responds cautiously, but like he welcomes the suggestion. We agree he will come home earlier than usual.

I am a little nervous, and more excited than I care to admit. Is it possible to rekindle our flame?

Seven o'clock. Talk about reminiscent of the old days. I open the bubbly, indulge in just one glass to calm my nerves.

Seven-fifteen. I expect Angel to roll into the driveway any minute.

Seven-thirty. I call Leo's cell. "Hey, where are you?"

"Still at the office. Got delayed."

"But I thought we agreed..."

"I'm busy, Lily. Don't be such a nag. I'll be there as soon as I can."

In a heartbeat, I am dismissed. Romantic evening gone to hell.

I pour another glass of champagne And another. Nine o'clock. I hear Angel come into the garage.

Leo walks in the door. I'm too damn horny and inebriated to argue. I greet him with a sloppy kiss. Then drag him into the bedroom and have my way with him. He doesn't resist. What man would?

It isn't lovemaking, at least not the way I had envisioned it, fantasized about it, all afternoon. It is clumsy, awkward, drunken (at least for my part) sex. Period. And when it is over, there is no cuddling. None of our old lying in each other's arms, talking the idle lovelies of the afterglow. He leaves the bed, and disappears into the bathroom. I roll over, and fall asleep.

Probably more accurately I pass out. I think on some level we both know it is the end. We never voice it to each other, but our souls know we have grown apart, moved past the point of no return. The fairy tale is over. My quest to find love, to feel adored, ends in a blur of arguments.

His oft repeated line? "Whatever I do, it's never good enough to please you." It must be a terrible way to feel. I am saddened by the thought.

And what do I say far too many times? "You never listen." Or at least if he does, he doesn't respond. I know, deep down in my gut, I have to get out. I just don't know how. I can't face another move, but I know he and I are over.

Guess he isn't my prince. And I'm far from being his princess. More like the ignored, lonely sister, cleaning the floors. The one in rags, in her corner, with soot on her face. How does that story go?

Chapter 61

We remain in separate bedrooms, and function like roommates, or I guess I should say housemates. Poorly matched ones.

I wake up alone in my bed, the day before my fiftieth birthday, here in my multi-colored room.

For the past year I've told myself the way to turn fifty and feel good about it is to be fiercely intentional about forty-nine. Clean up the loose ends of my first half century. Get rid of the cobwebs. And the ghosts. I've done a fairly decent job of it in most areas of my life, except for the obvious one I haven't had the courage to do anything about.

I lay here this morning, and know, in the deep gut way I have of knowing sometimes, I have one more thing I need to do before I turn fifty.

I get out of bed, surprised by how calm I feel. I walk into Leo's bedroom, formerly our bedroom. He has just gotten out of the shower. I sit on the edge of the bed, and pat the space beside me. He understands. Sits down next to me, still wet, towel wrapped around his waist, there on our old bed. The place where for years we made love, until the last time.

"What's up?" he asks.

"I think it's time we figure out how to exit gracefully from this."

"Okay."

No discussion. No argument. Just...okay.

We hug. Hold each other for a moment. No more words are spoken.

Until he says, "I have to go to work now."

And I reply, "I know. We can talk later."

He gets up. Walks back into the bathroom to finish his morning routine. I walk out into the living room, not sure what to do next.

I finally got the courage to speak my truth. Now what am I supposed to do?

Chapter 62

This isn't going to be easy, at least not for me. I can't say what it will be like for him. He owns the house, so it is up to me to move out. Again. Move my things, and my work things, and eventually my daughter's things.

The good news, if there is any, is that it's February. Hard to believe it took an entire year to get to this point, but it did. And once again, Leo is headed to Florida, which will allow me some time alone, to think, to figure out where I should go.

The bad news is that he is supposed to leave tomorrow, on my birthday. Again. I guess maybe it's good news this time.

Except there is a significant nor'easter moving up the coast. There is already talk on the news about flight delays and cancellations.

I want him to go, to leave me alone in peace on my fiftieth birthday. Funny how just last year I was so angry with him for leaving on my birthday.

Today I plan to enjoy lunch out with a small group of woman friends I refer to as my inner circle. All of the important ones, minus Sarah, who is in Florida for the winter. They will be the first to hear my news.

We gather at Gill's, just as the snow begins to fall.

"Well, ladies, I'm glad we're all together. Saves me the need to make three separate phone calls."

"About what?" Kiki jumps on it first. She senses something exciting about to happen.

"Well, it's like this. I woke up yesterday morning, my last day of forty-nine, and laid in bed staring at the ceiling asking myself what else I needed to do before I turned fifty."

"Yeah, so?" This from Celia, ten years my senior. She's the one who told Rose about Florida. How appropriate she is here today.

"So, I got up, went downstairs, and when Leo came out of the shower..."

"You threw him down on the bed and had your way with him?" says Kiki, with a wink.

"Nope. I told him we needed to talk."

Karen, happily married for thirty-two years, chimes in, "Uh oh. Aren't they the four most dreaded words in a relationship?"

"Yeah, pretty much," I say. "So, I told him I thought it was time for us to figure out how to exit gracefully from our relationship."

Silence.

Then, like a well rehearsed Greek chorus, they ask in unison, "What did he say?"

"He said okay."

"That's it?" says Celia.

"Yup. Just okay."

"Well, that's odd." Karen is visibly upset. She always look for the bright side, and I think I've left her without one.

I continue, "I know. Exactly what I thought. But that was it. No fight. Nothing. So I guess he must've been thinking about it, too, and just waited for me to be the one to say it first, so I could be the bad guy in the story. I get to be the one who broke us up."

Kiki is all over this. "Hey, you might be the one who asked for it, but he's not exactly been Mr. Warm and Fuzzy for the past year, the prick. He probably already has someone else on the side and was just waiting for you to do this."

Ouch. Cut right to my core, but I can't let it show. I glance at Celia, the only one who knows the truth about Leo and me. She's playing with her salad, avoiding eye contact.

"Where will you go?" asks Karen, ever the practical one.

"I'm not sure yet. I'm thinking I might try to turn my studio into an apartment." I had kept the studio over Sarah's barn, even while living with Leo. It was a place of my own where I could go to paint, to write, and to think, away from the house. It later became a place to go on the weekends, when he was home too much. Apparently I had been trying to separate myself from him long before I even realized I was. Or more accurately, I had never fully moved in with him.

"But there's no shower there, and no kitchen. You can't live there," says Celia.

"I know. But I love being there. And maybe it will inspire me to paint more. You know I haven't done much of that lately. Been too distracted by the Leo drama. I can shower at the gym, or at Sarah's house. It'll be good for me, to make sure I keep working out. And there's a sink, an extra one, not just the one in the bathroom, so I can use a hotplate or something and make it like a kitchen. I'll improvise. It's just for a little while." I'm not sure who I'm trying to convince - them, or me.

They fall quiet. Do they think I'm crazy? It's the first I've voiced my plan out loud, and I'll admit it sounds whacky, leaving the three thousand square foot castle to squat in my studio.

I need to break this awkward silence I've created. "I think a toast is in order! Champagne anyone?"

We're all relieved to move on to other topics, snippets of lives other than my own. Laughter. Friendship. Confidences shared. The good stuff of life.

I've done it. Said it out loud. It makes my plan more real somehow. Of course I can do this. I think. Why not?

As lunch winds down, the snow picks up in intensity. With Leo gone to Florida, I'll be alone in the house for a few days surrounded by a blanket of white. Snowbound, and quite content to be so. The perfect place to think, plan, and dream.

My phone rings. It's Leo. I answer, "Well, hi there. I didn't expect to hear from you yet. Are you at the airport?"

"Nope. I'm calling to ask where you'd like me to take you for your birthday dinner."

What the hell? He's supposed to be wings up by now. "But I thought..."

"My flight's been cancelled. Nothing moving until we're on the other side of this storm."

Thud. Snowbound with my soon to be ex is definitely not part of my birthday plan.

I repeat myself. "But I thought..."

"Yeah. I know. Sorry. You're stuck with me. So we better make the most of it."

"Oh." Reality is sinking in. "Thanks for the offer, I guess. How about if we meet at the house around five and decide from there?"

"Sure. So hey, did you have a nice lunch?"

"Yes. Thanks for asking. We're still here."

"Good. Well, tell them all I said hello. Though I guess my name has probably already come up, and likely not in the most glowing of terms."

"No, Leo. It's not like that."

"Okay, well, whatever. I'll see you back at the house."

We hang up. I'm stunned. Confused. Torn.

It isn't because I don't love him anymore. I never stopped. I just wanted him to love me more. To cherish me the way he used to.

A few months ago, the way tonight is working out would have made me hopeful. Instead it feels like a trap. I have worked so hard to close my heart to him. I don't dare open it again. Not now.

By five o'clock, road conditions are bad enough to force Leo to come home early. Still our home, together, yet separate, until I move out.

By six o'clock, the wind is howling. Snow is heavy and wet. They're calling it a blizzard.

By seven o'clock, the electricity has gone out.

Great. Dinnertime on my fiftieth birthday, at the kitchen island, the one I built when I renovated the kitchen a few years ago and now must leave behind. Leo and I sit here together in the candlelight. In an alternate version of the tale, it would be wildly romantic. The irony of it is palpable.

"So, what do you want to do for dinner?" Going out is no longer an option. The roads are bad, and most of the town is without power.

I open a can of beef stew. Light the gas stove with a match. Uncork a bottle of Malbec. *Careful, Lily, you know what wine does to you.*

Power still out, the house grows cold. The thought of the night alone in my frigid bed turns into a thought of how much warmer it would be to have Leo's body next to me. *No. Not now. It wouldn't be right.* Or would it? Must be the wine talking. I wonder if he is thinking the same thing. Is this some sort of cruel joke, or is it fate, and God has a different end of our story in mind? The perfect romance movie formula. The couple falls apart, then miraculously find their way back to each other in the end. Maybe...

As I begin to allow a slice of fantasy to enter my heart, to allow my body to warm up to the possibility, parts of me starting to warm up in ways I can't tell you about, the power comes back on, and I'm snapped back to the present reality. Out of the darkness into the light. Figuratively and literally.

Leo gets up from the table. Puts his dish in the sink. Pours a glass of Jack, walks over and gives me a kiss on the top of my head. "Happy birthday, princess. Guess I owe you a dinner out." He leaves the room, headed undoubtably to his den, leaving me alone to close my heart back up tight.

I've been given the gift I asked for. I have time alone on my birthday, time to figure out what it is I truly want. Yet now I'm not sure I still want it.

As I wash the dishes, a wine glass gets carried away by a slick of water on the counter, skates to the edge and falls to the floor. There's a loud crash. The sound of a glass slipper as it shatters into irreparable pieces.

Chapter 63

Three weeks later, I spend my first night out of the house in my new place. I've created a makeshift apartment, just like I told my friends I would. A refrigerator, a bar sink, and a microwave define my kitchen. There's a bathroom with a toilet and sink, but no shower. Most days I will likely use the one at the gym. Sarah will allow me to use the one at her place, but she hasn't returned yet from her winter in Florida, so the water is turned off in the main house. I keep a bag of toiletries ready in the back of my car, call it my gypsy bag, in case I end up at a friend's house in the course of my day. I casually ask, "Might I please use your shower while I'm here?" and hope they will oblige. I wonder if they take pity on me.

Funny thing is I don't feel like I need their pity. Sure, it's kind of a glorified camping experience, living in this loft over a barn, but it's fun. Yes, I said fun. Definitely not a Bohemian, woe is me, look at the poor starving artist living in her studio kind of thing. I don't feel like a victim. Leaving Leo was perhaps one of the bravest things I've ever done. I stood up for myself, was willing to leave the castle to camp in the woods for a time. I remember the night in the apartment with Grace years ago, the one with the ugly carpet and ceiling, when I said "we won't be here forever" and it turned out I was right. I tell myself the same thing once more. I'll live in a real house again someday. This time I know I deserve something better. Though for right now, where I am is just fine. I have the feeling I may even look back on these days with fondness. It's mine. All mine.

For the first time in twenty years, I am living alone. With Grace off on her own, it's just me, and a dog. Clarence. He was our dog, Leo's and mine, we got him together as a puppy, but I got custody. Told Leo he can visit when he wants to, or have Clarence stay with him occasionally, but I doubt he will care for very long.

Life is more simple, living alone. I can eat what I want to, when I want to. I can stock my kitchen with nutritious options, or sugar snacks, without anyone to judge me. I no longer need to be the one who sets the good example for the rest of the house. Lucky Charms cereal for dinner? No problem. Who needs a stove or oven? I learn to cook complex meals with an electric frypan. I can stay up late, or go to bed early, whatever hours I choose. And much as I miss a warm body in bed next to me, I don't miss the growls in the middle of the night. Nobody else's alarm going off. No misplaced blame.

I am free.

Well, almost, sort of.

The studio space isn't large enough for all of my stuff, so Leo has agreed to allow me to leave what I need to at the house until I get more settled. Which is kind and gracious of him, except it means I still have to go back there, to continue to sort, toss, and pack. I have his permission to use the shower when I'm there, or run a load of laundry. And while these are lovely conveniences, it also means I come face to face with what I left behind. And I don't mean the stuff.

It's the place. And the memories.

The heart takes far longer to move out than the physical body.

I knew I needed to leave, knew the way he treated me, oh heck, the way we treated each other, was unhealthy. Yet if I'm going to be one hundred percent honest, I also have to admit I still loved him. No, make it present tense. I still love him. A love with the intensity we shared doesn't go away overnight. But I've learned that loving someone, in and of itself, isn't always enough.

At some point, I will need to hire a moving van to get the larger furniture items. Just not yet. I don't have a place to put them, and I'm not sure if I'm ready, yet, to pull the door shut for the last time.

Because of the torch I still carry for him. Okay, maybe it's not a torch anymore. More like the size of a Bic lighter. But there is still a little flicker of a flame.

I give it my best try to redirect my energy into imagining a new love who moves me the way Leo used to, once upon a...

Oh, hell. I almost said it.

I feel stuck. I need to purge Leo from my life, from my thoughts, from my heart. Because every time I go back to the house, it rushes back at me.

It's Saturday morning, about a month after my move into the studio. I take Clarence for a short walk. Figure I'll shower at the gym after my workout. I call Leo and ask if I might stop by on the way to throw a load of laundry in the machine. He says sure, come on over.

We avoid each other when I'm there. Which these days is best, I think, for both of us. On many levels. Until after the gym, when I go back to move the wet clothes into the dryer. I'm not sure how we get into it. Maybe I ask him how he's doing, or he asks me the same. To which I reply, honestly, I'm okay. But it's hard. And I miss him.

It was stupid of me to be so honest. Instead of compassion, I get his anger. He starts to yell, sitting in his chair at the head of the dining room table. My mother's old cherry table, one of the pieces I haven't been able to move yet, with his papers scattered all over it. Left to his own in the house, his inner slob has been allowed full rein.

Most of his words just fly by me too fast to remember, to even comprehend, until he hits the punchline, hard, and loud. "But this is what you wanted."

Which sets me off. I look him straight in the eye, and respond, "No, Leo. This was never what I wanted. What I wanted was for us to work out. What I wanted was for you to love me the way I wanted to be loved, the way I deserve to be loved. But you couldn't. Or maybe you just wouldn't."

He stares back at me. Says nothing. He isn't going to respond, because there is no response. I grab my things out of the dryer, still wet. I need to get out, fast, before he sees how rattled I am. Shaking and on the verge of tears, I refuse to allow him to see me cry, or to give him the satisfaction of knowing how hurt I feel.

Safely in my car, on the way back to the apartment, I scream and yell and pray out loud. Let the tears flow.

I'm home now. My funky little place I call home. I let Clarence out of his crate. He wobbles sideways, almost falls over. He's panting, heavily. I give him water. He drinks, much more than usual, still panting. Something is clearly wrong with him.

It's a little past noon. I call the vet's office, praying they are still open, and ask if I can bring him in. "Yes. Come right over."

Thankfully it's only a few minutes' drive across town. Clarence is lying down in the front seat, resting his head heavily on the armrest, continuing to pant, hard. And there's pain and fear in his eyes. He's the perfect mirror to how I feel.

I'm still in my gym clothes. I must look horrible, after all those tears, but it doesn't matter. Not now. I pray out loud. "Please, God, let my boy be okay." I hope God is still listening, that I haven't used up my prayer quota for the day.

I have to call Leo. It's the right thing to do. He's the last person I want to talk to right now, but I have to let him know. He answers, clearly still angry. "What?"

"Something's wrong with Clarence. We're on our way to the vet." I tell him what happened.

"Well, keep me posted." His only words. No offer to come be with us, with me, or with Clarence. *Unfeeling prick.*

I hang up. We're at the vet's office. Clarence can barely walk. The receptionist takes one look and leads us directly into an exam room.

I'm doing everything I can to try to calm the dog. To calm me. Rubbing his ears. Still praying out loud. "Please, God, let him be okay. I can't lose him, too. Not now." Seventy-five pounds of dog lying in my lap, here on the floor of the vet's office.

The minutes crawl by until the vet appears. He listens to Clarence's heart. "He's having a heart attack. His heart rate is out of control. Ventricular tachycardia. You need to take him right away to the emergency clinic on the other side of the bridge. They might be able to do some things for him I can't. I'll pull together his records and meet you at the front desk."

How can my healthy eight year old handsome boy dog be having a heart attack? "Please, God, don't let him die. Not now. Not today." Too much loss already. I can't handle any more.

I try to call Leo, but the call goes to voicemail. Shouldn't he be by the phone, waiting for an update? I know I would be. No, correction. I would be here, with the dog, not waiting at the other end of the phone. I have no choice but to leave a message. "Clarence is having a heart attack. I have to drive him to the hospital on the other side of the bridge. Please call me, right away?"

We walk out of the exam room to the waiting area. It's too much exertion for Clarence, those final steps. He collapses, right there in front of the receptionist's desk, at twelve-fifty pm on this beautiful sunny Saturday afternoon, with a waiting room full of people to witness it.

This isn't a library in the Keys. There is no ambulance. No med-flight helicopter. And no Leo.

There is a rush of people. The vet and the vet tech together pick up Clarence and run, not walk, his seventy-five pound limp body to a surgical table in the back. Thank God they know me well enough here to allow me to follow. The vet listens for a pulse. They put an oxygen mask on him. My hand rests on his back. I won't let go of him. Won't let him do this alone.

I look at the vet. "Is he gone?"

"Not yet. There's a faint pulse." But even though the vet hasn't said it, somehow I know.

"If he's gone, Doc, please, no heroics. Just let him go." He nods. The flurry of activity stops. Maybe it was all just for show, with me there. They back away. "May I have a minute alone with him, please?" They unplug the oxygen and whatever else is in the way. Silently. Then just as silently, they leave the room. I still haven't let go of Clarence. Amazed I have sufficient tears left to cry after this morning, I watch as they roll down off my cheeks and land in his fur.

I'm standing here alone with my dead dog. How did this happen? How did my beautiful day go so wrong so fast?

It's too quiet. Something's missing.

Leo hasn't called back yet. It's been twenty minutes, maybe, from the time I first called to tell him we were in the car on our way here. Maybe ten more, not even, since I left the voicemail update, and he hasn't called.

I reach for my phone, still holding onto the dog. It goes to his voicemail again. "He's gone. We just lost him.

Clarence is dead. Please call me." Where the hell is he? Why isn't he on the other end, waiting for an update? What could possibly be more important?

The vet comes back into the room, wants to know what I want to do with Clarence's body. "I'll take him home with me. I can't decide this alone."

They help me load him into the back seat of my car. I drive to my apartment. Pull up to the backdoor. Somehow I have to discreetly move seventy-five pounds of dead dog out of the car and into my apartment. I want to clean him up, brush him, reverence his body, as I have with each of the other two cats and a dog who passed before him in the last two years. I've learned all too well how to do this. Too much loss in far too short a time.

I've also learned there is a reason dead weight is called dead weight. I use the blanket they wrapped him in to help push and pull him out of the car, across the stoop, and into the bathroom, the coolest spot in the place. Cool air is best when storing a dead body. Another lesson learned.

The day drags on. Still no call from Leo. Stunned by his cold heart, I've given up on calling him. Around five o'clock, my phone rings.

"Lily. I'm so sorry."

"Where the hell have you been all day?" The cumulative effect of today's pain rises back to the surface as anger, and I direct every bit of it at him. "You knew we were on our way to the vet. Didn't you get my messages? Don't you even care?"

"I was on my way into the office when you called. I left my phone in the car. Just got your messages."

"And you never thought to call to check on us? You weren't worried?"

"Of course I was."

No matter what he says, one fact remains. He didn't call. For four hours, I went through hell and back, alone, held our dead dog in my arms, carried him by myself into my apartment, and Leo couldn't even lift a damn phone to call me. He's trying, in his own way, but it's lost on me. He says, "I'm here for you, if you want to come over."

Bull shit. It's what comes to mind to say, but lucky for him, or maybe for me, my filter is in place. "No, thanks. I'll be fine." I pause a moment. Take a breath. "Though we need to decide what to do with him. Cremation, or bury him somewhere?"

"Why don't we bring him back to the house?" Leo says. "I'll get someone to dig a deep hole. We can put him in the ground tomorrow afternoon."

"I guess so. I need to go now." Though I don't. I have nowhere to go, other than to get away from him. The pain is too deep. I can't bear any more today. While part of me wants to run to him, I know I can not. I'm far too vulnerable.

Meanwhile, there are two baskets full of wet laundry in the back of my car. I call Celia. "Can I come over, please, for an hour? I need to use your drier."

"What's wrong, Lily? You sound awful." My voice gives me away. Obviously there is something more urgent going on in my life than wet laundry.

"Clarence just had a heart attack and died."

"Oh my. Come right over. I'm here for you."

A good, dependable, woman friend to the rescue is what I need tonight. And a place to dry my clothes. Need to be consoled, without any drama. I must attempt to regain a sense of normal life after all that has happened today. I'm alone again, more fully than before. I'll be okay. I know I will. *Sure, Lily. Keep telling yourself that and maybe it will come true.*

Chapter 64

Alone, without a significant man in my life, is something I don't do real well. Don't get me wrong. I love my independence. I don't feel I need a man to complete me. Definitely not. I just enjoy having someone to cuddle with. And I'll admit it, I enjoy sex, but I'm not a casual, jump into the sack just for a ride kind of girl, in spite of how it may appear. I find it more comfortable to be in a relationship, so when I feel an itch, there's someone around to help me scratch it.

I consider calling Jack. Dear, decent, honest Jack. One great date, then I dumped him. Such a wonderful man, and I treated him so badly. He probably wouldn't want to hear from me. Besides, I don't think I can handle more rejection. No need to set myself up. So no, I won't call Jack. I can do without, for a while.

I wonder what it would be like to be courted. To be wooed, slowly, respectfully, the old fashioned way. Because it occurs to me that I have been the pursuer far too many times in my life, chasing after the unattainable or emotionally unavailable. I set my sights on one, then pursue until until I emerge victorious. Not always with the most desirable outcome. What might it be like instead to be allowed to relax, to let him be the one to try to win my affection? It's such a foreign idea to me.

There's not a day goes by I don't think of Leo. I wonder if he thinks of me, too. Our last shared experience was burying Clarence. It was, well, pick the adjective of your choice. Tragic? Heart breaking? Ironic? Not just because of the dog. But there we stood in the yard of our old home, the one we bought together, in spite of the horrible fight in the driveway the first time we saw it. putting Clarence's lifeless body into the ground. A surreal physical manifestation of the death of our relationship.

There's still the last batch of furniture I need to remove from the house, but it can wait. He's not living there. They haven't put the house on the market yet, but I'm sure they will sometime soon. By 'they' I mean Leo and Elizabeth. Turns out she was always part of the trust that owned the house. It appears he's gone back to her. Not surprising, somehow, at least to me. Leo and I randomly text each other for a while, but it, too, ends, eventually. His words "our love will never end" became a mockery of what was.

Summer comes and goes. Now autumn. I'm getting the knack of living alone, but with winter approaching, I become aware of how cold it is in the studio, and that I need to start to think about finding someplace to live where I can be warm and comfortable. This loft over the barn was never intended for full time winter living. I got by last year with a space heater, when I came here for just a few hours at a time to work, but it won't be safe to do overnight.

There's a knock on my door one October afternoon. It's Sarah.

"I only have a minute, but I want to let you know the tenant in your old place just gave notice that he's leaving. I know how fond you are of the house, so I thought I'd let you know first. Are you ready to stop playing the starving artist living in your garrett and move back into your home?"

"Oh, Sarah, would you be willing to rent to me again?"

"Of course I would, silly. Why else do you think I just knocked on your door to tell you about it? The house should be empty by the first of January. Can you wait until then?"

"Absolutely. Yes! Perfect." Not a moment's hesitation. A new year. A new start. God has apparently been listening to my prayers. "And Sarah, thank you. You have no idea what a blessing this is to me right now."

"Of course. Hey, come to think of it, I'm heading over there later today. Do you want to refresh your memory on the place?"

"Sure!" I say yes because I want to see it, not because I have to. I know it like the back of my hand. We agree to meet there at two o'clock.

This is exciting. I'll have a real kitchen again. And a garage. I'll have an attic, and a basement. A shower. A washer and dryer. Room for the furniture I left behind at Leo's. I can finally have closure.

I pull into the driveway. So familiar, as if I never left. The mums are in bloom by the front door, the ones I planted here, years before. We walk into the porch. There's the stenciling I did, over the back door. I'm home.

We walk into the kitchen. Sarah flicks the switch for the overhead light, but nothing happens. She says, "I guess the bulb is burnt out."

I look up at the fixture. There's mistletoe. I hung it there the first Christmas that Leo and I shared together. It survived all the years in between, even though he and I did not.

I experience my first rush of doubt. So many memories here of our early years together. So many ghosts I need to rid from my life. This place smacks me in the face with our past. Maybe this isn't such a good idea.

Sarah reaches up to take the old fluorescent bulb out of the fixture. The mistletoe crumbles in her hand. Maybe it's that easy, to let go of the old remnants of us. I can only hope so.

We wander down the hallway. Past the bathroom, where I remember spending an anxiety filled night when he told me he had asked for his divorce. The night I knew there was no turning back for us, and I couldn't sleep. Sat there on the commode, and held myself in something resembling a fetal position, rocked gently back and forth, tried to calm myself with my breath.

"Oh look," she says, pulling me back to the present. "They've painted the bedroom pink." The bedroom. Where we discovered our passion in those early days. Where he promised he would always love me. Promised we would make love again, the day after he left the note in the garage.

Oh no. The garage. *It's just a garage, Lily, get over it. Are you going to let the memories of this guy rule you, or are you ready to be strong now?* Time to put on my big girl shoes. Take charge of my life. I am overwhelmed, in awe, at the thought of being given a second chance to do what is best for me.

I hug Sarah with tears in my eyes. "Thank you. You have no idea how much I need to be here right now."

I hope I'm right. Between you and me, I have no idea how much I need to be here right now, or if I even should be. But it showed up, just when I asked, no, begged God to show me the way. I have to say yes. I need to learn to trust again. Trust it will all be okay.

The timing becomes a challenge. There are delays. The other tenant tries to postpone his move out date. I start to worry and wonder if I've made a bad choice. It certainly wouldn't be the first time in my life I misunderstood God's directions for me. Back in the early days I used to think God had a hand in my relationship with Leo, and look how that turned out.

I start to look at other rental options, but come up empty. Nothing matches up to my little home by the sea. Our first love nest.

Love nest? Really, Lily? Do you not remember those fights in the early days? To think of this house as our love nest is, as Leo would say, revisionist history. That thing when we look back on something and change the details, obscure some of the truth, to make the event align more closely with our idea of how we wish it had happened. Or we change the details to justify our version of the story. Of course he would also say that perception is reality, which is ridiculous. Reality is reality. Perception, on the other hand, depends on the lens we use to look at the facts. The stories we tell ourselves about someone, the assumptions we make, all color what we allow ourselves to believe is real.

I do a lot of revisionist history with the early years of our relationship. I remember the lovemaking. How exquisite it was. And indeed it was. But I forget so much of the other stuff. Like how it felt to be the other woman. The media and popular fiction make us look like selfish, glamorous, spoiled, well kept women. I tell you, it's not that simple. We spend more time, too much time, alone, not with him, while he's with her, the wife, doing his best to be the dutiful husband, so she doesn't suspect anything. Some might say it serves us right. But they don't know how it feels.

I wonder, sometimes, what it was like for Leo during those years, to enjoy our lustful times together, then go back home where he was cared for and tended to. I think it must have been a wonderful time for him.

Except for the guilt. I know he felt he wasn't giving enough to either one of us. Maybe it's what was behind the line he would say over and over again, "no matter what I do it's never enough to please you." I thought it was a reference to something specific, like when I would nag him to put his laundry away instead of leave it out in the middle of the bedroom, but maybe that wasn't it. Maybe it was much larger.

This house is where we had our first kiss, in this kitchen. We had our first ugly fights here, too, and broke up here on more than one occasion. There was the time he left the envelope in the garage. And the other one. The one with the water bottles. It was our first horrible, terrible fight, almost broke us apart, long before he decided to leave her. I should have known then. If only I'd been paying attention.

It was a summer weekend. Grace was away with her dad, so Leo and I had an entire weekend together. It was heaven.

Correct that. It was a disaster.

One of our issues at the time was a difference in, how shall I say it, socioeconomic status? I was a single mom, trying to raise my child while working various part time jobs and launching my painting career. I grew deeper in debt with each passing month, and worried every penny. So stuff, my stuff, was important to me.

Leo, on the other hand, well, let's just say given his marriage to Elizabeth, or perhaps I should say to her money, he didn't worry about the same things I did. I would ask him to not leave his water glass, sweating around the bottom, on top of my paperback book or new glossy magazine I'd just purchased as a treat to myself. They were simple things, yet special to me. I'd ask him to not throw away the plastic water bottles so I could refill and continue to use them. He called me a control freak. I felt disrespected.

Ask him what the big fight was about, and he'll likely have no idea. Though I guarantee you he will remember which fight I'm talking about. As for me, I remember clearly what it was about. The damn water bottles. God gives us signs. We choose to ignore some of them.

We'd been squabbling most of the weekend. With Grace away, he stayed in my bedroom, not the guest room, so his messiness was in my personal space. His underwear on the floor. Little whisker remnants of his morning shave in the bathroom sink. Dirty spoon from his morning coffee on my white kitchen counter, leaving a stain. Bugged the hell out of me. Little things, to be certain, but I felt more like his maid than his lover. Perhaps maid seemed like a step up from mistress, but I still didn't like it. I grew more annoyed with each minor violation.

We'd gone out on his boat in the afternoon. He packed a cooler, complete with smelly dead fish bait. I watched him grab two brand new water bottles out of my freezer, and toss them in to keep the bait cold. Plastic absorbs smells. Made me nauseous just thinking of what the water would taste like. They weren't expensive. So it wasn't so much about the cost. It was about his disregard for my stuff. He assumed he could take whatever he wanted.

I didn't say a word. In hindsight, it probably was my first mistake of the day. Never, ever hold something like that inside, because it grows larger, festers like an oozing sore. Better to speak your mind at the time.

We had a pleasant enough afternoon on the boat, except I was unusually quiet. I pull in when I'm afraid to speak up. We showered afterward, naked, together, as was our routine, but not touching.

We decided to go to dinner at one of those places so typically Cape Cod. Screened in porch overlooking the water, where the specialty is fried seafood, with French fries and an ear of corn, served up in a red plastic dish lined with waxy paper in a red and white checkerboard pattern, the kind meant to resemble an old fashioned picnic cloth. Quaint. Family style.

It should have been a lovely evening together. Except I was ready to boil over. What I didn't know was that he was, too.

I don't remember how the conversation began, but I couldn't hold it in any longer and ended up saying something about the now stinky water bottles. Without thinking I made this gesture with my hand, for emphasis. He perceived it as a finger pointing in his face.

He blew up. Right there on the screened in porch amid moms and dads eating dinner with their kids on a blissful summer night.

"Don't point your finger at me," he said. No, he didn't just say it. He raged. His face grew dark and stormy. His eyes scared me. As he pushed back from the table, and stood up from his chair, he said, "That's it. I'm done with this." Conversation at other tables stopped. He stomped his way to the door. I had no choice but to stand up and follow him, the quiet, humiliated, dutiful little mistress, following her master.

C'mon, Lily, you had no choice? Well, it seemed so at the time. I wonder why I didn't let him leave alone, and call a girlfriend to come get me and drive me home. But I couldn't, because none of them knew about him. Or about us. How would I explain to my friend why I was there?

Instead, I followed him out of the restaurant. Gave new meaning to the phrase walk of shame. On the drive home, he pushed Angel's twin turbos like a mad man possessed. Twisting back roads meant for leisurely summer jaunts in the breezes became a frightening roller coaster ride for me. I remember feeling terrified, trying to sit as far away from him as possible in the front seat, not unlike the night Ray drove me home in his pickup truck.

Leo hadn't laid a finger on me, but once again I felt violated and unsafe in the company of a man I thought I loved.

I don't remember his exact words. I could make some up right now, but it would be more revisionist history. At a stop light, he said something about how he was tired of me always correcting him, trying to control him.

I do remember what I said. "Then take your shit out of my house and go home to your wife." I meant it as sarcasm, but it came out as truth.

Partly to distract myself from his driving, and partly out of practicality, I walked mentally through the rooms of my home, making a list in my head of the stuff I wanted him to take with him. So that when the scary ride was over, and we were back there, I could without a moment's hesitation put those things out in the driveway.

What was on the list? A bottle of his Chardonnay in my refrigerator. Tastes like canal water to me. Get rid of it. A can of his coffee. I only drink decaf, remember? His suitcase. I'm sure he'll pack that himself. Some of his fishing magazines on the coffee table in the living room. Put them in the bag with the wine. And those damn water bottles, the ones he fouled earlier in the day with the fish bait, then put back in my freezer.

There wasn't another word spoken in the car after I told him to go back home to Elizabeth. Just the roar of Angel's twin turbos until thirteen horrifying miles later we were back in my driveway.

I unlocked the door, and we walked into the house, still silent. He made a straight line to the bedroom, to gather his clothes, pack his suitcase, pick up the dirty laundry from the floor. I cleaned his things from the kitchen, and the living room, and laid them in the driveway next to his car. Then I went into the bathroom to avoid him, to not have to confront him or watch him leave.

The next thing I heard was the sound of Angel, headed back to Boston.

I walk outside to the driveway. Dark and empty, just like how I felt.

Except for those two fishy frozen water bottles, left behind like two dead soldiers, casualties from our war. Left standing alone, in my driveway.

Just like me.

Chapter 65

You know, I could have let it end right there. Could have spared us both a great deal of future pain and guilt. But I was weak, remember?

For a few days, there were no phone calls. No emails. Just dead air. This was back in the early days of our relationship. To end it there would have been clean and simple. We would have gotten away with our affair with no one ever needing to know about it, no one else being hurt by our actions.

I'm sorry to admit I was the one who called first. Simply missed him too much, and didn't know what to do with my feelings of loss. In spite of how ugly our last time together had been, I wanted him back in my life. Somehow we moved past it. Enough to eventually buy the house together, get engaged, and break up again, once and for all, forever.

Oh, I held on to the fantasy for a long time. Continued to believe our fairy tale would win out in the end. Like every classic romantic movie ever made, we would follow the pattern. The great misunderstanding and breaking apart, followed by the scene at the end where all is forgiven, both characters having evolved sufficiently in their time apart to come back together again, healed, new and improved. They kiss. The music swells, and everyone walks out of the theater happy for the happy ending. It's what you're hoping for, isn't it?

Don't believe it for a second. It's just another set up. Real life doesn't go that way. We're human. We're not perfect. We screw up. We may forgive, but we don't necessarily forget.

In spite of the ugly, I wanted him, and wanted to feel his love. I didn't value or respect myself enough to be patient, to wait for the real thing.

I don't mean to sound quite so harsh. Leo and I did love each other. I know we did. He tried, I know he tried, to please me.

On a certain level, I suppose he was right. No matter what he did, it was never enough. If I look deeply into my heart, I could even forgive Florida. He was scared, too. He covered his fear with anger, just as I do.

But how could I expect him to love and respect me fully when I didn't love and respect myself enough to stand up and speak my mind when I knew something was wrong?

It wasn't Leo's fault. Maybe it's all working out as it is meant to. He's back with Elizabeth. They got their happy ending. See, the romance formula does hold up. I just wound up on the wrong side of it. They can cast all of the blame on me. They now share the clean relationship, the one that carries no guilt.

I still hope to find that for myself someday. An honest relationship that begins with open hearts.

In the meantime, there's still a lot I don't know, and a lot I need to learn.

But I do know one thing. My next love needs to be able to love me fully, completely, without strings, and without reservation. I don't expect perfection. Just honest, respectful love.

I also know I have a deep capacity for love, but for some reason from the earliest days, beginning with Ray, I've begged and groveled and accepted crumbs. I know now I deserve more, and I need to hold out for the one who will be able to accept the love I have to offer, and then mirror it back, beautifully, to me. I want the whole enchilada next time. No more settling.

For now, until someone new shows up, if someone new ever shows up, it's just me. And I get to move back in to my old home sweet home. Just in time for my birthday.

Chapter 66

It's good to be here. It's familiar. It's home.

I wonder if Leo knows where I am. It's been a while since we've had any contact. I do my best to pretend he doesn't exist.

My birthday is tomorrow. One year ago today I told him I thought we needed to split.

This will be the first one in years we haven't been in touch at all. I've planned some special treats for my day. Nobody else to do it for me, so I will celebrate myself. I'll go to the pool for a long lap swim. The same place where I went the day the Florida drama began to unfold. Swam my way through my fears, while at the same time they were loading Leo onto a stretcher, out of the library, into an ambulance.

I wonder if he will remember it's my birthday.

I go to bed early, looking forward to the day I have planned. I'm awakened by the sound of a new text message, just after midnight. I assume it's from Grace.

"Happy birthday, Lily! WOW! May this year be your best yet. Leo."

Oh my. I'm shocked. It's casual, not too personal. But at this hour? Where's Elizabeth? Isn't she with him? Did he disappear into the bathroom to write this? Or maybe he's in Florida.

I write back a simple 'thank you.' As I begin to drift off to sleep, I allow the door to open on old feelings. Maybe he does still love me. Maybe our love didn't end. Maybe someday we will make love again. Maybe we do not, after all that has been, have to say goodbye. Damn fairy tale blindness.

I roll over onto my side and hug my pillow. I imagine his arms around me. We are us again, the good us. I indulge in the fantasy one more time. Fall asleep with a smile on my face, and a feeling of contentment. *Sweet dreams, Lily.*

Morning comes. I wake up slowly from a deep sleep, and do a quick mental inventory of what lies ahead this day, while still warm under the covers. Oh, yeah. It's my birthday today. Happy birthday to me! Then I remember last night. Check my phone. No, it wasn't a dream. There it is. His text.

What last night sounded vaguely romantic reads modestly congenial in the morning light. A birthday wish from an old friend. Nothing more.

I feel like a fool. Again. How did I ever let this man have such control over me? And even worse, why do I still allow him to?

No more. Because I also remember, in the light of the new day, those birthdays spent alone. When he was still married. And later when he chose Florida instead of me.

Again it occurs to me he probably wrote this without her knowing. She'd be furious. How dare he? And how dare I be his accomplice, again? No. I will not.

The rest of the day is smooth. I promise myself this will be a year to look forward, not back. Let him go. For real this time.

One task remains. I still have some furniture at the old house. A door I need to close behind me for the last time. At some point I'll need to contact him to set up a day and time. But not right now. It can be number one on the list of things I don't have to do today. There's been enough drama already for one day.

At the end of the day I decide to go to the beach to take in the sunset. Our beach. I wonder how long it will take for me to allow it to become my beach instead. I go there today to honor a decade old tradition. A toe dip. Just for me.

I take off my shoe, and put my foot in the frigid water. A crazy thing to do in February, but I do it because I can. Because I live here. Because I want to celebrate the mere fact of being alive, with so much of life, and love, yet to be experienced.

The sunset glow is divine. I am truly happy in this moment, by myself, celebrating me. There's a lightness to it. I don't need to justify my joy to anyone else. I did that far too much with Leo. Maybe it comes from the guilt I've carried with me all these years. So maybe if I let go of him, I can let go of the guilt, and move forward more joyfully. Be more content on my own.

Toe dip done, I head back to the parking lot.

Unbelievable. There sits Angel. Why is he here? He's already provided evidence he knows it is my birthday. He knows my routine. Did he come here on purpose at sunset to look for me? Is it a sign, or maybe just a coincidence?

I have to walk past his car to get to mine. No way to avoid it. His window is down. I stop. He winks, then says, "Well, hi there."

It's been months since we've been this close, since I've looked him in the eye. I say, "Fancy meeting you here." *Honestly, Lily, is that the best you can come up with?*

"Have you had a good birthday?" He grins.

"Yeah, pretty good, in spite of being woken up out of a sound sleep just after midnight." *Touché, Lily.* He says nothing, just winks.

I choose to ignore it. Time to take control, and turn this chance meeting into an opportunity. "Hey, I need to talk to you about something." I realize he hasn't bothered to get out of the car. I invite him to do so. "Want to walk with me for a minute?"

"No. Probably best not."

I look at him with a question on my face. He adds, "Someone might see us."

"Seriously? We've known each other for what, like twenty years, and you can't get out of your car to walk with me? Are you kidding me?"

"Nope. I'm forbidden from having any contact with you."

"Well, that's just plain insulting." *Didn't seem to matter to him last night when he sent the text.* But I've just been given the fuel to say what I need to say next. No more procrastination. "I'm ready to get the last of my stuff out of your house." *Good girl. Stay on task.* "When might you suggest I do that, maybe sometime you won't be there, so we don't upset anyone?" I attempt to say it without sarcasm. And fail.

"I'm leaving for Florida next week, on the fifteenth." *Of course he is.* "I'll be gone for two weeks. You've still got a key. Help yourself."

"Perfect. Thank you." Then it dawns on me. "The fifteenth? She's got you to stick around for Valentine's Day. Wow. Must have some serious power over you that I obviously did not."

He looks at me, part pain, part sadness. "Lily."

Yes, it was a cheap shot on my part, but I couldn't help myself. I say, "Well, goodbye then. I'll be fully out by the end of the month. Hope your Florida trip goes well. You know, without anything shocking."

I get a faint smile in return. I walk away, before he has the chance to say anything else. Head held high, I do my best to look confident and happy, even as I risk melting, just a little, inside.

I've got my marching orders now. The end is in sight. It's too late in the day to call the moving company, but I will, first thing tomorrow. I'll need their help with the last batch of heavy furniture. Help in moving forward to my new life.

Goodbye, Leo. Hello, single Lily. You're going to be just fine by yourself.

And you know what? If I'm honest with myself, truly honest, which is what I've promised to be as I move forward, I'm a little excited by the thought of being alone, of opening myself up to a new and better way, a more honest life.

Chapter 67

Living alone. Parts of it are joyful. Parts of it are scary. I worry sometimes I might allow myself to like it a little too much. What if someday the right guy does show up and I'm so happy about being here alone in my sweet home that I don't want to share my life with him? What then?

I'm trying the dating thing again, but meeting men here on Cape Cod, or at least meeting ones who are single, gainfully employed, don't drink or smoke to excess, and carry minimal baggage, well, they are few and far between. Haven't found one yet. And as to meeting women to date, well, let's just say I gave that up, too. It wasn't about wanting to be with a woman. It was about Sarah. Just Sarah.

So I've settled into the single life. I enjoy my friends, and devote myself to my work. My painting is flourishing. Galleries in Chatham, Nantucket, and Provincetown want me. Woman friends tell me to stay positive, to embrace the single thing. They say my life shouldn't be defined by whether or not there's a significant partner in it, like there's something wrong with having a strong desire to find my own Mr. Right. But you know what? The ones who tell me that are all settled into their own long term relationships. "Sure that's easy for you to say," I want to scream at them. But I don't. I smile, tell them I'm quite fulfilled in the single life I've created for myself. And part of me wonders if they might be jealous of what I have. Maybe they'd rather be single than be in the relationships they have.

My single friends are just as guilty of it. We get together and tell each other how happy we are to be alone, to not have to deal with some man's dirty laundry or dishes or messes in the garage. I wonder, when we do, how many are lying, to each other, or to themselves, because deep down they still want a handsome prince to make love with at the end of the day.

I know I do. I don't want to spend my senior years all alone. Oh, he doesn't have to be a handsome prince, but sure, I want someone to talk to over morning tea, to lay my head on the pillow next to at night, to share a smile with when we wake up. When did it become a bad thing to want to be in love?

I prefer to look at this time as a transformational, re-birthing time. It's what I envisioned for myself when I first moved to Cape Cod. Until the phone rang, at the end of moving day. I screwed it up that time. Perhaps God is giving me a second chance to get it right.

I can make better choices now. More empowered choices. After I move the rest of my stuff out of Leo's house.

Chapter 68

It's moving day. Again.

The van backs into my driveway. Just a few items, but heavy as they are it's worth every penny to have the help. This van's roof is intact. There are no stuffed animals, just a few large pieces of furniture. The dining room table. My old piano. I don't need Noah's ark this time. There's no flood, and the sun is shining on this spectacular late February day, the kind that gives us a tiny taste of spring to come, in spite of the fact that we know there is still a lot of winter to be endured.

It doesn't take long to unload. I say thank you, then send them on their way with generous tips. Walk back into the house, and close the door. Sit down on the couch. My couch. I exhale, long and deep. Finally, everything I own is under one roof.

Life with Leo is behind me. I'm ready to start my next chapter now.

Until the phone rings.

I pick it up without looking at the caller ID. "Hello?"

Chapter 69

Stop right there. I know what you're thinking. Well, no, honestly I don't, but I think I can guess. There are two obvious directions in which this story can go. So I'm stopping to ask you, where do YOU want to see it go? This is the test of your own belief in happy endings, and what you think would make a good one right now.

Remember the romance formula? We met. We fell in love. We fell out of love. He went back to her. We spent our time apart. So now maybe it's time for us to come back together, to live happily ever after. Are you hoping it's Leo on the phone?

Seriously. Please stop for a moment. Before you turn the last pages, I ask you to consider this question. Do you want Leo to come back to me, or do you have something else in mind?

Nope, not so fast. Take a few minutes. I mean it. Right now.

Dum dee dum dee dum...

Still thinking?

Okay. You now have my permission to read the last chapter. Cue the ringing phone again.

I pick it up without looking at the caller ID. "Hello?"

"Lily."

With just one word, I know it's him. "I thought you were supposed to be in Florida."

"Yeah. I am. I'm here, back in my favorite campground."

"Well, at the risk of being blunt, I'm in the midst of moving, so this isn't a good time for me to talk. The van just arrived, and..."

"I know. But, Lily, I need to talk to you. It's important. Please. Call me back as soon as you can."

Flashbacks of another Florida trip jump into my brain. "Are you okay?"

"Yes, I'm fine. Never better. Just call me, please? I need to talk with you."

"Okay, I will. But it probably won't be for a few hours."

"That's alright. I'll be here with my phone waiting for your call."

Yeah, right. Just like he said he would be the day Clarence died. This can't be happening. Not now. I've just packed all my remaining stuff out of the house, onto this moving truck, to be back in one place, under one roof, for the first time in too long. So why is he calling me now? Is he just trying to mess with my head, or, more accurately, my heart?

This is risky, because if I'm honest about it, absolutely 100% like you gave me truth serum and I had no choice but to be honest, I'm still hoping for my happy ending. And try as I might to tell myself how much I despise this man, and have been hurt by him, there's still a part of me wanting to believe otherwise. I mean, how romantic would it be? Back here in my house, a new fresh start for us. What if. *Snap out of it, Lily. Let it go.*

I focus back on the move. I've planned it well. The morning flies by with the busyness of it all.

It's three o'clock. He's called three times since this morning, leaving voicemails I've chosen to ignore. Because I don't know what to say. I need time. I'm not sure I can deal with this, with him. Temptation. But I'm resolved to get it right this time.

Seven o'clock. The hour continues to haunt me. I go out into the backyard with my phone. Sit in my favorite green chair, wrapped up in a blanket. It's dark out, but the flood lights on the back of the house light the area. The ones he installed for me so many years ago. So many remnants of him remain here.

Seven thirty. I still haven't returned his call. Though I do listen to his voicemails.

The first one. At noon. "Hey, Lily, please call me back. I know your day is busy. But this is important."

The second one. At two o'clock. "Yes, it's me again. I know you're busy, but Lily, I think this is something you're going to be happy to hear."

And the third. At three o'clock. They were starting to come closer together, like labor pains. "Please call me right away. Why are you ignoring me?"

Why, Leo? How dare you ask? Do you not understand what I've been through?

Eight o'clock. I take a few breaths. I'm calm. *Yeah, right.*

I pick up the phone. Dial his number. He answers immediately.

"Hey."

"Hey."

"I've been waiting for your call."

"Yes, I know. You said that on your messages."

"So, how did the move go?"

"It went great. I'm all in."

"Good. How does the old place look?"

I remember the day he referred to it in less than glowing terms. "It's beautiful. I think I'm going to be quite happy living here."

"Well, that's good, I guess."

He falls silent now. But I don't fill the space. Not right away.

Until my curiosity gets the better of me. I say, "So, what's this big news you wanted to talk to me about?"

"I'm single again."

"What?"

"I said I'm single again. Or at least I will be, soon."

"Okay. Good for you. But why are you calling me?"

"Because I still love you, Lily. I realized the other day when I saw you at the beach that I never stopped loving you."

"You can't do this to me now, Leo. I've been through too much."

"C'mon Lily - it's you and me. How can you say no?"

"I can say no because I'm stronger now, Leo. I need to be on my own for a while. We can't go back. There's been too much hurt, pain, anger. I love you. I always will. But we both know we're not good for each other. Not anymore. Enjoy Florida. I gotta go." I hang up.

Seriously. Did you buy that one? You give me far too much credit. It wasn't him on the other end of the phone. I just made up the whole thing. Because I'd like to think it could go that way. Maybe he might still carry a torch for me, and come crawling back some day. And I'd have the strength to stand up to him, to say no thank you.

But it's not going to happen. He's happy with his new life. Or perhaps I should call it his new old life. I can be happy for him, and for her. And I pray he never does try to come back to me. Because as strong as I might like to believe I am, I worry I wouldn't have the strength to tell him no. In spite of all of the pain, and the anger, and the insults, and the salt, well, I worry about what I might do for the sake of the fairy tale. Though certainly within a short period of time I would know I was wrong, in so many ways, to have gone backward instead of forward.

See, there was another part of the romantic movie formula I changed, a bunch of pages back. It occurred to me last night, while watching someone else's movie on the television.

Somewhere about two thirds of the way through the story I was supposed to enable you to find Leo endearing. Yes, the guy who had been the source of my pain and anger was supposed to do something charming so that in spite of Florida or the water bottles you would want it to work out between us. You'd want us back together, to live happily ever... oops. I almost said it. You know the thing.

But I couldn't do it. I wouldn't do it. Because in spite of the formula, life doesn't necessarily go that way. Which is also why I stopped letting Leo talk for himself. Seriously, did you want to hear him justify his side? Wasn't it enough to hear me limp on with my own justifications for something I knew in my heart was wrong, when I didn't have the strength to walk away?

Maybe the damn formula was the reason I allowed Ray back into my life so many times, even though he attempted each time to push me beyond my limits. I gave him one more chance. And one more. And yet one more. Because I was taught from an early age to believe in the romantic ending.

And as for Leo? It wasn't the dirty dishes, or the laundry on the floor, or the coffee stains on the counter that drove me away.

Remember the end of the day I retrieved his van? Remember how he yelled at me about how screwed up I was? A man isn't supposed to call the woman he loves crazy. I tried to justify it. Allowed myself to believe that maybe I had in fact overreacted. Maybe he was scared and frustrated, and I should have been more compassionate.

Maybe my ass. If that was true, there would have been an apology at some point when he realized what he'd done. I waited for it, but it never came. I accused him of verbal abuse. And he reacted with more anger. That's the part that drove us to counseling. And the part that drove me away.

But we see what we want to see, don't we? And we are more than capable of ignoring what we choose to not see. Maybe that's what I've been doing all along. I call it self induced fairy tale blindness. An incurable belief in happy endings that allows us to justify just about anything.

Fairy tale happy endings are just stories we make up to bring hope to our broken hearts. So let's try this another way. Cue the ringing phone, again.

I pick it up without looking at the caller ID. "Hello?"

"Hi, Liliana, remember me?"

Only one man I know still uses my full name. The prettiest form of my name. I'd like to say I'd forgotten about him, but honestly, he's been on my mind a lot lately. I promised myself I wouldn't call him. I'm secretly delighted to hear his voice on the other end of the phone.

"Well, hello Jack, what a nice surprise to hear from you."

"Yeah, well, you've been on my mind for quite a while. I'm not sure why. It didn't go so well the last we saw each other, but I'm a glutton for punishment. Back then you said life was complicated. Maybe it still is. I just thought I'd take a chance and call you."

"It's okay, Jack. That's over. All over." And for the first time, saying those words, I believe it is true.

"Really?"

"Yeah, well, it's a long story."

"I'd love to hear about it. I'm going to be on Cape this Saturday. Want to try this again? I'll buy you lunch if you'll tell me your story."

"I'd love that, Jack. Yes. Thank you. I know the perfect place. Water view down in Woods Hole. Called Quicks Hole Tavern. I absolutely love their soups. *Okay, Lily, you're doing that nervous babbling thing. Spare him the details and stay on topic.* Yes, Jack, let's have lunch."

"Where are you living now? I'll pick you up."

"Believe it or not, the same place where I was the last time you saw me."

"No way! I thought you might have moved on by now."

"Well, I did, and then came back again. Like I said, it's a long story."

"Okay, well, I'll have plenty of time this weekend to listen. See you in your driveway at noon?"

"Perfect. Oh, and Jack..."

"Yes?"

"I'm so grateful you called. You have no idea. Thank you."

"My pleasure. See you on Saturday."

Time to move forward. Here's to smoother sailing ahead, on more honest, open waters.

This ending works better than the Leo one, now doesn't it? It's the one you expect at the end of the movie. But I'm not satisfied with it.

Because if the story goes this way, I, Lily, haven't learned much from all I went through with Leo. I've still allowed a man to provide my happy ending. I haven't learned how to stand on my own, to be joyously independent.

So give me another chance, please. Just one more. Cue the ringing phone, just one more time.

Chapter 72

I pick it up without looking at the caller ID. "Hello?"

"Hello. I'm calling for Liliana Daniels."

"This is she. Who's calling, please?"

"Liliana, this is Helen. I'm calling from the Copley Society of Art."

Oh my. I'd forgotten, well, not really, but sort of, about the application I submitted to become an artist member. I forgot about it because this was my third time trying to get in, and I guess I assumed it would fail like the first two times.

I'd discovered it that snowy magical day, back before, well, before everything.

"Yes," I say, "so lovely to hear from you, Helen." She's the same one I spoke with that day I walked Newbury Street. I remember, because Helen was my grandmother's name, and I remember at the time I thought it was a sign.

"I'm calling to let you know that the jury committee wants to extend full artist membership to you. Congratulations."

"My goodness, thank you! You've made my day." We continue on with discussion of next steps. A new member exhibit to which I am invited. And a list of future opportunities.

Talk about a dream come true.

Not about a man.

Just about me. And my paintings.

And I decide that for at least a little while, I will do my best to redirect the energy I used to spend on worrying about my relationships and focus instead on my art. And trust that when the time is right, if the time is right, that someone will show up with an open heart and respect me for who I am.

New life awaits. Time to head to the studio, right next door. My happy place. On my way out the door, I utter one more prayer. "Thank you, God, for being patient with me."

Epilogue

It wasn't about the water bottles.

It was about respect. And my need to learn to give it to myself, before I could expect to receive it from others.

What Leo and I did was wrong. Period. We were doomed from the start.

The lie was easy. Living with the consequences nearly impossible. A relationship rooted in dishonesty has a hard time growing past its origins. I am stunned by how wanting something to come true with all of my heart and soul led me to do things I would normally never consider.

Great sins are not committed just for the thrill of the moment. They are the culmination of a lifetime of hurts, disappointments, and losses, that we hope we can cure. That's not an excuse. Simply an observation.

Those of you who know me will ask how much of this story is true. You'll pull me aside, and whisper, "So hey, you can trust me. Did you really do this? And did he really do that? What's the truth?"

I'll whisper back to you, "Can you keep a secret?"

You'll say, "Yes, of course."

And I will look you in the eye, wink, and say, "Well, so can I."

ACKNOWLEDGEMENTS

A.K.A. Oozing gratitude

Ask me what fiction I've read in the past two years, and my answer is PAINTING LILY. Over, and over, and over again, under a variety of titles, with several different openings, but essentially the same story. It's been my stay at home, curl up in bed with a good book, Friday and Saturday night date on more nights than I care to admit. And I have loved every moment of it. Except for the times I worried it might never see the light of day beyond my own computer.

The writing of this book has been a labor of love. But writing a book is not a solo effort. I have so many to thank.

Thank you first to Alan Watt for his book *"The 90 Day Novel."* It was my daily guide and companion as I wrote the first draft, longhand, in the front seat of my car at the beach for two hours nearly every weekday morning for three months.

Thank you to Toben, for buying the first copy of the book when it was barely an idea. Your twenty dollar bill stayed on my bulletin board as a reminder.

Thank you to the Cataumet Arts Center Artists' Circles, for my first opportunities to read out loud.

I finished the first longhand draft while camping in Truro. Thank you, Bill, for toasting that moment with me.

Then there was the first round of agent query letters. Thank you to each and every agent who said "pass." I am truly grateful you did, because the book wasn't ready yet. Not even close.

Thank you to my readers - Jill, Jo, Eunice, Danielle, and Lee - for your thoughtful comments and questions of Lily and Leo.

On to more revisions, more query letters, more rejections.

Thank you to the next round of agents who said no "thank you." And the next round after that.

The story continued to evolve, as did Lily.

Then, dear Edmund, you stepped in, willing to read, and offer a man's perspective. When you told me how Lily exasperated you, I knew I was onto something, because you were more caught up in character than in sentence structure or syntax. You've helped so much in your role as "just some guy down the street." Thank you.

Thank you, Laura. You ALWAYS believed in 'the novel' but refused to read it until you could hold the real thing in your hands in print. Well, ta da! Here it is!

Thank you, my beloved, beautiful, amazing daughter Anna, who surprised me on my birthday in the midst of it all with flowers for Lily. You inspire me, every day. I am proud of you beyond words.

Thank you, Jill, for our late night two hour phone calls. Thirty years of friendship, and I still learn from you every time we talk.

Thank you to Joan, my emotional ambulance when I needed one.

To Stephanie, for fried pickles at the Pickle Jar, asking me again and again about the book's progress. Your early encouragement helped more than you know.

To Pamela, who I pay to listen when I know others are tired of hearing me prattle on. You offer pearls of insight every time.

To Ellen, for taking me sailing, or joining me skiing, when I needed to get away from it all for a while. Bless L'Escargot.

To Pat, so fun to share God signs and miracles along the way.

And to Melissa, for keeping me centered and adjusted on the mat.

Thank you to Laurie (and Anne and Phil) for first introducing my family to the magical place we know as Megansett.

To Tina and Dave and Ursula, for my beloved "Mimi house."

And to Cyndi, for my other home.

Thank you, Lori, for the workouts, the wine, the job, and the martians. (No, that is NOT a typo for martinis! I meant martians. Don't ask me to explain.)

And thank you to Joe, dearest Joe, for the cookies, and oh so much more. I am quite certain you thought me crazy when I told you "there's a novel." But here it is.

Thank you to Christ Lutheran Church, and Cape Cod Church. To Dunkin' Donuts and Starbucks. To *The Silver Palate Cookbook*'s best ever chocolate chip cookie recipe. To *Cape Cod Life* magazine, and *mvyradio*, and to more musical artists than I could ever mention for the special tunes that provide the soundtrack to my life.

Thank you, Beth Colt, for your delightful marketing wisdom and delicious soups.

And thank you, Amy Rader, for taking the best darn professional headshot of me ever.

Thank you, HUGE thank you, to Chrissy Caskey, for the gorgeous cover design to make it "real." You're awesome!

Thank you to my father, Ralph, gone too soon. I miss you, and wish I'd taken the time to ask you more questions to know you better.

To my brother, Bob, for reaching out to help at the right moments, and perhaps not even knowing how much he did.

To my Aunt Eleanor, for asking again and again "when do I get to read it?"

And to my mother, Mary, for healing and understanding when it mattered most. I miss you more than I ever knew I would.

Thank you to Jeanie, and to Evana, whose passings nudged me on to know that I could no longer wait to write the story I'd been holding inside. You are my angels.

Thank you to Nora, for allowing me to take you to the airport in my little car some thirty years ago. And to Delia,.for your Tweets that allowed me to feel connected.

To Dora, crazed cat, who too often refused to move off the keyboard, and is willing to take full responsibility for any typos found within.

To Rosie, cutest dog ever, for asking me to take her on walks when she knew that I needed them.

And thank you to the ones who provided the inspiration for the characters in this book. If I painted any of you with too rough an edge, please forgive me. This is fiction, after all.

Last, but not least, I thank God, the true muse of my life, for being there, offering grace, every time I cried for help, shed fearful tears, fell on my knees, and managed to get back up again, with joy. You never cease to amaze me.

Thank you, every one of you who reads these words. For you are the ones who give life to the story.

May you feel my gratitude, and enjoy abundant blessings, grace, and joy in your own lives.

Mimi

Mimi Schlichter is an artist, musician, and author.
She lives on Cape Cod, where she can walk the beaches,
swim, paint, or write as the mood and muse call to her.

More information at MimisArt.com.

Ta da!

CPSIA information can be obtained
at www.ICGtesting.com
Printed in the USA
FFOW02n1701121115
18487FF